The Perfect Couple?

Also by Robyn Sisman

A Hollywood Ending
Weekend in Paris
Just Friends
Perfect Strangers
Special Relationship

The Perfect Couple?

Robyn Sisman

First published in Great Britain in 2010 by Orion Books,
an imprint of The Orion Publishing Group Ltd
Orion House, 5 Upper Saint Martin's Lane
London WC2H 9EA

An Hachette UK Company

1 3 5 7 9 10 8 6 4 2

A CIP catalogue record for this book is
available from the British Library.

ISBN (Hardback) 978 0 7528 9890 2
ISBN (Trade Paperback) 978 0 7528 9891 9

Typeset by Deltatype Ltd, Birkenhead, Merseyside

Printed in Great Britain by Clays Ltd, St Ives plc

The Orion Publishing Group's policy is to use papers
that are natural, renewable and recyclable products and
made from wood grown in sustainable forests. The logging
and manufacturing processes are expected to conform to
the environmental regulations of the country of origin.

www.orionbooks.co.uk

Part One

∾ ∾

Chapter 1

∾ ∾ ∾

Kate eased one black fishnet stocking up her bare leg, then the other, and fastened the suspenders. Straightening up, she slid her feet into patent-leather dominatrix heels and teetered round the bed to the full-length mirror that was fixed to the inside of one of the wardrobe doors. Hmm. Her blonde hair still looked a little wild, having been washed and hastily blow-dried upside-down. Her winter-pale skin contrasted starkly with the deep satiny red of her basque – or bustier, or whatever it was called – and minuscule matching briefs. She turned sideways, first one way and then the other, admiring her flattened stomach and enhanced bosom, then put her hands on her hips and struck a pose. This outfit certainly made a change from the barrister-black and starched white she wore to work every day. Rikki was in for a surprise.

She had been planning this evening for the past couple of weeks, after they'd gone to see a steamy new film by a Spanish director, starring a sensational spitfire with cascading dark hair and a cleavage like the Grand Canyon. As they sat munching pizza afterwards, Rikki had made a decent attempt to contain his admiration for the gorgeous girl, but had let slip a wistful remark about 'adventurous' sex that had rankled at the time and gnawed at her ever since. Well, she would show him tonight.

Kate checked the time: six forty-eight. She consulted her schedule, which she had carefully devised, typed and printed out for instant reference:

5.30: leave work
6.00: arrive flat. Turn up heating. Draw curtains
6.05: shower/wash hair/brush teeth
6.15: dry hair. Hide toys. Affix handcuffs
6.30: make-up; perfume; get dressed (!)
6.50: candles. Turn off mobile
7.00: R arrives. Action!

Outside, gusts of winter wind flung raindrops against the bedroom window like handfuls of gravel, but inside the flat was warm and snug. Kate scanned the bedroom. Everything was ready. She shut down her mobile, lit the 'pheromone candle' and turned off the overhead light. Time for the handcuffs. It was a bit of a problem that their bed didn't have a headboard, let alone the fabulous brass bedstead that had been depicted in the film. Even Kate had been struck by the sight of the Spanish girl's wanton writhing, her beautiful brown arms pinioned above her head. Fortunately this little hiccup had been foreseen by the handcuff manufacturers, who also supplied an 'Eezyfit Door Kit', consisting of a metal bracket which fitted over the top of a normal door ('No drilling! No screws!'), from which the black velvet cuffs now dangled. They were adorned with fetishistic buckles, but these were just for show, disguising a more convenient Velcro fastening. The idea was that Rikki would come home, notice her coat and briefcase, left in prominent view in the living room next door, and come looking for her. He'd open the bedroom door, see the candle, turn round in puzzlement – and there she'd be, pressed helplessly to the door in her fancy underwear, ready for the taking. Stretching her arms above her head, Kate slid her wrists into the cuffs and pulled them tight, just as the bells of their neighbourhood church struck seven o'clock.

୭୬

She had researched all this paraphernalia online, which had certainly been an eye-opener. There were devices for everything imaginable — and some things she preferred not to imagine. Mainly, though, she'd laughed. There was a bizarre variety of 'fantasy' outfits that made her question what went on in other people's minds: cheerleader, nurse, policewoman, airline pilot, Mrs Santa and even a football referee's costume, its tiny shorts emblazoned with the phrase YOU'VE SCORED, which came complete with a whistle, and red and yellow cards imposing different penalties. In the end she'd settled for lingerie, fancy but not too tacky – though her basque had what the catalogue called a 'fuss-free' zip down the front. She'd agonised about ordering online because she was worried about the labels on the parcels, so earlier in the week she'd ventured into the Pussy Cat shop after work one day, wearing a beret and dark glasses in case she ran into anyone who knew her. 'Did you want to go on our mailing list?' the girl serving her had asked. 'No!' Kate was horrified. 'I – I'm leaving the country, actually. Charity work in Africa,' she'd added firmly, seeing the girl about to enquire further. 'You know, famine and stuff.'

Now, as she sagged against the door, eyes closed and hands dangling above her head, her thoughts began to wander. She must remember to nip out one lunchtime and buy a present for her godson, six-month-old offspring of her old friend Sam. This weekend she and Rikki were driving down to Somerset to check out Sam and Michael's new country house and for a general worshipping-at-the-shrine number. The trouble was that she never had a lunch hour. It was only in television dramas that barristers sat around in quaint Dickensian pubs, swapping Latin tags and ordering another bottle of champagne to toast their own utter brilliance in court. Kate thought anxiously of the brief she'd stuffed into her bag this evening with some hastily scribbled notes, rather than the meticulous dossier she usually prepared, with key facts and questions picked out in colour-coded highlights. She was meeting the client at ten tomorrow morning, along with a solicitor who was potentially a rich source of future work and therefore needed to be wowed. Never mind. If she set the alarm for six, she could be in chambers by seven and be ready in time. The case itself was bread-and-butter stuff. Three hours should do it easily.

What was that? At the sound of a slammed door she tensed, raising one shoe towards the stirrup. But it was only the woman from the upstairs flat, returning home. Kate recognised the familiar pattern of footsteps across bare floorboards overhead, accompanied by ecstatic cat miaows and shortly followed by the signature tune of a soap opera. That was a relief: the television would mask the noise they made. These Victorian warehouses were generally very solidly built – that's what her stepfather had said, anyway, having once worked as a surveyor (before he started drinking). The flat was 'enviably situated' in what the estate agent had described as 'the doorstep of trendy Shoreditch'. It would be nice to live in one of the penthouses, with nothing but sky and pigeons above, but those were way out of their league. Even this third-floor flat – basically two large rooms plus a tiny kitchen and 'Manhattan-style' bathroom – required a frighteningly large mortgage. But she loved the big windows that flooded the flat with light on a sunny day, and the fact that she could walk or cycle to work if she wanted. Having grown up in the bleaker outreaches of a dull Midlands town, whose most glamorous attraction was a shopping mall, it was exhilarating to live in the heart of a great city.

Outside the shaded window, London roared and rumbled and tooted, alive and full of promise. Rikki would be home any minute. She pictured him striding up from the Tube station, coat billowing romantically behind him, with his arms full of goodies. Tonight he had promised to cook her a celebration dinner. He had two specialities: stir-fried prawns with cinnamon rice, and a curry that used every pan, bowl, utensil and machine in the kitchen and took all day to prepare. Prawns, then – and champagne. There might be a present, as well: nothing too extravagant, she hoped. They were only just beginning to dig their way out of a mountain of debt.

A burst of raucous female giggles suddenly exploded from the pavement outside. She heard a squeak of brakes and the whirr of a taxi engine, a stampede of high heels, more laughter and a shriek of 'Wait! My balloon!', before the door clicked shut and the taxi took off. A balloon in a taxi? Well, why not? London was awash with balloons, red roses, heart-shaped chocolates and cards ranging from schmaltz to smut. It was Valentine's Day, after all.

Kate leaned back and closed her eyes. On this exact day, two years ago, she and Rikki had met, arguing against each other in Croydon Crown Court. He was the most beautiful man she had ever seen. Even when he'd been wearing a wig and robe, she'd found him instantly attractive. His mother was Persian by birth, his father English. The combination had given him fine-boned features, impossibly dark hair that curled sexily when it got too long and extraordinary green-grey eyes that lit up his face. His proper name was Rustom – Rustom King, whose initial letters had given him the nickname of Rikki since schooldays. They were arguing against each other in an inheritance case, which had turned into a delicious flirtation, all the more exciting for being played out in public in front of a crusty old judge. 'I think My Friend has failed to note the significance of *Grieves* v. *Harbottle 1985* regarding intestacy,' said Rikki – or something like that. 'Irrelevant, Your Honour,' Kate retorted. 'That judgment was superseded in 1991 by *Rudge* v. *Gulliford*. And I believe My Friend will find that the date of the case he cites was 1986, not 1985.' She had been on top form, and won the case. Male barristers often disliked being trounced by a woman, but Rikki had been charming about it – even impressed. 'Wow. You really know your stuff,' he'd said afterwards, when they met in the robing room. He was even better looking without his wig, with smiling eyes, straight jet-black hair and the most incredible golden skin. Since they were both returning to their chambers, it had seemed natural to walk to the station together and carry on talking in the train. Arriving at London Bridge, neither of them wanted to stop, and he'd suggested a drink together.

That was the beginning of a whirlwind romance – the best

kind, in her opinion. As well as taking her to films and dinners he'd shown her all sorts of special places in London, which he knew much better than she did, having grown up here: the view from Parliament Hill, a candlelight tour of the John Soane Museum, a tiny Lebanese restaurant that looked like a cheap café but had food to die for. He was full of energy and ideas. He loved surprises.

Two months after they'd met, he took her to the Amalfi coast for a long weekend. He'd organised everything, not even telling her where they were going except that it was 'somewhere warm'. Kate had never been to Italy before, and even at Naples airport was enchanted by the emerald-green palm trees sprouting into a cloudless blue sky and the sensation of heat on her sun-starved skin. A taxi had driven them for an hour or so through a steadily more mountainous landscape and finally into a village up a steep, cobbled street. She tried not to be disappointed when it stopped in front of an unprepossessing hotel entrance, just a dark doorway in a white wall: she would forgive Rikki, of course, if it turned out to be a dump. They were dragging their suitcases down a high, tiled hall when the middle-aged manager, trim and elegant as a ballet dancer, appeared from a side office. With a snap of his fingers he summoned a porter to take charge of their luggage, then ushered them out onto a large balustraded terrace with geranium-filled urns and ornately wrought tables and chairs. It would be his great pleasure, he affirmed, to bring them a drink, personally, while they enjoyed the view.

Stepping outside, Kate caught her breath. Greenery spilled vertiginously from the edge of the terrace into a sea of bright, heartlifting blue that stretched for miles to a hazy horizon. She could see a part of the rugged coastline with terracotta-roofed villages perched high on the cliffs or squeezed into tiny harbours. An ancient tower decorated with brick arches poked up from among the pines immediately below her. Even as it caught her eye, bells inside began to ring, as if in celebration.

Everything about their stolen days together was perfect. Their room was in a private turret, with huge windows to the sea, where their love-making could be uninhibited. By day they roamed the ancient goat paths in the mountains, explored churches and villas, kissed on shingly beaches, all the time talking, arguing, finding out about each other. At night they gorged on seafood and proper Calabrian pizzas before tumbling into their high, white bed. On their last night they were sitting together in a little restaurant on the hill-town square. They'd been swapping confessions about their previous girlfriends and boyfriends, and why the relationships had blown up or fizzled out. Rikki told her that he had been in love several times. 'But,' he added thoughtfully, 'there's only been one girl I wanted to marry.'

'Oh?' Kate was piqued, but curious. 'Who was that?'

'You.'

She remembered how the clatter of plates and buzz of conversation receded to an eerie silence in which she could hear nothing but her own heartbeat. The pink tablecloths and bustling waiters dissolved into a blur. For a few moments she may have stopped breathing altogether, unaware of anything except Rikki's handsome face smiling into hers and the warm clasp of his legs under the table.

He reached for her hand and leaned forward, eyes locked with hers. 'Let's do it. Marry me, Kate. Tomorrow – next week! Let's surprise the world and be happy for the rest of our lives.'

I love this man. That's all she could think. She loved his open, impetuous heart and his optimism that all things were possible. She loved it that he had chosen her above all other women and wasn't afraid to say so. Marriage was not on her agenda, except as a vague future probability. She was still only twenty-seven, and she'd always thought it vital to establish her career first, so that a man would take her seriously, not try to turn her into a 'support' and free housekeeper. But that night something within her shifted, as if a stone had been rolled away from her heart, leaving it open and vulnerable. Quite suddenly she saw marriage not as a surrender, but as an adventure. It was like that psychological test where you could decipher an inkblot either as a household vase or two people kissing. There were a thousand reasons to say, 'Not yet.' But this was the moment. She saw herself reflected in Rikki's eyes as a confident, opinionated woman who ran her own life in her own way, a fit partner who would relish the boldness of his proposal.

'OK.' She felt herself blushing like a teenager. Then, seeing the excitement leap in his face, she started to laugh. 'Yes! Why not? Let's do it!'

'Kate Pepper, I adore you.' He pulled her across the table into a kiss in which she could feel his pent-up passion.

They stared at each other in wonder, laughed, kissed, stared again. It was madness! But, Kate told herself, remembering a bit of Socrates, it was the madness of Aphrodite – a gift sent by the goddess of love herself – and one must never scorn gifts from the gods. In the absence of anyone else to tell, they shared their news with the grizzled waiter, who threw his arms joyfully into the air, shook Rikki's hand, kissed Kate soundly on both cheeks, and brought them a glass each of pink Prosecco.

They'd been married that summer. In his wedding speech,

Rikki had described how they had met, vowing that this would be the first and only time they would appear against each other in court. 'From now on, we're on the same side, and in any case, we intend to do all our arguing at home,' he quipped. Everyone laughed. Everyone agreed that they were the perfect couple.

It hadn't all been plain sailing. Giving up her single, independent life to move in with Rikki while they searched for a place to buy together had been oddly unsettling. She remembered a moment almost of panic when she realised that this was it: that she couldn't escape, that she couldn't walk out and do as she pleased, even for a day, without explanation. Kate shook her head, dispelling the memory. She'd simply felt swamped by the sheer chaotic volume of his possessions – piles of yellowing magazines, scrolls of posters dotted with Blu-tack from his university days, tennis rackets with broken strings that he couldn't bring himself to throw away, perished football boots held together by the solidified mud of yesteryear which he 'might need one day'. As soon as they had moved together into this flat the anxiety had vanished.

People talked such nonsense about marriage: that somehow it 'changed' you; that couples inexorably fell into stereotypical gender roles; that romance faded into compromise, and other agony-column drivel. She and Rikki were exactly the same people as before, pursuing their own careers, holding their own bank accounts, seeing their own friends and thinking their own thoughts. They'd even retained their own copies of the same book, which sat side by side on the shelf like Siamese twins. The trick was to insist on a relationship of equals. Occasionally this meant arguing, but sometimes arguing was good. Romance was as much a matter of the mind as of the body. Though the body was good too ... *Where was he?* Kate snapped out of her reverie. The bedside alarm clock showed that it was seven fifteen. Her arms were aching. And the telephone was ringing.

She tried to undo the handcuffs but her fingers had gone numb. As she struggled with the Velcro, the answer machine kicked in. It was Rikki, sounding hassled. 'Hi, it's me. I thought you'd be home by now. Maybe you got held up.' Kate writhed in fury. 'Anyway, I'm running late. See you about eight. Gotta go. Love you.' *Click. Beep.*

Well, great. Finally freed, Kate exercised her fingers and flapped her arms until they tingled with restored circulation. What was she supposed to do for the next forty-five minutes? She blew out the candle (which did not appear to be working – at least not on her), switched on the lights and wandered into the sitting room, absently pinging her suspenders. She rearranged a cushion and straightened the TV on its stand, but basically she'd already tidied up in here. But the kitchen was still a mess from last night's supper and this morning's breakfast. Kate surveyed the pile of dirty crockery in the sink. No time like the present She found the apron that Rikki's mother had given him last Christmas – dark blue with a crown and the words 'His Lordship' stamped in gold – and tied it on over her sexy underwear, then snapped on some rubber gloves. By the time she had washed and dried the dishes and put them away, and cleaned all the surfaces, she had used up twenty minutes. What else could she do? The carpet was looking a bit grubby. When had anyone last cleaned it? She wrestled the unwieldy vacuum cleaner out of the hall cupboard, plugged it in and set to work. If their love-making was so 'adventurous' that they ended up on the floor, at least they would be rolling around on something *clean*. By the time she stowed the vacuum cleaner away, it was ten to eight. Better make sure, this time. Turning on her mobile again, she tapped in a text: How long now? A minute later she had a reply: Just left tube. Back in 5.

Five! She dashed into the bedroom, ran a comb through her hair and gave herself a final shot of perfume. OK: lights, candle – apron! For a panicky moment she couldn't undo the apron string. Oh God! What if Rikki came in now and found her like this? It would be worse than the referee outfit. She plucked furiously at the knot, which finally came undone. She pulled it over her head and stuffed it under the duvet. Help! There was his key in the lock. She closed the bedroom door and did up the handcuffs in record time. Right. This was it. Come and get me.

The front door slammed. 'Kate?' called Rikki. 'Hey, Mrs Impatient, where are you?' His voice was joyous and eager, as if it had been weeks rather than hours since he'd last seen her. A ripple of excitement ran through her body. She wasn't going to answer; let him find her.

A strip of yellow appeared under the bedroom door as he switched on the living-room lights. She heard the jingle of keys, tossed onto the hallway table, and the thud of his briefcase hitting the floor. He was the one who sounded impatient.

Rapid footsteps crossed the floor. The doorknob rattled. Then he flung the door open, propelling her through almost a hundred and eighty degrees so that she had to do a kind of running tiptoe and nearly crashed nose-first into the wall. With his other hand he had switched on the bright overhead light. The next moment he had flipped it off again, and she was dragged backwards, heels helplessly scything through the carpet pile as he swung the door shut. She dangled from the handcuffs, trying to regain her balance as her bottom banged against the back of the door.

For goodness' sake! Why are men so stupid? Kate blew out her breath, wondering what to do next. She was feeling a little foolish. And annoyed. Once again she undid the handcuffs, and after a moment's thought jerked them free of the bracket and stuffed them out of sight under the mattress. She retrieved her kimono from the wardrobe and wrapped it tight, then opened the bedroom door and sauntered into the living room.

'Oh, there you are.' Rikki's face broke into a smile. His black overcoat sparkled with raindrops. Radiating masculine vitality he strode over to her and pulled her into a damp hug. Kate put her arms around him. It was still not too late.

'Guess what?' he said excitedly. 'I have big news.'

'You have big everything.' Kate peeped up seductively through her hair, waiting for him to kiss her.

'No, seriously – listen.' He pushed her away from him and held her by the shoulders. 'Snape wants me to work with him on a case! He's chosen me specially.'

'Oh.' Kate was thrown. Nicholas 'Snape' Fonthill, as he had been dubbed by *Private Eye,* was a very senior and very terrifying QC in Rikki's chambers, whose saturnine looks and icy sarcasm irresistibly evoked the Harry Potter character.

'And guess who we'll be acting for?' Rikki paused dramatically. 'Cassandra Carnaby.'

'*What?*'

For years the marriage between the singer Cass Carnaby and Jeremy Benson, TV megastar, had kept the celeb media afloat on a tide of gossip about wild parties, reckless expenditure, infidelity and whether or not their second child was really his. A while ago it had disintegrated in spectacular fashion when she had thrown a glass of something over him onstage at an awards ceremony. Since then the rumour tom-toms had gone crazy: Jez had changed the locks on all his houses, leaving Cass and their children homeless. She was having an affair with a twenty-four-year-old rock star, and had demanded a fifty-million-pound divorce settlement. He had offered five. On one of the *Starmaker!* talent shows that had made him famous, you could distinctly see the vertical lines scored into his cheek by her fingernails, despite thick make-up. It was something like the tenth most popular YouTube video ever. If they were now going to the High Court to argue a financial settlement, the case would be huge.

'Rikki, that's fantastic,' Kate told him, though she couldn't help feeling a stab of jealousy. Nothing this big had come her way yet.

'Yep. You are looking at a man who is on his way up, baby.' Rikki threw off his coat and collapsed onto the sofa, hands clasped behind his head, looking incredibly pleased with himself. A strange buzzing noise came from under the seat cushion. 'Christ! What's that?' He jerked upright.

Bugger! He'd sat on the battery-operated Love Glove, which she'd hidden under one of the seat cushions. 'It's ... a toy I bought for Sam's baby,' she improvised. Quickly she whipped it out and switched it off. 'You know, a kind of ... vibrating ... octopus.' She stashed it in her briefcase, then sat down next to Rikki, putting her arm through his. 'But why you?' she went on quickly. 'I mean, how come old Snape chose you?'

'Because I'm brilliant, of course.'

Well, yes. Though *she* was the one with the first-class degree and an 'Outstanding' in her Bar exam. Kate nibbled a nail.

'God, I might really be successful,' Rikki burst out. 'I could become a QC – a judge! You'll have to call me "My Lord".' He leaned over her, chuckling. 'Go on, call me "My Lord".'

'Don't be silly.' Kate pushed him away, feeling unaccountably irritable.

His eye fell on her fishnet stockings and high heels. 'Are we going out?' he enquired doubtfully.

'No.' She stood up.

'Hey, what are you doing?'

'I need to get dressed.'

'Think what it could mean for us, Kate.' He grabbed her hand. 'If this case puts me on the map, I could start to make real money. We could move to a bigger flat – maybe a house. We could go on exotic holidays. Even think about having kids.'

Not that again. She stood passively with her hand in his, eyes down, wanting to escape and yet shamed by her feelings. This was Rikki, her husband, whom she loved. It was Valentine's Day, the anniversary of their first meeting. Not that he seemed to have remembered. Upstaged by a bloody court case!

'Speaking of "exotic",' she said brightly, 'what are you cooking us?'

'Oh shit.' Letting her go, he sank his head into his hands. 'I didn't have time to get anything,' he confessed. 'Snape didn't even ask to see me until six, and I couldn't say I had something else to do. I'm afraid your present's going to have to wait another day, too.'

Kate felt a yawning disappointment which she knew was unreasonable. She'd have done the same. In fact, more than once she'd stood him up because of work. 'That's OK,' she said in a dull voice. She headed for the bedroom. As if aware that he'd somehow missed a trick, Rikki followed her and leaned against the door-frame while she made a pretence of looking for something in a drawer.

'Tell you what, we'll go out! Anywhere you like. Bugger the cost.'

'On Valentine's night?' She threw him a sour look. 'Rikki, every single place in London will be booked.'

'Oh … Well, I'll cook you something anyway. What about *oeufs scramblés*?'

'Whatever.'

'OK. Bad idea.' He raised his palms in surrender. 'I know! What about that Thai place you like so much? They do takeaway, and it isn't all that far to walk.'

'It's raining. Really, you don't have to.'

But Rikki was fired with energy now that he'd made a Plan. 'You get yourself all glammed up' – he fluttered his fingers at her – 'and I'll hunter-gather us a banquet. When I get back we'll celebrate.' Mischief danced in his eyes. 'Of course, you don't have to wear any clothes at all.'

Oh, ha ha, thought Kate. To her alarm she saw that Rikki was peering round the door at the metal bracket. 'What's that?' he asked in a puzzled tone.

'That? Oh, you know,' she replied vaguely, 'more hanging space.'

'Ah.' His brow cleared. He strode into the living room and grabbed his coat. 'I'll be back soon,' he promised. 'Oh – and happy Valentine's Day!'

She watched him let himself out. The front door slammed. Kate gave a howl of frustration. Pulling off one of her heels, she hurled it after him.

Chapter 2

❧❧❧

'"To love and to cherish till death us do part." What rubbish! What sanctimonious, hypocritical drivel.' The woman's faded eyes momentarily flashed with fury. 'I looked after that man for *twenty-five* years.' She stabbed the mock-ebony conference table for emphasis. 'I decorated his houses, cooked his meals, brought up his children. I even ironed his underpants! Now he's proposing to dump me on the rubbish heap with barely enough money to feed the cats.'

Kate smiled sympathetically. 'I do understand, Mrs Mitchinson.'

'*Mitchison.*'

'Of course.' Kate flushed at the correction, especially given the watchful presence of Mrs Mitchison's solicitor, a tough-looking cookie in a lime-green suit and chunky gold jewellery. She herself wore black, as always, a rather niftily cut trouser suit that made her feel feminine as well as professional. Her hair was pulled back and twisted up into a clip. The three of them sat on moulded plastic chairs at a large table in one of the smaller conference rooms, located in the basement of Old Court Chambers. At one end of the table stood bottles of still and fizzy water and a stack of plastic cups – together with a box of paper tissues (most clients cried sooner or later). Apart from the table and chairs the basement room was empty. A few nineteenth-century prints hung irrelevantly on the walls. The sole window, heavily barred, provided a view of a stairwell choked with soggy leaves.

Surreptitiously Kate consulted her notes. Harriet Mitchison, aged fifty-three. Husband Martin, aged fifty-five, who provided 'executive coaching for presentational skills in the healthcare industry', whatever that meant. Two daughters, one at university (Chloe) and one on a gap year in Australia (Tara). It was the usual story. Middle-aged man panics as his status and virility slip, encounters firmer-fleshed female who flatters his ego, and does a runner. One couldn't altogether blame him. Harriet Mitchison was at least a stone overweight and wore the dowdy uniform of a Home Counties woman up in town for the day: mid-calf pleated skirt teamed with a checked jacket, court shoes and a lumpy, unfashionable handbag. Kate could confidently predict its contents: a packdown umbrella, two pairs of glasses (one for driving, one for close work), a paperback to read on the train and home-made sandwiches and a water-bottle filled from the kitchen tap to outmanoeuvre London's rapacious restaurateurs. Her hair was dull in both texture and colour – mid-brown streaked with grey – and hung limply in a pudding-basin style. Angry red spots blotched her cheeks, clashing with the traces of carmine-pink lipstick that had lodged in the wrinkles of her mouth. She looked worn, tired, used up.

Mind you, the husband was probably no Romeo. Not like Rikki … Kate felt a qualm of anxiety about yesterday evening. Perhaps she'd been a bit brusque after his return from the takeaway. He had bought far too much food, as usual, and was bouncy to the point of tactlessness, going on and on about his big new case. After dinner she'd pointedly continued working and eventually he'd gone to bed, telling her that he needed a good night's sleep in order to stoke up his energy, now that he'd acquired such a major new client. Rikki had the enviable ability to fall asleep within about ten seconds of his head hitting the pillow, and by the time she slipped in beside him he was deep in dreamland. Cuddling up to his warm body, she regretted her own coolness and even thought about waking him to tell him so. Instead, she planted a soft kiss on his shoulder, then lay awake for an hour or more worrying about her career and her future and whether Rikki would still love her if she wasn't as successful as him.

She dragged her attention back to the present. 'Tell me a little bit about your husband, Mrs Mitchison,' she said.

'He's bald. He can't boil an egg. He stinks out the loo. I hate him.'

'Yes, I do understand.' God! She was repeating herself like a parrot. 'But I was thinking more in terms of his personality. You see, if it comes to a cross-examination—'

'Basically, he's a selfish bastard,' cut in the solicitor. 'Thinks he's God's gift, and that Harriet should be grateful for any old bone he throws at her. Obstinate as a two-year-old. Whines when he doesn't get his way. Emotional blackmail a speciality.'

'Oh, Lexi, you always put everything so well.' Harriet Mitchison's admiring tone suggested that, if was up to her, she would dispense with Kate's services altogether.

Well, tough. That wasn't the way the legal profession worked. Solicitors could deal with many legal problems, but when it came to a dispute that could be resolved only by a judge in court, they had to hand over the problem to a barrister – like Kate. She was the one trained in advocacy, who knew how to put a favourable spin on her case while picking holes in the opposition's, whose cross-examination skills could make someone look good or bad, who was familiar with the quirks of the judges and could tailor her submissions accordingly. She had spent the last six years fighting her way up, and she was good at what she did. But it was impossible for a client to hire a barrister directly – not in family law, anyway. Complex and enraging as the system appeared to outsiders, you had to hire a solicitor first, who would in turn 'instruct' a barrister, if required. The relationship between the two was close but tricky. Solicitors couldn't solve their clients' problems without barristers. But without solicitors to feed them work, barristers would starve.

Lexi (Alexis) Kaufman was a potential goldmine, whom Kate had schmoozed at the lavish party hosted by Lexi's firm in Somerset House last Christmas. Their actual offices were in Weybridge, strategically placed amid the leafy suburbs and gated communities of Surrey, which provided rich pickings. Lexi was adept at hoovering up discontented or cast-off husbands and wives, and could disgorge them into the lap of any barrister who won her favour. Over mulled wine and mini mince pies she had been unabashed in explaining to Kate how she had joined five local reading groups and several up-market gyms and country clubs in order to stalk her prey. Discussion of almost any novel, she maintained, could be steered into a discussion of marriage in general and then, with the aid of cold white wine (women) or beer (men), a litany of complaints about marriage partners. Similarly, an unfit, middle-aged man sweating on the pec press had very likely just found himself a new woman, and it was amazing how many women, relaxing with their fellow-sufferers after an hour of ashtanga yoga, smoothie or hot chocolate in hand, yielded their innermost secrets. Lexi always had her business card to hand – 'just in case'. It all seemed a bit vulture-like to Kate, but she could see how women might find Lexi's 'let's get the bastard' approach empowering, and how men would appreciate her tough-talking while ogling her cleavage. She certainly made a dynamic contrast to poor Harriet Mitchison, though the age difference was probably narrow.

Determined to wrest attention back to herself, and show Lexi that she was on top of the brief, Kate patiently began to lead Harriet Mitchison through the details of her marriage. The couple had met and fallen in love at art school. He had trained as a designer before moving into marketing, and she had become an art teacher in a secondary school. Initially, their earnings had been similar, but she had given up her job after the birth of their first child. Thereafter, the husband's job had involved relocating several times from city to city as he was promoted, with the wife each time sorting out schools and domestic arrangements. 'You see, I thought it was a partnership,' Mrs Mitchison said bitterly. 'I took care of everything to do with the house, paid the bills, got the cars serviced, went to parents' evenings, leaving him free to concentrate on his work. In fact, it was me who typed out his so-called motivational speeches half the time. He said that word-processing interfered with his higher brain functions.' She scowled. 'Nothing seems to have interfered with his lower functions.'

'Ah, yes. I see you have petitioned for divorce on the grounds of adultery with a named co-respondent, Miss Desborough—'

'Miss Desperate, I call her. Some kind of marketing assistant. They met at a conference last summer while I was getting

Tara through her A-levels. She's probably not much older than you are.' To Kate's consternation, Mrs Mitchison was giving her a brooding, critical look, as if she were the one who'd run off with Old Baldy. 'If he marries her, I'm going to take back my maiden name.'

'Good idea,' Kate said ingratiatingly.

'I suppose you've kept yours, have you?' Mrs Mitchison nodded towards Kate's wedding ring. 'Career woman and all that?'

'Well, yes, as a matter of fact I have. But of course things are very different these days.'

'Oh, are they indeed?'

Kate glanced nervously at Lexi, and ploughed on. 'As I understand it, your husband is not contesting the divorce, but he finds your financial demands excessive. He has made you what he considers to be a reasonable opening offer.'

'Reasonable! He's offered me half the value of the house and four per cent of his salary until he retires. *Four!* How am I supposed to live on that for the rest of my life? He has at least three pensions, plus a large sum he inherited ten years ago, which I find he's stashed in a separate bank account and intends to keep all to himself. "For richer, for poorer" – just so long as he's richer and I'm poorer.'

'And you yourself have no pension, is that right? No funds of your own, or means of support?' Kate was ticking off items on a checklist in front of her.

'No, I haven't. I've been *his* means of support for all these years.'

'You haven't, for example, taken employment outside the home?' The euphemism slid easily off her tongue.

'Have you been listening?' The woman glared at her. 'How on earth could I have managed a job when I had my husband

and the girls to look after, and kept having to pack up and move every couple of years?'

'I quite understand, Mrs Mitchison. But you must appreciate that these are the kind of questions our opponents will ask you in court. It's never pleasant, which is why litigation is the last resort. You need to be certain that this is the route you want to go down.'

'Well, I do if you're going to get me the money I'm entitled to.'

'There's no strict entitlement, I'm afraid. I can only present the facts in the most favourable light – and of course your husband's barrister will be doing the same. The judge will evaluate both arguments and come to a decision which is binding on both parties.' Kate smiled to soften the blow, but this seemed to enrage Mrs Mitchison further.

'Do you have children?' she demanded abruptly.

Annoyed and taken aback, Kate shook her head, hoping to quell further enquiry.

'Well, you wait. All that equality malarkey goes right out the window. It's you that has the baby, you who breastfeeds it, you who stays at home when the children are ill because he is *far too important.*'

'I'm quite sure I'll be able to make that point to the judge,' Kate said stiffly. 'What the opposing barrister may question, however, is why you couldn't take a part-time job once your children were at school. Or indeed why you can't find some employment now, since you're separated from your husband and your children have left home.'

Mrs Mitchison gasped with outrage, as if she had been shown some especially offensive pornography. 'Oh, this is so humiliating.' Mrs Mitchison turned pathetically to Lexi. 'Why have I got to defend every detail of my life? She doesn't know how it feels when your husband sets your worth at four per cent of his own. He says I can get a job stacking shelves in a superma-ar-ar-ket.' She dissolved into hiccupping tears.

Lexi handed her the box of tissues with sisterly sympathy. 'I don't think this conference is going the way we want it to,' she said coldly to Kate. 'My client is experiencing considerable emotional distress, and it's important that she feels properly supported.' She stood up. 'Come on, Harriet.'

'But ...' Kate was aghast. What had she said? Surely they weren't going to walk out on her?

'I'll be in touch.' Lexi led her still-sniffling client out. Kate followed them up the stairs and into the reception area, dismayed at this turn of events and conscious of curious stares as they passed the clerks' office. In a final, desperate act to redeem herself she darted ahead to open the outer door. Mrs Mitchison paused to face her, red-eyed, as she was leaving.

'Don't think you're immune, with your nice job and your smart little suit. I was young and pretty like you once, and one day you'll be fifty-three like me. Well, I've been dumped, and now I'm dumping you.'

Kate stood in the doorway watching the two women walk away arm in arm. She wanted to shout after them that she would never look as frumpy as Mrs Mitchison, even if she lived to a hundred and ten – that Rikki would never leave her – that she would always be able to earn her own living, thank you very much. But doubt had lodged in her mind. She felt shaken. The heavy door slipped from her fingers and slammed resoundingly shut.

Chapter 3

ꪖ ꪎ ꪖ ꪎ

'Forget the old bag,' Rikki told her, changing down into second gear as they approached yet another motorway tailback. 'She was probably just jealous of you because you're young and beautiful, and have your whole life ahead of you while hers is kaput.'

Beautiful. Did he really think so? Kate covertly checked herself out in the wing mirror. Did she look a bit silly in the tweed cap bought specially for their weekend in the country? Maybe it would be better to save it for when she actually had to go outside. Removing it, she fluffed out her hair, dragged a heavy blonde lock across one eye and gave her reflection a smouldering look.

'I expect Cass Carnaby will be the same,' he added.

The smoulder turned to a scowl as she twisted round to face him. 'What – beautiful?'

'No,' he laughed. 'Bitter and twisted. Out for revenge. Divorce is always first and foremost about thwarting the other party.'

'Just like marriage, then,' she said teasingly.

'No. Not like marriage.' He reached for her hand. 'At least,

27

not like ours. Have I ever stopped you from doing anything that you wanted, or made you do things you didn't?'

A list began to scroll through her mind, like a computer scanning documents. The ordeal of Sunday lunch at his parents; watching football when there was a chick flick on another channel; delaying her shower because he'd locked himself in the bathroom for a ten-minute crap (what did men *do* in there?); the way he said, 'There's no bread,' meaning she should buy some, and, 'This needs to go to the dry cleaners,' as if the garment in question might walk there on its own little feet; his hurt look when she told him it was cheese on toast for supper because neither of them had been food shopping; the fact that, even when he did go to the supermarket, it always had to be an Event. Rikki couldn't just buy the food and put it away, as she did. First, the front door would crash open dramatically: 'Kate, I'm back!' This was the signal for her to drop whatever she was doing and rush to meet him, so that she was in time to witness him carrying fistfuls of shopping into the flat, huffing and puffing as if he were dragging a freshly killed two-ton bison into their cave. Next, she would have to compliment him on each item as he drew it triumphantly from the bag. 'Butter – brilliant! ... Washing-up liquid – well remembered, Rikki!' Halfway through, he would give up. 'Right, I'm exhausted. You can unpack the rest.'

The image she had conjured up made her smile. 'Not really,' she said in answer to his question.

'I doubt if there's another husband in England who's less demanding or better-tempered than me,' he said, complacently gazing ahead at the traffic.

Suddenly she loved him so much that she raised his hand to her lips and kissed it.

28

He grinned. 'I hope there's a nice, big bed for us at this new pile of theirs.'

'You know Sam and Michael. They're bound to have everything.'

ᏩᎤ

The house was even grander than they expected, approached through a pillared gateway with rampant stone lions and a driveway that curved round a lawn dominated by a magnificent cedar of Lebanon. In awed silence they clocked the golden stone, the sash windows, a porch in the shape of a scallop shell over the front door, and a generous sprinkling of outbuildings. It all seemed terribly grown-up.

They had arrived very late, since their satnav had abandoned them in the middle of a muddy lane with the announcement that 'You have now arrived at your destination.' There was no mobile signal, and Rikki refused to ask for directions until they'd been driving round in circles for twenty minutes and Kate had stopped speaking to him. One yokel on a tractor advised them to 'turn left just before where the old cement factory used to be'; another reckoned it was 'over t'other side o' Long Barrow'. By sheer luck Kate spotted the words 'Manor Farm' chiselled into one of the entrance pillars, just as they whizzed past.

'Relax, darlings,' called Sam as she came out to greet them, still steaming with frustration and fury, in the gravelled parking area. 'You're in the country now.'

Oops, Kate had just plunged one of her new suede boots into a muddy puddle. As she bent down to inspect it, a black labrador accompanying Sam sniffed her bottom with interest. 'It's lovely to be here,' she said, hugging her old friend.

And once they were inside, sitting in the vast kitchen at a table spread with food and drink, chatting at top volume, it was rather lovely. She'd been friends with Sam since they'd found themselves on the same corridor in their first term at university: Kate determined to study hard and get a first, Sam equally determined to have a good time and study as little as possible. A little dynamo of five foot nothing, with a fringe of dark hair falling into her eyes like a wild pony's forelock, and the naughtiest smile Kate had ever seen, Sam had undermined Kate's best intentions from Day One, turning their first night into a party with vodka and home-made brownies. Sam was everything Kate was not: outgoing, boarding-school educated, free with her money (and of course she had more to be free with), secure in her stable family background with two parents still married, four siblings and a childhood with dogs and ponies in a ramshackle house in Oxfordshire. Kate found her *joie de vivre* irresistible. Under Sam's influence, Kate began to relax. It was Sam who had persuaded her that she would not turn into a raging alcoholic if she had the odd drink, and Sam dragged her along to the university drama group, where Kate had discovered, to her great surprise, that she enjoyed performing in public. Their high point was a sell-out production of *Chicago*, with Sam playing Roxie to Kate's Velma. Since then, there were few secrets they had not shared, including Kate's ambition to become a QC and Sam's determination to find a rich man to marry, have lots of children, 'and never be stuck in a sodding job'. Five years ago she had triumphantly become Mrs Bunyan, having tied the knot at an extravaganza of a wedding, at which Kate was a bridesmaid and the ring had been delivered by an owl specially trained to fly down the church aisle and land on the best man's forearm (suitably protected by a falconer's glove).

Kate was not so sure about Michael, an Old Etonian who did something fiendish and very lucrative in the City when he wasn't flying off to Dubai or Hong Kong. On those occasions on which they had met before, she had never quite got on his wavelength. Although tall and good-looking, with an old-fashioned air of courtesy, there was something unnerving about his perpetual, slightly superior smile, as if other human beings were an amusing species not related to himself. Possibly this was down to the age difference, since he was in his late thirties, getting on for ten years older than they were; but he was a very good host, kept the wine flowing, and after lunch helped to lug their bags in from the car and up to a bedroom that was very nearly the square footage of Kate and Rikki's entire flat. There was a king-sized four-poster bed, hung with shot-silk curtains. 'Bliss,' murmured Kate. If anything needed patching up between her and Rikki, this looked like the perfect place.

Sam had gone to check on the baby, who'd been asleep during lunch, and by the sounds of things had now woken up. Kate rummaged in her suitcase for the present she had brought, an unbelievably naff-looking but surprisingly expensive plastic toy, which, so the sales assistant had assured her, was ideal for a six-month-old.

'What's its name?' Rikki stage-whispered.

'Milton.' Then, as his eyebrows rose incredulously, 'Shush. They like it.'

A peculiar crooning noise approached down the long corridor. 'Who's a gorgeous boy, then? Who's Mummy's Milty-wilty-woodle? Look, here's Katey-watey, come specially to see you.'

'Oh, Sam, isn't he adorable?' Kate gushed, mainly in response to her friend's expression of pride and beatific joy. The baby itself looked much like any other baby: a lumpy, tightly packed parcel with a Tintin quiff and the round, unblinking eyes of an alien being.

'Do you want to hold him?'

'Well, I, er ...' The next second, Milton's present was withdrawn from her hands and substituted by the baby himself. He felt hot and solid and exuded a sweet, unfamiliar smell. She held him awkwardly while he gazed implacably into her face. 'Hello, Milton,' she said in a village-idiot tone. His face crumpled. Huge tears welled in his eyes. He began to wail. 'Oh dear. Better hand him back.' Kate tried to make a joke of it, but she felt a failure. To redirect attention, she pointed at her gift instead. 'It's supposed to be good for his motoring skills,' she told Sam.

Sam and Rikki burst out laughing at her mistake. 'I doubt that this little guy's going to be driving for a while,' said Rikki, stroking the baby's cheek with the back of his finger. Milty-wilty gave him the same stare to which Kate had been subjected and then broke into a huge, toothless, irresistible smile.

'Oh, Kate, you are hopeless,' Sam told her fondly. 'Comes of being an only child, I suppose.'

'What about that other toy?' Rikki asked Kate. 'You know, the vibrating—'

Cutting across him, Kate put a hand on Sam's arm. 'What about giving us that tour you promised?'

◦◦

It took almost an hour to view the entire property, with running commentaries by Sam and Michael about what they had done so far and the improvements they planned. There was the attic that would become a children's playroom, the suite of rooms destined for a nanny, the boot room, the laundry room, the workshop, the walk-in larder, bedrooms galore, spanking-new bathrooms and wet rooms. 'Wow ... fabulous ... amazing!' chorused Rikki and Kate, privately exchanging raised-eyebrow glances.

Michael must be even more stinking rich than they had thought. Outside was a coach house that would become Michael's home office upstairs and a private gym downstairs. A swimming pool was shortly to be installed in one of the old farmyards, with showers and changing facilities in the former game larder. One of the walled gardens had already been laid out as a vast *potager* ('veg garden', Sam translated for her guests), complete with miniature box hedging and decorative iron benches from which, presumably, one could view the gardening staff at work. 'Just think, Kate!' Sam pointed to some leafy patches amid the mud. 'Tonight we'll be eating our own home-grown organic leeks and purple-sprouting broccoli.'

'Great. I'll help you cook,' offered Kate – not without some effort, but reckoning that Sam must be exhausted by the baby, and that even peeling potatoes together would be fun.

'Don't be daft. I'm having it catered. We've invited some local friends round as well. You'll love them.'

৩৩

'... and that was the last fox he ever saw. Had to put him down, poor old fellow. Knees completely buggered.'

'Oh dear,' said Kate. There was a silence while she dredged desperately for something to say to this man. He probably wasn't all that much older than her, but with his talk of hunting, the perils of parapet roofs on old houses and family skiing holidays he seemed from a different generation. She'd spent ten minutes trying to find out what he did before realising that the answer was nothing much. Some dabbling in antiques ('a bit slow at present') and intermittent trips to London to 'sort out' a couple of flats he owned which were rented out to tenants. Slowly it dawned on her that he lived on inherited wealth. The concept of money simply trickling into one's bank account, year after year, was new to her. What would it feel like not to have to work?

Accustomed to the cut-and-thrust of London dinner-parties – well, supper with friends, really – where everyone talked across each other, casually picking grapes from the communal fruit bowl while they argued passionately about films, books, politics, whether bicycle lanes were a good thing or Amy Winehouse a genius, Kate felt at odds with the present company. Not a single person had asked her about her recent triumphs in court. The dinner itself, though cooked to perfection by a tremendously posh woman of about forty-five called Anastasia, seemed over-elaborate and formal. So far there had been four courses, not including pre-dinner nibbles and a palate-clearing sorbet, and dessert was still to come. Or desert, she thought as the silence lengthened. She wondered if she might join in one of the other conversations. Rikki was in full flow at the far end of the table, with one of the female guests hanging on his every word, flushed with laughter and obvious attraction. Well, OK, she was used to that. What about Sam? She was looking very animated, nose to nose with another woman, but when Kate tuned in she discovered that they were talking about local nursery schools.

'Have some more wine,' a voice murmured in her ear, 'and

tell me what you've been getting up to in court these days.'

She turned gratefully to Michael, sitting on her other side, and began telling him about one of the High Court judges who liked to play online chess on his laptop during hearings, and had once been subliminally tricked into ruling in her favour when she used the word 'checkmate' in her summing-up. Michael appeared to be just as amused by her company as Rikki's dinner partner was by his.

'I suppose you've heard the old joke about the two solicitors who arrive at the Gates of Heaven?' Usually Kate was not very good at telling jokes, but Michael encouraged her to continue. 'Well, they're rather surprised to be there, obviously, but before they go in one of them says to St Peter, "I just want to make sure that we won't find any barristers in here." St Peter reassures them that they have nothing to fear. So they go in, and a little later they come across an old man with a long beard and a wig, wandering about with a set of law reports under his arm. "I thought you said there were no barristers in here," they say to St Peter, rather annoyed. "That's right." So the solicitors describe the old man. "Oh, that's God – he just *thinks* he's a barrister."'

Michael burst out laughing, making Kate feel that she'd scored a success. He complimented her on her dress, telling her that very few women carry off that particular shade of red. At one point she caught Sam's eye and read her pleasure and relief that her old friend and her husband were getting on so well. After that she tried even harder, while Michael steadily refilled her glass, and even heard herself enthusiastically inviting him over for supper one evening if he was at a loose end in London.

'I'd love that,' he said, in a deep, conspiratorial tone that made her feel slightly uncomfortable. Then, unmistakably, his hand grasped her thigh under the table and squeezed it meaningfully.

She froze, not daring to shove his hand away or to say anything that might alert Sam. The wine she'd drunk rose in her gorge and scalded the back of her throat. She stood up abruptly, saw faces turn to her in surprise. 'Shall I help clear the plates?'

Sam smiled at her. 'Nice offer, Kate darling. But let Anastasia do it. She's being paid for it, after all.' Everybody laughed.

It was a relief when all the goodbyes had finally been said, and she and Rikki went upstairs and closed the bedroom door behind them. 'God, I'm exhausted,' she said, kicking off her shoes. 'Can you unzip me?'

He did so, then lifted the weight of her hair to kiss the back of her neck. The pleasure of it made her smile. She wouldn't tell him about Michael's pass, she decided. He might be upset; Rikki had an unpredictable temper. Probably Michael had been a little drunk. Maybe it hadn't been a pass at all, just a friendly pat. Besides, Sam was one of her favourite people, so it was important that the four of them got on.

'Ooh, linen sheets!' she exclaimed as she slid naked into bed. She could hear Rikki brushing his teeth in the ensuite bathroom, then gargling mouthwash.

He sauntered naked into the bedroom, looking like a Greek god stripped for a race. 'Funny old evening. The woman next to me talked virtually non-stop about some flash new country club that's opened up around here. Kept talking about "pampering".'

'Yeah, Sam said something about going there for lunch tomorrow.' Kate yawned. 'Anyway, I got a fox-hunting bore.'

Rikki climbed into bed and drew her into the crook of his arm.

'Budge over,' he said. 'You're hogging the warm bit.'

'It's *my* warm bit.'

'Not now it isn't.'

They tussled playfully under the duvet until Rikki rolled on top of her and stopped her giggles with a long kiss. Kate felt his hands begin to explore her body, and she grabbed him eagerly. Suddenly she wasn't feeling tired any more ... Her eyelids fluttered shut.

'*Waaaaaaaah!*' They snapped open again.

'Christ! What was that?' asked Rikki.

'That bloody baby.'

'Maybe it'll go back to sleep again.'

'*Waaaaaaaah!*' Another shriek, even more penetrating than the last, shattered the momentary silence. Then another. And another.

Rikki rolled off her. 'Milton, thou shouldst be sleeping at this hour,' he murmured. The two of them lay side by side, listening tensely to the sounds of doors opening, footsteps running up and down the hall, cupboard doors banging. A bright strip appeared under the bedroom door as lights were switched on. Amid the hubbub Kate recognised Sam's voice raised in alarm. 'I'd better go and see what's happening,' she said.

'You don't need to interfere.' Rikki grasped her hand. 'I'm sure she knows what to do.' But Kate was already out of bed. Noise, particularly crying, always made her anxious.

A wild-eyed Sam, baby straining rigidly against one shoulder, confronted her in the corridor. 'I don't know what's wrong with him,' she told Kate fearfully. 'He's been fed. I've changed his nappy. He hasn't got a rash.'

'Poor little thing,' said Kate, gingerly touching the puce-faced monster, who was emitting cries of quite astonishing volume. 'He's awfully hot, isn't he?'

Her casual words had an electrifying effect. Sam's eyes and

mouth flew wide with horror, as if Kate had just told her the baby had one minute to live. 'Michael! *Michael!* Where's the Calpol? Please can you fetch it now? *Now!*'

It took another half an hour of sympathy, standing around, opening and closing childproof bottle-tops, and jiggling the baby before Kate felt that matters were sufficiently under control for her to leave Sam and return to her own room. Needless to say, Rikki was sound asleep.

∾

'I hope this little chap didn't keep you awake last night?' Michael gestured towards a face surrounded by a baby suit in the carrier on his back. The two men had just left the house, wrapped up against the cold wind in coats, scarves, gloves, hats and wellington boots, and Michael was carefully climbing over a stile that led directly from their garden. Rikki looked askance at the ploughed field on the other side. There was no sign of a path. The sky was grey overhead. Their large black lab ran back and forth, waggling his tail with disgusting energy.

'Er, no, don't worry, thank you,' he mumbled, not knowing what to say. He could never understand the English compulsion to leave a warm house no matter the weather, but he had accepted Michael's invitation, feeling that it would be rude to refuse. In reality he would have much preferred to have gone with Kate and Sam to the nearby country club for a swim and a sauna. He didn't really know what to say to Michael.

'I expect you were otherwise engaged,' Michael suggested roguishly. This innuendo reduced Rikki to complete inarticulacy, and he could only manage a grunt. What could you say in response to such a remark? For the umpteenth time since they arrived he felt awkwardly metropolitan, out of place in this environment of Agas and Barbours.

'You don't mind the cold?' Michael looked at him with apparent concern. 'I mean, I expect it's a lot warmer where you come from.'

Oh God, thought Rikki, that one again. He decided to play it straight. 'Hammersmith can be pretty cold in winter, you know.'

Michael laughed. 'You know what I mean.'

What did he mean? It was the same old thing: Rikki looked 'foreign'. It was true that he had an Iranian mother, and that his parents had lived in Tehran before the Revolution. But Rikki was born in Charing Cross Hospital, and had never been further east than Cairo. He had found Egypt just as hot as any other Englishman would. But he knew from experience that it was no good saying that sort of thing to Michael; he was incapable of absorbing the concept.

Fearing that he was in danger of becoming curmudgeonly, Rikki attempted what he hoped was a safe conversational gambit.

'So, erm, how long have you lived in the country?'

'Almost six months now. Never looked back. Can't think why we didn't come here earlier.'

'And do you commute every day?'

'Bloody hell, no. I've got a pied à terre in London. I stay there in the week and come back here at weekends. So I get away from this little monster and catch up on my beauty sleep. Suits us both.'

'Ah.'

'We must meet up for a boys' night out one evening.'

'Yes.' Rikki tried to sound enthusiastic.

Michael adopted a knowing grin. 'Girls do their thing; we do ours, eh?' Rikki thought of Kate luxuriating in a hot tub and wished that he was a girl.

They trudged across the sticky mud. Rikki's boots felt heavier with every tread. 'It's only about three miles,' Michael said reassuringly. They passed out of one field and into another almost identical. 'Do you see that tree in the distance? Once we're there, we're almost there, if you see what I mean.'

He broke off to call the dog, which had bounded ahead and disappeared. This continued for about five minutes, with plenty of shouting. The baby watched stolidly from the carrier, its cheeks now ruddy from the cold air. Rikki experimented with a smile. The child stared back at him, impassive. Suddenly something shot past them from behind, spattering Rikki with mud as he passed. 'Good boy,' crooned Michael, bending to rub the dog's belly like an over-attentive masseur.

They resumed walking. Michael had begun to talk about his work, and was banging on about the 'financial illiteracy' of those who complained about bankers' pay packages. 'What these people don't appreciate,' he said, gesturing expansively in each direction as if to indicate deferential peasants toiling in the fields, 'is that talent goes where the money is. If you try to cut bonuses, or raise taxes, the best people will just go somewhere else, simple as that.'

Rikki decided to be provocative. 'This talent you're taking about,' he responded, 'is that the same talent that brought the banks to their knees, and required all the rest of us to bail them out? Or is that some other talent?'

Michael looked at him, amused. 'I can see that you don't understand high finance,' he said indulgently.

Rikki muttered assent. They continued in silence for a while, before Michael opened the conversation again. 'Kate was telling me a bit about your line of work last night,' he confided. 'I wondered what it must be like to be in the same game as your wife. I suppose that it could be a bit of a problem?'

'How so?'

'I mean, when one of you is more successful than the other. I'd hate to be in competition with Sam.' He rolled his eyes in mock horror, inviting Rikki's complicity.

'The issue hasn't arisen.'

'Really? I'm surprised.'

They lapsed into silence. To Rikki's relief, Michael opened a gate out of the field onto a relatively mud-free lane. The dog disappeared again and there was a lot more shouting. Eventually they started off. Rikki tried desperately to think of something to say, but his mind had seized up.

'We're doing bloody well in the cricket,' Michael said suddenly. 'Carry on like this and we'll absolutely slaughter the Pakis – oh, sorry, Rikki, I wasn't thinking.'

Rikki groaned inwardly. How much longer?

೧೦

'God, Sam, this is utter heaven.'

Kate was lying at one end of an enormous bath, up to her neck in warm, scented water. Through half-closed eyes she could see Sam looking equally contented at the opposite end. Soothing music played in their small, private 'Relax Room', whose floor-to-ceiling window offered a view onto a peaceful garden, stylishly designed with clipped lollipop trees and terraces where you could sit in summer. Her body was smooth and blissfully relaxed after a full-body massage with some kind of special essential oils. The therapist had talked incomprehensibly about 'working on your meridians' and 'increasing the flow of chi in your body energy channels', and promised that the Soaking Tub would aid detoxification, purification and various other -ations, but early on Kate's brain had switched off. All she could say was that she felt fabulous.

'Mmm ... That's why Michael and I wanted to buy a house nearby.' Sam sounded half asleep. 'Great food ... swimming pools ... tennis courts ... uh ...'

'Private cinema,' Kate reminded her, having been shown round the club before they clocked in for their treatments. 'Crèche.'

Sam's legs stirred under the water. 'I hope Michael doesn't let Milty lose his bootees. It's as cold as a witch's tit today.'

Kate felt a tiny flicker of irritation. On her own, Sam was just as much fun as she'd always been. But when the baby was around, it was as if her brain had undergone a seismic shift. This morning, a perfectly straightforward question like 'What's the time?' elicited the answer 'Don't worry, he's not due another feed for two hours.' At breakfast she had cut Kate's toast into soldiers.

'What's it like, having a baby?' she asked idly.

She'd meant *living* with a baby, not giving birth, but before she could clarify this Sam had embarked on a vivid, blow-by-blow account. '... insides *ripped* out ... screaming so hard I couldn't breathe in the gas and air ... all this *gunge* leaking out ... absolutely *begging* Michael to shoot me in the head ... sadistic doctor, blood *dripping* from his hands ... never walk again ... *agony* going to the loo.' Kate must have tuned out through sheer self-preservation, for the next thing she heard was, '... most marvellous moment of my entire life.'

Huh?

'I just totally fell in love,' Sam continued complacently. 'Honestly, Kate, you should try it. Rikki would make a brilliant father.'

Kate waited for her to say that she, Kate, would make a brilliant mother, and felt mildly put out when she didn't. 'I couldn't possibly have a baby at this point in my career,' she said briskly. 'Do you have any idea how difficult it's been to get even this far as a barrister?' Without waiting for a reply she began to list all the hurdles that had to be cleared, and the statistics of success. '... preferably a first, preferably from Oxbridge ... Bar exam, at least a "Very Competent" ... one-in-six chance ... *incredible* competition for pupillage ... unless you're *very* clever, of course ... tenancy like absolute *gold dust*. And at the end of all that,' she concluded, 'you're self-employed, with no salary or pension or maternity leave, scrabbling for the juicy briefs. *Cases*,' she amended, catching Sam's lascivious grin.

'But surely Rikki could earn the money for a bit,' Sam suggested, after a pause. 'Just while you're having babies, I mean. When you're ready. If you want to.'

'But I like my job,' Kate protested. 'I love being in court. I want to earn my own money, not be dependent.'

'Like me, you mean.' Sam was giving her a wry look.

'Gosh, no! I didn't – that is, I—'

'Don't worry, darling. I'll never have your brains in a million years. Mind you, I can do *this*.' She heaved one blue-veined breast out of the water, placed a finger on the enlarged nipple as if cocking a gun, and sent an arc of breast-milk spurting ten feet across the room.

'Sam, that's disgusting!'

'Yeah. But awesome.' She slid back down into the bath. 'Quite honestly, I'm thrilled to be a kept woman.'

43

'But don't you miss Michael when he's away in London?'

'Of course I do. But it works for us. He's happy doing deals and meeting his "contacts", whoever they are. Men like that stuff. It makes them feel important.'

Kate remembered Michael's hot hand on her thigh last night, and felt a twinge of anxiety.

'Plus it means I can get on the sofa with Milty and the dogs and watch crap television, without him tut-tutting. It's a win-win situation.' Sam grinned. 'Shall we turn on the water jets?'

While getting dressed Kate reflected on their conversation, weighing up the facts as if summing up a case. Her lovely, madcap friend was turning into a yummy mummy. Consider the evidence, My Lord: Mini-Boden catalogues on the coffee-table, a shiny new four-wheel drive with top-of-the-range child seat; girlfriends who debated the merits of nursery schools. Judgment concluded.

As for herself, she could not hear even the whisper of a ticking biological clock, and didn't intend to listen. She was already looking forward to getting back into court next week and nailing her opponents. A baby would just get in the way.

Despite Kate's protests, Sam insisted on paying for both their treatments – which was just as well given the prices that were discreetly listed in a leaflet Kate picked up in the luxurious waiting area. She was hanging around said luxurious waiting area while Sam did the credit-card business and booked herself a pedicure for next week, when her glance fell on the cover of a magazine. Her attention sharpened. Wasn't that Cassandra Carnaby? She studied the dark tumble of hair, wide cat's eyes and dazzling white smile. Not a wrinkle in sight. Digital enhancement, no doubt. But the pre-divorce

PR was clearly kicking in already, since instead of depicting Ms Carnaby in some sexy outfit, the photograph showed her wearing a flower-sprigged dress, cuddling two children. CASS CARNABY – 'MY CHILDREN ARE EVERYTHING!' read the shoutline. Oh, puh-leeze.

The image niggled away at her as she and Sam walked up to the main house to meet their husbands. Rikki had told her that he was meeting the Carnaby woman next week. His excitement was palpable – over the case, that is, not the woman, who must be at least forty-five and no doubt looked it in real life. She couldn't help comparing his sudden career-boost with her own failure with Harriet Mitchison. Rikki was going forwards just as she seemed to be going backwards. That was all wrong. *Get a move on, Kate!* First thing on Monday morning she would find a moment for a little chat with the Head Clerk, whose job it was to allocate briefs, and persuade him to steer more work her way.

'There they are,' Sam pointed, as she and Kate entered the entrance hall of the club house. 'Aw, isn't that sweet?'

Kate looked across the room to where Michael and Rikki were standing together in front of a glowing log fire. In one hand Rikki held a beer glass. In the other, casually nestled along his forearm, was the silent, utterly relaxed form of Milty-wilty.

Chapter 4

ᏇᏇᏇ

'Good of you to come,' Fonthill said in a dry monotone, as Rikki shouldered open the panelled mahogany door to the chambers' conference room, bearing a stack of papers up to his chin. 'It is King, isn't it? Only I can't quite make you out behind that lot.'

Nicholas Fonthill, QC gazed coldly up at Rikki from his seat at the head of the conference-room table. His comments were invariably ambiguous; somehow he always managed to sound sarcastic even when making the most routine observation, as he was doing now. After all, Rikki wasn't late. They had arranged to meet here half an hour before Cassandra Carnaby and her solicitor were due to arrive, at ten thirty this morning. Rikki glanced nervously at the clock above Fonthill's head. Ten o'clock precisely. Of course, that was always Fonthill's tactic: to make you feel small. Severus Snape.

'Sit.' Fonthill gestured to a chair beside him, with an imperious flick of the hand. On that side of the conference room three full-height sash windows offered a panoramic view across the garden square below. The interior of the room was in complete contrast to its classical proportions, being decorated in contemporary colours and fitted out with ultra-modern furniture chosen more for its looks than practicality or comfort: pod chairs on steel stalks, curvaceous armchairs with no arms and undulating sofas that caught you nastily in the middle of the back. Rikki lowered the pile of papers onto the smoked-glass surface of the table, etched with the chambers' logo, and sat down. 'Push all that stuff aside, will you?' said Fonthill. 'It's blocking the light.' Standing up again, Rikki divided the stack into several smaller piles and spread them out on the table. In contrast, Fonthill had only a pad of chambers paper and a fountain pen in front of him.

'Let's get down to business,' he said. 'First of all, let me make one thing clear, as we haven't worked together before. I'm the brains in this partnership. I do all the talking. Your job is twofold. First, you're here to look decorative and to make the client happy. If she's happy, then I'll be happy. Second, your duty is to ensure that you have to hand all the documentation I need, when I need it, which is straight away. Got that?'

Rikki swallowed. 'Got it.' This was not at all what he had envisaged.

'Good. This is a big-money case and I don't want any mishaps. So, I assume that you have read the solicitor's brief?'

'Of course.'

'Good. Now, tell me, what do we need to ascertain at this conference?'

'OK … First of all, we need to know what the client wants and what she'll settle for. Issues of custody and access to the two children, both of whom are minors have already been decided. Aged ten and eight, a boy and a girl, they will continue living with their mother. What remains to be settled is the financial settlement. We need to find out how much she knows about her husband's financial affairs, in case he tries to hide anything from us. Of course we'll need an audit.'

'Mmmm ...' grunted Fonthill. 'So far, so obvious. Let's try to be a bit more creative, shall we?' He looked up at the ceiling, as if in search of inspiration. 'Here is a talented, beautiful woman who has chosen to sacrifice her career on the altar of her husband's ... no, perhaps not "on the altar" ... to put aside her own needs and dedicate herself to her husband's career ... a wife and mother ... a companion ... a soulmate ... heartlessly cast aside.'

'I seem to remember that it was she who left him,' Rikki said mildly.

'Details,' snapped Fonthill. 'Perception is all. We're not talking about reality here. All that matters is what happens in that courtroom. Our task will be to portray Mrs, er ... Benson, as a wronged woman, abandoned without means of support, unable even to pay the heating bill.'

'Is that entirely accurate?' asked Rikki. 'Mr Benson seems to have been coughing up rather generously since he lodged the divorce petition. His wife even threw a party to celebrate.' Rikki decided not to mention the celebrity rag from which he'd gleaned this information. Apparently Ms Carnaby had ordered a pastiche wedding cake, with black icing instead of white and a marzipan figurine of a groom lying on top, impaled on a silver toothpick.

'Yes, well, he's just trying to give a good impression, isn't he? We'll find a way to make him look bad. Of course, what's even more important is how she comes across. Her past doesn't matter, so long as she appears suitably humble now. There's nobody the public likes more than a star willing to be ordinary.' He put on a voice: '"She's just like us, i'n't she?"'

he scoffed. 'Let's see, now … hmmm … I wonder what she should wear in court? Something smart but plain, I think.'

Not for the first time, Rikki wondered how much of this was an act, how much Fonthill played up to his cynical, calculating image. It was his manner and his looks as much as his brain that had brought him success. Six foot two, with a cadaverous face, hawkish dark eyes and black hair combed across his scalp from a side parting in a style apparently unchanged since his schooldays, he was an imposing figure. Since he was now in his early fifties, the juniors had opened a book on whether his hair was dyed. He was certainly vain enough, but Rikki reckoned it was real. Quite how the matter was to be settled was still in debate. There'd been a female pupil last year whom Fonthill had seemed rather keen on, judging by the way he puffed out his chest when she was near and gave a wolfish, yellow-toothed smile that was, if anything, more intimidating than his habitual sinister expression. The whole of chambers had speculated that the two were having an affair and hoped she would spill the beans. But either she had eluded the Fonthill Fondle or she had been too smitten to divulge.

'There are not going to be any *children* in court this time, are there?' asked Fonthill. 'I suppose you know that, thanks to the Thought Police, we have been forbidden from wearing court dress in front of the little bleeders in case we give one of them *nightmares*?' Rikki reassured him that neither of the children of the Benson marriage would be present – which, of course, he knew perfectly well.

'Thank God for that. I do so hate *slumming* it.'

A telephone on the wall sounded. Rikki jumped up and answered. 'They're here,' he announced as he replaced the receiver.

Fonthill swung his head round and looked up at the clock. 'Good,' he commented, his voice rising so as almost to indicate enthusiasm. 'Five minutes early. They *are* keen. So, are we ready?'

'Ready when you are,' replied Rikki.

'Ready when you are, *sir*, I think, King.'

'Ready when you are, sir.'

'Have them shown up.'

Fonthill placed his clasped hands behind his head and closed his eyes, shutting out further communication. Rikki rose to his feet and mooched over to the window to quell his nervousness. He always enjoyed gazing out at the square. Mature beech trees spread their branches over a picturesque nineteenth-century wrought-iron bandstand and a delightful miniature rose garden. He noticed that someone was using one of the two tennis courts even at this time of day. In summer Rikki liked to get in early and play a set with one of his colleagues before starting work. There was nothing like bashing a tennis ball for an hour or so to set you up for a long day in the courtroom. He liked working here. Though Fonthill might be the exception, this was in general a progressive chambers, informal and unhierarchical, as its name – Nexus – suggested. The sleek Italian furnishings and contemporary artworks on the walls reinforced the impression of businesslike modernity. Instead of clerks they used 'practice managers' and 'staff', and there was an active policy of recruiting from minorities or non-traditional backgrounds: perhaps another reason why Rikki felt comfortable here. The ethos of Nexus was utterly different from Kate's ramshackle old chambers, which looked as if it had hardly changed in the last few hundred years. He labelled hers 'Jarndyce & Jarndyce', while she branded his 'Ikea'.

As the door opened to usher the visitors in, Fonthill broke into a grimace of welcome. 'Justin, how splendid to see you again,' he greeted the solicitor, a dandyish figure in later middle age, in a voice that was obviously intended to sound friendly.

'And you, Nicholas,' said Jenkins, though without much warmth.

Rikki was curious to meet Justin Jenkins in the flesh. He was famous in matrimonial-law circles, with a reputation as 'the ladies' choice' – the ladies in question being invariably heiresses, celebrities or trophy wives. His route to success had been unconventional. He had never gone to university, and had not even taken up the law until he was thirty, after divorcing his own first wife. Evidently the experience had put fire in his belly. By the time of his second divorce he had qualified as a solicitor and was on his way to acquiring the nickname 'Jackal Jenkins' for his rapacious pursuit of large financial settlements. His mouth smiled, but his eyes did not. Encased in an immaculately tailored pin-striped suit with a silk handkerchief protruding from his breast pocket, he struck Rikki as just a little *too* well dressed and too well manicured to be entirely trustworthy.

But there was no more than a fleeting moment to explore this reaction before his attention was captured by his client, the famous Cassandra Carnaby, standing patiently at the door. He caught his breath. Rikki was familiar with her appearance because she was so often in the papers, or more usually the magazines, but the reality was much more impressive. She looked like a million dollars ... no, make that ten million dollars. Luxuriant black hair, smooth glowing skin, big dark eyes, full red lips ... the curves of her voluptuous body disturbingly evident beneath a slinky dress ... long legs, slim calves and high-heeled shoes. As she sashayed into the room Rikki felt certain that he could hear the rustle of her stockings. Of course he remembered seeing her on *Top of the Pops* back in the last century, while he was still at school. He'd had a bit of a thing about her then. There was that poster of her, surrounded by adoring male dancers, lashing a whip ...

'May I introduce my client?' the solicitor said.

'Mrs Benson ...' Fonthill's smile reached horror-film proportions. 'I am honoured that you've chosen me to look after your interests in this distressing matter.'

Cassandra Carnaby accepted his outstretched hand. 'I'm not distressed about anything except the possibility that I may not get what I'm due,' she said. 'I'm only too pleased to be getting shot of that bastard.' She laughed. 'And please call me Cass. No one's called me "Mrs Benson" since I was last in court,' she chuckled. 'Possession of Class B substances, as I seem to remember.'

'No need to dwell on that,' said Fonthill. 'We have all those details on file, of course.'

'Hmm, yes, I expect that you know all about me,' she said coyly. 'And I know so little about you.'

Was Fonthill blushing? Rikki took a mental snapshot of this moment-to-be-savoured.

'Aren't you going to introduce us to your friend?' asked Cassandra, gesturing towards Rikki.

Fonthill's manner changed abruptly. 'This is Mr King, my *junior*,' he said coldly, emphasising the last word. 'He will be doing all the fetching and carrying.'

Rikki stepped forward awkwardly, first to greet the solicitor, Justin Jenkins, whose glance skimmed over him, and then Cassandra Carnaby, who gripped his hand while she looked straight into his eyes. 'Hello, Mr King,' she said beguilingly. 'I hope you won't mind fetching and carrying for me.'

Rikki stammered a reply. 'Oh, no, of course not. That's what I'm here for.'

'Precisely,' interrupted Fonthill. 'Now, I think we should be seated.' He gestured for the two visitors to sit down on the opposite side of the table to Rikki, so that they had the benefit of the view outside. 'King, would you organise some tea and coffee for our guests?'

∞

Half an hour later, Rikki was still disconcertingly conscious of Cass's presence across the table. Every now and then their eyes met, as they listened while the other two dominated the conversation. At one point she actually winked at him. Even when he was looking away, he couldn't ignore the scent of her perfume. Of course he wasn't attracted to her – he couldn't be attracted to anyone so much older – but he was forced to admit that she was very glamorous. She must have been in her late twenties when he was still in short trousers. How old was she now? Forty? Perhaps even forty-five?

Fonthill had begun by outlining the principles involved. 'It used to be the case that divorce settlements were invariably settled according to need. It was incumbent on the wife to demonstrate her future needs or reasonable requirements. But since the landmark case of *White* v. *White* in 2001, courts have been instructed to assume an equal split of the matrimonial assets on divorce. Since *White* v. *White* judges have been advised to check their views on the distribution of assets against the "yardstick of equality of division". This is not to introduce a presumption of equality in all cases, but "to ensure the absence of discrimination", for instance, between a wage-earner and a childcarer, thereby recognising the non-financial contribution of the parent caring for children.'

'Don't waste the legal mumbo jumbo on me, Mr Fonthill,' interrupted Cass. It's the money I'm interested in. You know, I'm *very* expensive to keep.' She sat back in her chair (apparently a witty modern take on a medieval papal seat), crossed her legs, and swept them all with her irresistible smile.

'Indeed.' To Rikki's glee, Fonthill was disconcerted, and Rikki couldn't help acknowledging this with an eyebrow flash at Cass. 'In cases where the assets are substantial, like this one, it is important to ensure that they are all taken into account. In such big-money cases—'

'Is that what you call them? "Big money."' Cass let out a sensuous sigh. 'Hmm, I like that.'

'Yes, er, well, ahem – in such cases the husband may argue that it is unreasonable to divide the assets equally, arguing that it is sufficient to provide enough for the wife's every reasonable need. The wife may want to argue that she has sacrificed her career and thus her earning power in order to care for the children. She may also argue that she has made an unrecognised contribution to her husband's success.

'Mrs Benson.' Fonthill addressed her directly for the first time since they were introduced. 'Sorry, Cass.' Again he smiled his ghastly grimace. 'Mr Jenkins and I have reviewed the evidence, and I think that we have enough material here to draw up an affidavit. What happens then depends on what is said in your husband's affidavit. Do you have any notion of what his line of argument against you might be?'

'Oh, yes. I am quite sure that he will make me out to be a bad mother, an unfaithful wife, a disloyal companion, wilful, unstable, blah blah blah ...' Rikki immediately felt indignant, but Cass laughed loudly. 'There's plenty of shit he can throw at me. But then there's plenty of shit I can throw at him.'

'The trouble with throwing shit is that you tend to get your hands dirty,' Fonthill observed. 'It's important to show that you are putting the children's interests first. It doesn't make a good impression on the court if the parents are casting aspersions on each other in public.'

'You're right, of course – but what can you do? The press makes most of it up anyway.'

'I suggest that we should see if we can get his PR people to talk to your PR people,' said the solicitor. 'That way we can limit the damage.'

'I think we should talk a little bit about filthy lucre,' said Fonthill, putting on his most oleaginous smile. God, he really is appalling, thought Rikki. He tried not to catch Cass's eye. 'As I understand it, the other party has made a wholly inadequate offer.'

'Damn right he has, the tight bastard.'

'And this offer amounts to – five million pounds?'

'That's right.'

'Tsk, tsk. How much do you feel would be reasonable?'

'I was hoping for a package amounting to fifty mill.'

'Oh, I think that we can do a little better than that,' Fonthill said smoothly.

'Though we must remember that Mr Benson claims that his wealth has been much exaggerated,' Jenkins interjected.

'Surprise, surprise,' Cass replied.

'Do I understand you to suggest that he may not be telling the truth?' enquired Fonthill.

'He never tells the truth about money,' Cass explained. 'It's against his religion.'

'I see … But we must assume he knows that an audit will disclose all his assets?'

'My husband has a way of squirrelling money away – from the tax man, from his business associates and from his frigging family. Your accountants are going to have to be pretty smart to keep up with him. In fact, his biggest asset could be … invisible.'

'I see.' Fonthill was riveted. 'And do you have any idea where this "invisible" asset might be?'

'As a matter of fact,' beamed Cass, 'I do.'

Chapter 5

'... tied the so-called expert witness in knots. Judge found in my favour in about one minute. *God*, I'm brilliant.'

'Bollocks. Dotty Doughface, wasn't it? Mondays are her string-quartet night. She likes to get off early. Probably tossed a coin.'

'Well, *I* didn't even have to go to court. Managed to settle at the eleventh hour. Twenty-grand brief fee and a week off. By tomorrow lunchtime I'll be on the piste at Klosters.'

'Speaking of piste, has anyone else noticed that our new pupilette is suffering from a monumental hangover? ... Oh, sorry, didn't see you there. Pass over the choccy biccies, will you?'

Kate was standing in a throng of her fellow-members of chambers, at the institution known as Chambers Tea (much ridiculed by Rikki, whose own 'office' had abolished this anachronism in favour of Practice Meetings). Every afternoon, those who wished to could gather in the big conference room, under the po-faced gaze of various worthies (all male) whose portraits lined the panelled walls. Anyone from the grandest QC to a terrified university student on a two-day mini-pupillage might turn up. Kate's pompous Head of Chambers liked to claim that it offered a 'collegiate' atmosphere in which members could benefit from the experience of others – pitfalls to be avoided, clever tricks with injunctions, how a particular judge had interpreted a precedent or how to locate an opponent's Achilles heel. In reality it acted as an arena for shameless boasting and a thoroughly enjoyable gossipfest, as members blew off steam after a day in court or hours trawling through paperwork. At least, it was thoroughly enjoyable when you yourself weren't the subject of gossip.

Word had got around (as it always did) that Kate had been chucked by a client at the end of last week: no big deal, but a blot on her so-far excellent record. The best way to handle this was to turn it into an amusing, self-deprecatory story, ideally counterpointed by an account of a success big enough to eclipse the memory of any failure. Fortunately, this morning she'd received a favourable judgment on a complicated case of child abduction that she'd been working on for some time, which had caught the attention of the media – well, in the south-west anyway. Her colleagues frequently blew their trumpets about far less, so she was busily spreading the news. 'Yes, I'm delighted,' she trilled loudly to anyone who would listen. 'Did you see my client on BBC News?' (She didn't say that it was the local news – five minutes of largely human-interest stories about flooding, dustbin collection and unusual gatherings of toads, tacked on to the national headlines.) Kate had invited Lexi to lunch next week, when she would attempt to overcome any lingering awkwardness and rebuild their professional relationship.

Angus McLaren, her former pupil-master and mentor, had been particularly kind, going out of his way to congratulate her publicly on 'a fine piece of work', then drawing her aside to tell her 'not to worry' about Mrs Mitchison. 'These things happen. Best to learn whatever lessons you can and move forward.' But then Angus was of the old school – courteous, civilised and knowledgeable about subjects ranging from Greek philosophy to wildfowl, with an incisive mind that could dissect a case with a surgeon's skill. Almost as valuable as this last asset was his cherubic face, adorned about the ears with white curls, which frequently caused opponents to underestimate him. Though a top QC with a string of land-mark cases to his name, he never jostled for attention, and treated all members with equal respect, regardless of their status. His was the modesty of true success. No one knew anything about his private life, except that he lived on the river somewhere near Kew Gardens with his wife, who had never been seen in chambers but must be a terrible old tartar since the only thing that ruffled his calm, authoritative air were the words 'Mrs McLaren on the line for you, sir.' He himself referred to her as the Dragon.

'Must be off, now,' he told Kate, consulting an old-fashioned pocket-watch which he extracted from his waistcoat, 'or the Dragon will be breathing fire. Some sort of Residents' Association meeting. Presence required – or else.' He pulled one index finger across his throat, gave her a genial smile, and moved away.

Oh bugger, there was Milo Wittering-Coombe sidling towards her, usual smirk in place. There weren't many members of chambers she disliked. In fact, two or three were among her closest friends. But she detested Milo, arse-licker of his superiors and arse-kicker of those junior to him. Kate was neither, being the same age and from the same call year as him – though he seized every opportunity to patronise her.

Unfortunately, he also specialised in family law, overlapping with her in certain areas, and was therefore direct competition. Hoping to avoid him, she moved swiftly over to the window and stood with her back to the room, looking out. But she could see his reflection looming towards her.

'So, Ms Pepper, how's tricks?' he said archly, gazing down at her from his superior, masculine height.

'What do you want, WC?'

'Just coming to offer my humble congratulations.'

'Thank you.'

'And commiserations, of course. Hear you got blown off by a Weepy Wife. Kleenex at dawn.' He gave his hee-haw chuckle.

'And your point is?'

'Oh, nothing. Nothing. Ah, how pleasant this all is.' He let out a deep breath of contentment as he swivelled round to take in the scene. 'Panelled room, civilised *conversazione*, courtyard lit up outside. Takes one back to the days of heady youth, what?'

'What?' she demanded stolidly.

'Cambridge, of course.' He mimed surprise at her obtuseness. 'Port in the Combination Room. Dons scurrying across the quad.' He paused, and allowed his brow to furrow. 'Or were you at Oxford? I can never remember.'

'Neither, as you know perfectly well.' Even though more than ten years had passed, it still rankled that her school had never even considered entering their pupils for Oxbridge and, when she tentatively enquired, told her not to be so silly. Most didn't go to university at all, and Kate was the first member of her family to do so. But she had a lingering desire to know if she might have got in, even though Oxbridge turned out as many idiots as anywhere else. Like WC.

'Oh, yes,' he drawled. 'Somewhere "oop north", wasn't it?'

'Birmingham. Which I believe is almost as far north of Cambridge as Cambridge is of Oxford. Practically in Scotland, really.'

That knocked him off his stride, but only for a moment. He was drawing in breath for another dig when a brazen voice interrupted. 'Hey, Kate, congratulations!' With barely a pause it added, 'Get lost, WC.'

Kate turned with relief to find her friend Hayley at her side, red hair blazing round her strong, determined features. Hayley Ward was her chief ally, moaning mate and some-times advisor in chambers, about five years senior to Kate, who took no shit from anybody. As usual, she was looking amazingly glam in killer heels and a dark suit comprising extremely short skirt and fitted jacket bulging in all the right places, though men who took this as a come-on would be swiftly and pithily advised of their mistake. Hayley dressed to please herself. Moreover, after several trips around the block which she had recounted to Kate in hair-raising detail, she now had a steady partner to whom, so far, she appeared devoted. An outspoken product of a London comp, she was the one who had come up with the wheeze of calling the vile Milo by his unfortunate initials, and clearly terrified the pants off him since he slunk away without a murmur.

'Little creep,' she fumed. 'He wouldn't even be here if his dad wasn't some big-wig in the Bar Standards Board.'

She and Kate exchanged a resigned look. Everyone was wary of the BSB, which could discipline or even disbar bar-risters for professional misconduct, whether it was failure to pay a minor fine, filing late for bankruptcy or having an affair with a client.

On the whole it was better to have WC inside the fold, under an unspoken agreement whereby his discretion regarding minor infringements was delicately balanced against his continuing tenancy.

'Fancy a drink later?' Hayley asked Kate. 'I've still got some bundles to get through, but I should be free about six.'

'Sure. Come by my office when you're ready.'

'Rikki won't mind?'

'God, no. We both do as we please. It's not like he expects some little wifey with dinner in the oven.'

Hayley laughed. 'That'll be the day.'

⁊

The night was clear and starry when the two of them stepped out into the courtyard and began to thread their way, high heels echoing, towards the bar they usually favoured. The Temple often surprised Kate with its beauty. With its elegant buildings, clipped lawns, stately trees and the confident air of an enclosed community it *was* rather like an Oxbridge college, she conceded, though bang in the middle of London, sandwiched between the river and Fleet Street. Because no roads ran through it, and it could be approached only on foot via narrow alleyways, vaulted stone passages or forbiddingly grand gates, many Londoners didn't even know it was there, or didn't dare enter – at least, they hadn't before the wretched Dan Brown brought tourists flocking to the Temple Church. In summer, especially, it was almost impossible to get from chambers to the Hall at lunchtime without being stopped several times and asked inane questions.

At night the Temple was magical, with lamplight glowing from sash windows and old-fashioned lanterns, trees rustling in sudden, swirling gusts from the river and so few intrusions from the modern world that one could almost imagine oneself back in the days of Dickens. With legal reforms nipping at their heels, it was a dying world – and probably rightly so – but she was glad to have witnessed it. She didn't say so to Hayley, though, who would have called her a romantic idiot.

Instead, she allowed Hayley to get a rant off her chest about the virtual impossibility of getting any decent Legal Aid these days, and her frustrations with the bureaucracies that were designed to protect the interests of children but so often did the opposite. This was often heart-breaking work – and the least well paid – dealing with the lives of children torn apart by vengeful mothers and violent fathers, and neglectful or over-intrusive Social Services. Before she started at the Bar, Kate had assumed that she'd be good at this kind of work, since it was partly her experiences as a child that had driven her into the legal profession in the first place. But of course the opposite turned out to be true, and she now specialised in the easier and more lucrative option of divorce work. Kate admired Hayley not only for her fierceness and dash, but for being tough enough to do what she could not.

'You find a table, I'll buy the drinks,' she said, as they entered the tiny bar and were enveloped in welcome body heat and the roar of conversation. 'Vodka and tonic, as usual?'

Hayley hesitated. 'My throat's like sandpaper. I've been shouting down the phone all day. Think I'll start with a double tomato juice.'

Kate located her eventually at a table by the window in the upstairs room. She set down the drinks, took off her coat, and sat down. 'That's better,' she sighed, after downing a good mouthful of Argentinian Merlot. She placed her elbows on the table. 'So, finish telling me about that poor woman with five children in the B&B.'

'Oh, you don't want to hear. Anyway, I'd rather talk about something else.'

'I *do* want to hear,' Kate insisted. 'I'm your friend, Hayley. Let me help.'

'Well, it's just ...' Hayley stopped, as if unable to go on.

'I know,' Kate murmured sympathetically. 'Your work is *so* hard. I was thinking of Dickens earlier, actually. Sometimes I can't believe that in this day and age, in *England* for God's sake, there are still people who can't afford to buy their kids shoes, while others have them kitted out in designer outfits that they'll outgrow in a couple of months.'

Hayley took a slug of her tomato juice.

'I mean, we were in the country last weekend,' Kate continued, 'and went to this club that was absolutely crawling with yummy mummies and their little darlings. "Mummy, I want another dwink,"' she mimicked. '"Daddy, I don't like this pizza. I want a hamburger."' Getting into her stride, Kate assumed an indulgent parent's voice: '"Of course, sweetie. Whatever you want, my angel."' She waited for Hayley to laugh, or at least join in. Slagging off overindulgent, child-obsessed parents was a favourite game, and one of the many things that had cemented their solidarity as independently minded career women with more interesting things to talk about than rival brands of drinking cup.

But the only response she got was, 'I suppose it doesn't have to be like that.'

'It doesn't have to, obviously. It's just that women's brains turn to mush the moment they become mothers. Well, actually, even before that. You should have seen all the women at the club swanning around with their bumps on display and their smug, madonna smiles, as if no one had ever got pregnant but them.'

'Come on, be fair. It doesn't happen to everyone.'

'Yes, it does. Take my friend Sam, whom of course I completely adore ...' For the next few minutes Kate put all her energy into cheering Hayley up with amusing anecdotes about Sam's scattiness, self-absorption and inability to focus on any subject not involving children.

'They do require a lot of attention,' Hayley said feebly. 'Anyway, Kate, the fact is—'

'And babies are the *worst*, let me tell you,' Kate interrupted. She embarked on a lurid account of her disturbed night thanks to Milty-wilty, before concluding gaily, 'Please promise to shoot me if I ever think of having a baby!'

She felt a restraining hand on her arm. 'What?' she demanded. 'Who cares if people are listening? I'm only saying what we both think.'

Hayley looked her in the eye. 'I'm pregnant.'

Chapter 6

∾∾∾∾

Kate stared numbly into space, swaying with the movement of the Tube train as it rattled and jerked through underground tunnels. *Why can't you keep your mouth shut?* How could she have been so tactless, so obtuse – in short, a total plonker? Tomato juice, duh. Her eyes focused on her own reflection in the dark windows, and hardly recognised herself in that self-possessed career girl in her fashionable coat and expensive haircut, whose face betrayed none of the embarrassment and shame that curdled her insides. She jerked her head away.

Did it make it better or worse that Hayley actually wanted a baby and that her pregnancy had been planned? Kate wasn't sure. Her tirade had been equally insensitive, whether Hayley had been gearing herself up for an abortion or, as was the case, longing to share the exciting news. Or, more accurately, *break* the news. For Hayley acknowledged that she was defecting from the childless sisterhood, and had been almost apologetic to Kate. 'Maybe it's my biological clock, maybe it's my fabulous man – who knows? All I can say is that I'm ready. I'm looking forward to it – well, the good bits anyway.' Her honesty had been strangely chastening.

Why was that? Kate tried to analyse her feelings, and came up with the discomforting answer that, by comparison with Hayley, she felt immature – juvenile – schoolgirlish.

It wasn't true that she hated babies – though, frankly, children were much more interesting when they could walk and talk – or that she despised mothers. Her best friend was a mother. Kate wanted to be a mother herself one day, though only when she was ready, and she wasn't going to let herself be railroaded by Rikki. It was just that she'd drunk too much wine, too quickly. Rikki always said that alcohol made her dogmatic. Personally, she thought it made her more fun. She'd only dredged up those stories about babies and brainless mothers for a laugh, to entertain her friend.

Hayley swore that she would not turn into a yummy mummy – 'otherwise you can be the one to shoot me. I'm going to carry on working until August, when the baby's due, take the rest of the summer off, and be back just as work hots up again in the autumn. Everyone in chambers goes away in the summer. You won't even miss me. I'm certainly not giving up my job. For one thing I love it, and for another we need the money.'

'What about the baby? Who will look after it?'

'Nanny? Au pair? I don't know yet. Maybe I'll start lobbying for a Middle Temple crèche.'

'Dream on.' Kate's tone was sarcastic. Although women were now pouring into the profession, 70 per cent of practising barristers were male, some of whom still couldn't see the point of females in the Inns of Court, let alone babies.

For the first time during their conversation, Hayley's eyes flashed with annoyance. 'Look, Kate, I'm not stupid. I know the Bar isn't ideal for a woman bringing up children. Sure, you're self-employed, so technically you can work as much or as little as you want, but you have to pay the chambers rental regardless – which is expensive these days. If you don't work enough, solicitors forget about you, so you don't build up the experience to get the best work and the highest fees. Then there's the problem of getting a brief just as you're going home, which means staying up half the night to be prepared for court the next morning. Or maybe a case takes you to Newcastle, or bloody Bristol. But that's the way it is, and I'll deal with it.' She swept back her red hair abruptly. 'I know you want to become a silk one day, and so do I. But it's not everything. If I don't make it, that will be because something else was more important to me. Something *here*.' She pressed a palm to her heart.

Kate didn't know what to say. The consternation must have shown in her face because Hayley's expression softened. 'Having a child is one of the big experiences of life. It's like love, or death. These things change us. If they didn't, we wouldn't be human.'

The train pulled into a station, jolting Kate out of her thoughts. Had she missed her stop? No, one more to go. She watched people getting on and off, each with a private purpose, each inspired by hopes and anxieties she could not know. A woman laden with a briefcase and Sainsbury's shopping bags pushed past her knees to reach an empty seat. Even though she was wearing a bulky coat, Kate could see that she was heavily pregnant. Usually she never noticed such things, but Hayley's news made her look more closely. The woman sat down, and extracted a book from her briefcase to read. What would it be like, Kate wondered, to have a constant companion inside oneself, felt but unseen – to harbour that second, silent heartbeat and share the mysterious beginnings of a new life? How could the woman look so calm and unconcerned? With a pang she began to see the lives of her friends dividing from her own: between city and country, children and no children, between conversations about schools and work discussions. Would all her female friends cross this border, leaving her stranded? Or would she have to join in?

Suddenly she longed to be at home with Rikki, and to hear him tell her that she was marvellous, and that he loved her. She stood up and moved to the Tube doors, impatient for the train to stop and let her out. When they slid open she click-clacked through the passageways and onto the escalator, climbing the moving steps so that she would get to the top quicker. The air temperature cooled sharply as she neared the surface. By the time she had swiped herself through the barrier and reached the street, it had plummeted to freezing. Snuggling her chin into the deep collar of her coat, she turned into the biting wind, whimpering under her breath at the cold. It was only a five-minute walk to the flat, but she felt like Scott trudging across the ice floes. She started to fantasise about a cosy evening in, cuddled up on the sofa with Rikki and a favourite DVD. Warmth, comfort, familiarity – heaven! And maybe afterwards they could pick up where they had left off when Milty-wilty had interrupted them.

The block was already in sight when her mobile bleeped to tell her that she'd received a text message. She felt a stab of disappointment in case it was from Rikki, telling her that he'd gone off for supper with his mates. She didn't even want to look, in case it was. But what if it was a message from work? The clerks liked their barristers to be contactable at all times. Reluctantly she reached for the phone in her bag and thumbed the pad awkwardly with a gloved hand. The sender was not Rikki, or anyone from her contacts list, but a number that she didn't recognise. Her pace slowed a little as she brought the message up onto the screen. A passer-by muttered impatiently as, concentrating on her phone, she drifted across the pavement into his path. Then she stopped altogether, to peer at the illuminated screen which spotlit her bewildered expression.

Can't stop thinking of u in that sexy red dress. Meet me in Ritz bar Frid. 6.30. – M.

Who the hell was 'M'?

An icy blast up her skirt shocked her into movement. She slipped the phone into her coat pocket and strode on, considering possible solutions to the puzzle. Her first thought was that it was simply a wrong number. Miss-keying a digit was easily done, and she didn't get messages like this any more, from half-remembered strangers randomly encountered on nights out. She was a married woman, for God's sake. Mind you, the offer of drinks at the Ritz was a very superior version of the usual 'Found your number in my pocket – fancy a shag?' approach. She rather admired 'M's style.

No – wait! Could 'M' possibly be Milo W-C, trying to wind her up? What a pervert. As if! Reaching the communal front door of her building, she jabbed in the code and shouldered her way inside. Really! It was time she put WC in his eponymous place.

There was no lift, which was one reason why their flat was affordable – just. As Kate climbed the stairs her expression became thoughtful. She was pretty sure she'd never worn her red dress to any legal junket at which WC had been present. Usually she stuck to something more sombre if she was at a party in her professional capacity. It was only with Rikki, in the company of friends, that she let rip with the whole look-at-me number.

Oh, no! It couldn't be. Not Michael. Not her beloved friend's *husband*, and father of six-month-old Milton? She weighed the evidence. Michael had complimented her on her dress. He had put his hand on her thigh. Anger flooded through her. Right, that was it! She was going to tell Rikki. If he lost his temper, so be it. She pictured him confronting Michael in the Ritz bar and knocking him to the floor with a single blow. 'Never insult my wife again!' he'd snarl, before suavely departing under the admiring gaze of assorted cocktail-drinkers.

Kate was beginning to feel quite excited. She scrabbled for her keys and unlocked the door of the flat, preparing to unfold the drama. But the lights were off. Rikki wasn't home. She called his name, and checked the bedroom in case he was playing their special game in which one of them lay silent in bed waiting for the other, but everything looked as it had done this morning: duvet in a tangle, Rikki's trainers on the living-room floor where he'd kicked them off last night, unwashed coffee mugs standing in the kitchen sink. Feeling deflated, she hung up her coat, and then changed into jeans and an old cashmere jumper that had been rescued too late from the moths and was no longer fit for public outings. What now?

She was hungry, but there seemed no point in cooking without Rikki. She thought about ringing him up, but decided that would be too possessive. He was free to do as he liked, of course. But she missed him. And what was he up to, anyway? The text from Michael disturbed her. Did all men behave like that? She flicked on some music for company, and decided to distract herself by making a sandwich.

Just as she had put it onto a plate and was resigning herself to an evening alone, she heard the front door open. 'Honey, I'm home!' Rikki announced. 'Where are you?'

'In the kitchen, honey,' she sang back, smiling. Their parody of a traditional 1950s American couple was a silly routine they'd adopted when they first got married and found it hilarious to be 'husband' and 'wife'.

Thump! went Rikki's briefcase, followed by further thuds as he unloaded something onto the coffee-table. Then he breezed into the kitchen in a swirl of cold outdoor air. 'Hey, gorgeous.' He kissed her on the lips and wrapped his arms around her, running his hands up and down her back. 'Mmm, you feel so warm and delicious. Is that a new jumper?'

'No,' she laughed. Rikki must have seen it a million times.

'Well, it looks great. And so does that sandwich,' he added.

Kate took the hint. 'OK, you take a couple of beers next door, and I'll bring in the sandwiches in a minute.'

'Have I told you recently that you're a wonderful woman?'

'I love you,' Kate told him happily.

Rikki flashed her a smile, clinked the beer bottles together in a mock-toast, and disappeared.

Kate made another sandwich. Then she decided to add a side-salad – oh, and maybe some of those upmarket root-vegetable crisps – which she distributed artistically on their plates. Michael's text was forgotten. In the absence of any napkins, she folded a couple of pieces of paper towel, put the whole lot on a tray and carried it in. Rikki was sitting on the sofa, pen in hand, studying a sheaf of papers. Further piles of documents had been distributed over the remaining surface of the sofa and their one comfortable chair. A couple of lever-arch files were open on the coffee-table, and more were scattered on the floor, next to his gaping briefcase. He'd taken off his shoes, which had now joined his trainers in any untidy heap, laces trailing. An open beer bottle stood on the carpet by his stockinged feet. He'd wedged hers, still unopened, between the sofa cushions.

'Oh, Rikki,' she sighed, 'where am I supposed to put our supper? And there's nowhere to sit.'

He was so absorbed that it took him a moment to grasp what she was saying. 'What? Oh, sorry.' He leaped up to clear a space on the sofa, tripping over his beer bottle, which fell onto its side, gushing foamy liquid. 'Shit! My papers!'

'The carpet!'

She used the paper-towel napkins to mop up the beer, and in the end put the tray on the floor and ate off a plate on her lap, squished into a small space that Rikki had cleared for her at the end of the sofa.

'Great sandwich,' he told her, munching enthusiastically. 'Did you know that Cass Carnaby is *forty-five*?'

Kate was startled by this non sequitur, but only for a moment. Of course: Rikki's big case. All this paperwork must be his background reading. She glanced at the top sheet of one pile, which was headed 'Essential Annual Expenses', and just had time to make out the words 'Hairdressing: £100,000' before scrupulously averting her gaze. They had agreed never to look at each other's work unless their advice was actively requested.

'Why shouldn't she be forty-five?' Kate demanded. 'She's been around long enough.'

'All I can say is that she sure doesn't look it.'

Kate crunched a shard of crisped beetroot. 'You've met her, then.'

'Today,' he nodded. His face lit up at the memory. 'You should have seen old Snape oiling round her. He was practically rubbing his hands at the thought of his fat fee. She'll make him earn it, though. The woman is definitely not stupid.'

Kate grunted. 'Didn't I read somewhere that she had one O-level? Before she was expelled for having it off with the art master.'

'Actually she struck me as highly intelligent.' There was a cool silence. 'You don't mind if I go on working, do you? Only Snape wants me to give him a summary of all this stuff by tomorrow. I get the feeling that I'm going to be doing all the work, and he'll be taking all the credit. But that's OK. This could be my big break. I want to be absolutely on top of everything.'

'Not including Cass Carnaby, I hope.'

'For God's sake!' Rikki threw the remainder of his sandwich onto his plate, suddenly petulant. 'Niggle, niggle, niggle! Why can't you just be happy for me?'

'I am.' She sat in uncomfortable silence while he went back to his papers, then cleared her throat. 'It's just that I'm a little upset about something.'

'Her first top-ten hit when she was only *eighteen*! I never knew that. Sorry, what were you saying?'

'I just thought you'd like to know that Michael has sent me an extremely inappropriate text message.'

He looked up. 'Who's Michael?'

'*Michael*. As in Sam and Michael? The people we visited last weekend?'

'Oh, him. Dodgy bloke, if you ask me. I wouldn't have anything to do with him.'

'I'm not going to. Obviously. I simply thought you'd like to know that he invited me out for a drink.'

'Really? Did you know that Cass Carnaby is completely teetotal these days?'

'At the Ritz.'

74

'Apparently hasn't touched the stuff for two years.'

'And he, er, commented on my red dress.' Kate felt embarrassed to repeat his actual words.

'Cass Carnaby always wore white onstage. Very unusual.'

'His actual words were, "Can't stop thinking of you in that sexy red dress."'

Finally she had caught his attention. Rikki gave her a disgusted look. 'Why do men do that? It's so sleazy. Particularly when you're married to a terrific girl like Sam.'

'Don't you like my red dress, then?'

Rikki blinked in bewilderment at this change of tack. 'Of course I like it. But other men shouldn't make that sort of comment, even if they're just joking around.'

'Oh, it's a joke, is it?' She stood up, gripping her plate. 'Kate looks sexy in her red dress, ha ha.' Now she grabbed his plate, too, and clattered it noisily on top of hers.

'Whoa, where are you going?'

'To bed. I'm going to watch a movie on my laptop, since you're so busy.'

'Er, well, all right, if you're sure. I have got an awful lot to get on top— I mean, to get through.'

'Good luck,' she said succinctly.

Having washed up and wiped the kitchen surfaces with unprecedented vigour, Kate shut herself in the bedroom and sat up in the bed, arms folded, fuming. If Rikki was so busy defending Cass Carnaby that he could not even defend his own wife, she would have to do it herself. She pulled her mobile out of her jeans pocket, having earlier retrieved it from her coat, and considered it thoughtfully. *I will not be free on Friday – or ever. Please do not contact me again.* No, that would be too abrupt. *How can you make such suggestions when you have a wife and baby?* Too priggish. *No, thank you. I am happily married.* Was that even true, the way Rikki was behaving?

It would be better to phone Michael than to text. Then he would hear the implacable *froideur* in her voice. She would also have the opportunity to give him a brief lecture on the consequences of marital infidelity, a subject on which she was a professional expert. Finally, she would graciously offer to forget the whole incident, in view of the close and long-standing friendship between herself and Sam. (*Poor* Sam, with her engorged breasts and screaming baby, stuck in the country.) Having spent some moments running this scenario through her head, she keyed in the number and put the phone to her ear, feeling as determined as Joan of Arc riding into battle against the English invaders, with God on her side.

After three rings a foreign, female voice chirped, 'Hello, I am Eva. Can I help you?'

Kate was completely thrown. Had she got the number wrong? 'Oh. Um. Is Michael there?'

'Michael is in shower. Can I help you?'

'And who are you, if I may enquire?' Kate demanded through tightened lips.

'I am Eva,' the girl repeated, as if Kate were a little slow on the uptake. 'Can I help you?'

Kate tried again. 'Are you speaking from Michael's flat?'

'Yes. This is the flat of Michael. Can I help you?'

Michael in the shower and a strange girl in his flat: Kate did not like the sound of this at all. 'You do know that Michael is a married man,' she said severely. 'With a baby.'

'Oh, yes?' said the girl, unperturbed.

There was an eruption of noise in the background, the unintelligible rumble of a masculine voice, an outraged squeak, and the line went dead.

Kate was still sitting in a daze, phone held limply in one hand, when the bedroom door opened, making her jump guiltily.

'Is there a pen in here?' asked Rikki. 'Mine's run out.'

'Try the drawer.' Kate pointed.

'Who was that on the phone?'

'No one.'

He shut the drawer, and turned to give her a long look.

'A girlfriend,' she amended, adding inconsequentially, 'Hayley is having a baby.'

Something flickered in Rikki's expression. 'Good for her.' He left the room without a word, pulling the door shut behind him. Kate burst into tears.

Chapter 7

When life gets you down, work pulls you through. That had always been Kate's mantra, and accordingly she set off on Tuesday morning determined to get into chambers early and attack her in-tray. She didn't even bother with breakfast, since by the time she got up Rikki was already standing at the front door with his coat on, laden with the Carnaby files and bristling with purpose. 'Don't know how I'll get through it all! Thanks, but no time – I'll grab something at the coffee shop and eat it at my desk. Have a good day.' Kiss. Slam. Over and out.

At Temple Tube station she bought a huge bunch of yellow irises, which she arranged in a vase once she got to work and put on Hayley's desk, with a note that simply said, 'Congratulations and lots of love from Kate and Rikki.' Then she trotted back downstairs to see if there was anything interesting in her pigeonhole. These were not arranged alphabetically, but by order of seniority, each wooden box in the grid neatly labelled. When first working in the set Kate had practically been forced to crouch in order to reach hers, and her label had still only advanced to the third-from-bottom row. Along the top rows the QCs' boxes looked impressively stuffed. Would she ever see her own name in that elevated position? As she ducked down to snatch the meagre contents from her pigeonhole, she couldn't help noticing that WC's – which was right next to hers – was comparatively full.

'Nice lot of work coming in, miss,' said the Head Clerk, pausing beside her on his way to the clerks' office. A portly man of about sixty, with the deferential manner and immaculate dark suit of a head porter at an extremely grand hotel, he had solved the problem of married women retaining their maiden names by calling them all 'miss' (she was 'Kate' to the hair-gelled junior clerks). Like a head porter, he knew more than anyone about the workings of the establishment under his care, and kept an astonishing file-index of names, cases and legal knowledge in his bald head. This morning he was looking particularly pleased, actually rubbing his hands, but Kate knew it would be useless to ask the reason, such was his reputation for discretion.

'Oh, yes, I've got a *million* things to do,' she told him, meaning to make herself sound in high demand. 'Though I always have time for more,' she added hastily. 'You know me. Workaholic. No job too small. Or too big!' She gave an inane laugh.

'Indeed, miss.'

She climbed the five flights to her attic office, mulling over this unsatisfactory exchange, and shut the door. Coat off, laptop on. While it purred and beeped into life, she sat down to sift through the contents of her pigeonhole. Ah, here was a nice fat envelope.

Dear Ms Pepper,
Are you suffering from winter blues? Post-Christmas weight-gain? The stresses of clients and court? Then our

79

state-of-the art Wellbeing Centre, situated on the lower floor of the Royal Courts of Justice, is for you! Join now at the special discounted membership fee of ...

Kate scrunched the letter into a ball and slam-dunked it into the wastebasket at her feet. The 'Welcome Pack' followed swiftly. She tapped a few keys on her laptop, and started to open her emails while they were still stacking up in her inbox. There was plenty of drudge work but nothing exciting, just the usual updates and follow-up enquiries from solicitors, some information she'd requested from the library and an internal memo peppered with capital letters and exclamation marks about 'keeping the kitchens TIDY!' She took a shorthand pad from her desk drawer, wrote the date on a clean page and started to write out a list, prioritising her tasks for the day and giving each a time deadline. Flipping back to the previous day's page, she then incorporated any items that hadn't been ticked off. 'Thank Sam for w/e' was still outstanding, under the 'Personal' heading at the bottom. Kate pursed her lips thoughtfully, troubled by Michael's flirtatious behaviour towards her and even more so by the mystery woman in his flat. Could she possibly have been a work colleague – perhaps an international banker? This was wishful thinking. 'Eva' had sounded spectacularly dim, even for a banker. And it was surely not normal practice to conduct financial deals in your own flat – from the shower. Adding the reminder to today's list, Kate decided that the best thing to do was to rattle off a cheery email to Sam, if she had time at the end of the day, and keep her doubts to herself. Now: item one, redrafting the affidavit for *Davies* v. *Davies*. A slamming of doors, braying of voices and shoes clattering down the stone staircase indicated that those who had business in the High Court today were off. Bully for them.

There was a knock on her door, immediately followed by Hayley, carrying a coat over her arm and a bulging plastic shopping bag from which her barrister's wig protruded. 'Fabulous flowers. Really sweet of you. Shit, I'm going to be so late!' she said all in one breath. 'I just wanted to ask if you and Rikki want to come with us to the new Coen brothers film tonight. Seven thirty at the Curzon, pizza or something afterwards. Let me know.' Before Kate had time to answer Hayley had spun round and was out of the door again, leaving a trace of musky perfume. Kate smiled and shook her head, then reached for her phone. There was nothing on the agenda for tonight, and an evening chilling with friends was exactly what she needed – and Rikki, too, though she'd better check. She decided to ring him rather than text or email, telling herself that it would be polite to give Hayley an answer sooner rather than later, though really she just wanted to hear his voice. But her call went straight to voicemail. He was probably on the line to someone else: she wondered who, before reminding herself it was none of her business. *'Hello, you have reached Rustom King. Please*—' she cut off the impersonal message and sent him a text instead. For a moment she paused to look out of the window, imagining her message flying through the air to him on a winged arrow – a Cupid's dart. It was a foolish fantasy, but her gaze lingered on the heart-lifting view of the river, which redeemed the small size of her office. There was the London Eye, where she and Rikki had taken a trip on their first anniversary; flags flapping on top of the National Theatre, where they often turned up on spec after work; and somewhere beyond it, out of sight behind the looming grey buildings, the Oval cricket ground, where she had made him howl with laughter by getting LBW mixed up with LBD.

Back to work! She wrote up her notes for the briefs she did have, checking the courtroom number and presiding judge in the online listings, then turned her attention to the article she was writing for one of the legal journals on the Hildebrand Rule. Getting your name into such publications was good PR, and although any normal person would have found the contents as dry as dust she rather enjoyed researching and writing them. She relished the combination of meticulous detail and abstract thinking required, and could happily argue for hours over interpretations of a point of law – though it was much more fun to do so in court, on her feet. With divorce looming, Mr Hildebrand had secretly photocopied Mrs Hildebrand's personal papers, suspecting that she had never revealed to him the full extent of her wealth. A judge had found that, so long as Mr Hildebrand disclosed the fact that he possessed the documents and did not 'keep them up his sleeve' to be sprung on his opponent in cross-examination, he could use them in the court proceedings. However, all that was prior to the Human Rights Act and other developments in laws governing privacy and data protection. More recently, conflicting views expressed by judges about copying a spouse's entire hard drive, intercepting emails or even forcing entry into a spouse's office had muddied the waters in a fascinating manner – fascinating to Kate, anyway. She lost all sense of time until she heard Big Ben striking one o'clock, and realised not only that she had amassed far more detail than she could possibly squeeze into the article, but that she was starving.

Slinging on her coat, she decided to go out foraging for lunch. At the first-floor landing she was struck by a sudden thought, and instead of continuing down the stairs, turned towards a door leading to a long corridor. She punched in the security code, made her way down to an office at the end, and knocked softly. 'In!' called a peremptory voice. Kate entered, to find Angus McLaren standing by his bookshelves with a duster in his hand. It was one of his habits to polish his splendid mahogany desk and wander round his large room wiping the deposits of London air from his books and picture frames. Physical movement was an aid to thought, he had often told her, citing William Wordsworth, who had composed much of his great verse while walking up and down the gravel path outside his home, even in the rain, when he kept dry under an umbrella.

'I'm just nipping out for a sandwich and wondered if I could bring you anything,' offered Kate. 'Unless you're planning to eat in Hall. I can't face it today.'

'No, no. Far too noisy. And I think I've lost my pass again. Porter might chuck me out.' He gave her a rueful grin, though they both knew perfectly well that no one in the Temple would dream of stopping Angus McLaren, QC going wherever he wanted. 'A sandwich is just the ticket,' he told her. 'You know the sort of thing I like. Make it a surprise.' Kate was turning to go when he added, 'And come and eat yours with me, if you can spare the time. I want to talk to you about something.'

'Of course. I'd love to.'

Kate made her way towards a sandwich bar she particularly liked, just off the Strand, run by an Italian family who could process a long lunchtime queue with irrepressible good humour and astounding speed. She'd discovered it soon after starting her pupillage at Old Court, five or six years ago now, back in the days when she had addressed Angus as

'Mr McLaren'. Technically she was already a barrister, in that she'd acquired the necessary qualifications and had formally been admitted to the Bar on Call Night, the grand gradua-tion ceremony held in the Middle Temple Hall, with much speechifying in Latin and an audience of parents (though not hers) bursting with pride to see their offspring dressed for the first time in robes and wigs. But in terms of being a practising advocate, she was at square one – the lowest of the low. The system was that you were taken under the aegis of a pupil-master, a senior barrister who would show you the ropes. It was an intimate relationship. For the first six months of your pupillage year, you sat in your pupil-master's office, listened to his phone calls, accompanied him to court, read what he read. You knew what he ate for lunch, how often he blew his nose, and even when he went to the loo – and vice versa. There were plenty of horror stories about pupil-masters who shouted at their pupils or ignored them, or else used them solely as slaves to make coffee, photocopy documents, carry their bags and walk their dogs in Temple Gardens, armed with a pooper-scooper.

Kate had been lucky with Angus. He was intimidating, no question. Though invariably polite, he had no small talk, and the speed of his mind could sometimes make him appear brusque. She was expected to keep up without asking silly questions, and to begin with was so consumed with nervous anxiety that she'd lost half a stone in a fortnight. Pupils who did well would be offered a tenancy at the end of the year, i.e. a permanent position within the chambers, which meant that finally they could start practising – and make money! The unsuccessful were granted a further six months max to 'squat' – a brutally accurate description of the discomfort and peril of their position – and after that were out on their ear.

A good pupil-master could make all the difference. As the weeks went by Kate realised that Angus was one of the best, taking the time to discuss cases, teaching her how to write a succinct legal opinion, suggesting articles and books for her to read. He gave praise only when praise was due, but he did give it. His first quiet 'Well done', offered with a smile and an approving look over the top of his glasses, had sent her floating home on a cloud of euphoria. She was going to be a lawyer – a good one – maybe a brilliant one.

Then everything went disastrously wrong. In the second six months of their stint, pupils were let off their masters' leash and given a chance to get their teeth into some proper court work, usually low-level and routine as befitted their 'baby barrister' status. For a family lawyer this meant travelling all over the country applying for non-molestation orders, dealing with immigration and adoption issues, petitioning for contact orders so that a parent could see its child, or 'ouster injunctions' so that it couldn't. Kate could deal with this fine on paper. She knew the law; her research was thorough. After endless advocacy training and 'moots' where students practised their courtroom skills, she was itching to get onto her own two feet in front of a judge. But the grim reality of some of the family courts, their waiting areas crowded with desperate, angry parents and white-faced children – the aggression, the distress, the *noise* – came as a shock.

It was in her third week of this that she'd found herself in a stuffy ante-room in Leicester Crown Court, not so far from where she'd grown up, discussing a contested care order for a nine-year-old boy called Billy. His mother had a drug problem. Social Services wanted him taken into care; Billy didn't. He was frantic. The mother looked ill and unkempt, but Billy clung to her hand, his face taut with fear. Kate was supposed to be representing Social Services – the opposite side – in the squat, bosomy shape of a middle-aged social worker, utterly convinced of her own rightness. 'Well, I'm sorry, but that mother's had her chances,' she'd told Kate privately outside the conference room. 'It's her own fault, and I cannot allow the child to suffer further.' Her voice and manner had evoked an uncomfortable, elusive memory: where had Kate heard that bossy, self-righteous tone before? To Billy himself the social worker had been sugary and cajoling. Mummy needed 'a rest'. He would be much happier, wouldn't he, living somewhere neat and tidy, where he could get proper meals and proper sleep? Where someone would make sure that he went to school every day and didn't fall behind with his homework? She was sure he agreed, didn't he? *Didn't he?* The voice went on and on, implacable under that phoney sympathy. Kate's heart started to thump with panic, so loudly that she didn't hear the social worker ask her for some document, only saw her irritated frown as she repeated her question. Oh God, she had to get out of here. There was no air. She couldn't breathe. Her chair screeched against the hard, tiled floor as she stood up abruptly. Muttering an excuse, she ran out of the room, leaving her belongings behind, and pushed her way blindly through the throngs of people in the lobby. Once outside, she leaned against the cold granite wall, palm pressed to her breastbone to muffle the galloping beat beneath, gulping in draughts of fresh air.

'Hallo, my darling, 'ow are you? Egg mayonnaise on granary – eh? Watercress? Black pepper?'

'Er, yes. Great. Thanks.' Kate had reached the sandwich bar on auto-pilot, and now stood at the front of the queue. Guido himself was in charge today, helped by his son, whom she had watched transform from a gangly seventeen-year-old to a handsome young man. Granny ran the till. Kate forced herself to concentrate on the array of sandwich fillings spread out before her under a glass canopy, and chose something for Angus. In a few moments Guido put together the sandwiches, cut them in half, wiped the knife on a cloth tucked into his apron, and wrapped up the results as deftly as a conjuror, while singing out the prices to his mother. Kate counted out the money and handed it to her with a smile. 'See you – eh?' said Guido cheerily, placing a brown paper bag containing her purchases on the counter. 'OK, who's next?'

Kate made her way back along the Strand, hunched into the collar of her coat against the wind, resuming her thoughts. Of course, she knew why she had flipped out that day in the Leicester court. A bus roared past her, its front and then back wheels thumping over a newly asphalted patch in the road. Bang, bang. Knock, knock. Even now a peremptory knock on the door could make her stiffen with alarm. But she'd learned early on not to show it, when social workers first started turning up at home, with their prying eyes and false smiles. On the contrary, she'd put on her most polite manner, and invite them in for a cup of tea. Then they could see for themselves that the house was immaculate, except perhaps for her schoolbooks open on the kitchen table. But that was OK. So long as Kate seemed clean, well fed and happy, and the reports from school were good, she was safe. None of the social workers seemed to think they could be hoaxed by a smiling little girl in a uniform she had ironed herself. Sometimes her mother was drunk when they came – Kate couldn't always help that, no matter how hard she searched for bottles stashed in ever-changing hiding-places. But she was never an aggressive drunk. She threw the odd piece of crockery, but only out of frustration and never at Kate. Alcohol initially made her self-conscious and stiff, as if she was playing a part onstage, then resentful, then maudlin. 'Oh, Kate, what would I do without you? My little housekeeper … my clever girl … my only friend in the whole world.' And Kate would try to coax her to bed so that she could get on with cleaning the house, making supper and doing her homework so well that no one at school would ever have cause to suspect that her home life was anything other than normal.

It was sometimes tricky getting hold of her mother's money before she spent it. Sometimes she had to wash her hair in Fairy Liquid or use newspaper instead of loo paper. Often there was nothing to eat for supper but cereal, or crisps, or something peculiar for which her mother had developed a craving, like a jar of California olives. The worst was having to make up excuses why she couldn't invite friends home from school. The house was being decorated – her mother was ill – her mother was working – the plumber was coming. For the better part of five years, from the age of eight to thirteen, she'd managed to run her parallel universes, balancing on a knife-edge between the two. She got used to it. And once the difficult time had passed, she thought she had got over it.

On the day of the Billy incident she'd pleaded illness and gone home to the flat she theoretically still shared with Sam, though Sam had already half moved out to live with Michael. It had been difficult to ring up the clerk on the train journey back, to explain her failure to deal with the case, and she heard the justifiable irritation in his voice. Alone that night she'd struggled with the problem, and in the morning walked into Angus McLaren's room, now as familiar as a second home, to tender her resignation from her pupillage – the chambers – her career.

Kate was now entering the Temple through one of the

side gates. From her very first visit here, when she was a law student, she had fallen in love with its orderliness: the quiet dignity of its buildings and the pleasing proportions of its courtyards; its air of permanence and stability despite a turbulent history. Its calm imperturbability reflected the law itself, which was why she had been attracted to the profession in the first place. She liked its precision, and the way that it dealt with the knottiest problem by a series of logical steps. Human life, as she knew all too well, was chaotic and unpredictable. But the law taught you to how to impose control on seemingly uncontrollable events. It might not always come up with the right answer, but at least it had an answer. It de-personalised what was most personal and emotional by its insistence on facts and formalities. She liked the rituals, too, which reinforced the notion that she was not so much an individual lawyer as an embodiment of the law. That gave her confidence when she doubted her own abilities, or her right to belong.

As she passed under a stone arch, Old Court Chambers came into view. A large plaque outside listed the names of the members, each engraved on a brass plate. And here was her own name: KATE PEPPER LLB in elegant capitals. She owed Angus a lot. He hadn't exactly refused her resignation; nor had he pestered her for an explanation, though she suspected he had guessed the broad outlines. He simply took her out to lunch and talked with great delicacy and kindness about the law – its values, purpose and the many varieties of practice open to her – and about her own talents as a lawyer. The crisis passed. Angus subtly diverted her away from childcare work, and she had repaid his confidence in her with 100 per cent commitment. Despite the difference in their age and status they had become friends, of a kind, though they knew very little about one another's private lives. As she pushed open the door to chambers she wondered what he wanted to talk to her about. Whatever he asked, she would say yes.

Halfway up the stairs she remembered Mrs Mitchison. Angus had told her not to worry about it, hadn't he? But perhaps that was just to protect her from public comment. Currently her career wasn't perhaps as sparkling as it might be – by comparison with Rikki's, for example. Her face tautened with worry. The idea that Angus, of all people, might be disappointed in her made her so anxious that she'd lost her appetite by the time she'd returned to his office and handed over his small wrapped parcel. She sat down in a comfortable padded chair placed on the opposite side of his desk, fiddling with the sandwich bag on her lap while he investigated his surprise.

'Prawns – how lovely! Don't tell the Dragon about the mayonnaise. And do I spy black pepper? I've always said you had a formidable memory for detail.'

'Angus, is it about Mrs Mitchison?' Kate burst out. 'I feel so bad about it. I know I've let the whole chambers down. Somehow I antagonised her, though I simply wanted her to understand what she would be up against in court. But I did it all wrong, and—'

'Listen to me, Kate. Stop warbling.' Angus held up an authoritative hand. 'You have not let anyone down, except possibly yourself. Chambers will survive. Your only problem, if you have one, is wanting to control events instead of letting people speak for themselves. A little more empathy, perhaps? A little, dare I say, humility? The law is one thing, but never forget that ultimately we are dealing with human beings, in all their rich and flawed variety.' He gestured to the pictures on his wall, which were not the usual Victorian cartoons and bad paintings of legal luminaries but reproductions of portraits by great artists, from Velázquez and Titian to Gwen John and even Francis Bacon. 'My advice to you is analyse your mistakes, learn the lessons, then KBO, eh? Keep buggering on. And eat up your sandwich. You look peaky.'

'It's not just Mrs Mitchison, it's my whole career. I feel … stuck. I'm sure I can do more, handle bigger cases, but – but, well, what if I can't? What if I never get the chance?'

Angus McLaren looked at her steadily. 'In my opinion, Kate, you are a highly promising young barrister. That is precisely why I should like to ask you to consider acting as my junior in a case coming to the High Court next week that will require brains, organisation and nerve – all qualities I believe you to possess.'

Kate straightened in her chair. Her eyes lit up.

'I have arranged a meeting here in chambers with the client and his solicitor tomorrow morning. I should like you to sit in on that meeting. This is a case which will be of considerable interest to the media, and I must ask for your word that you will keep all details confidential.'

'Of course,' she breathed. She felt wildly elated. This was big-money work: she could practically smell it. Her big break at last!

'Right, then. Here's the instruction letter.' He pushed it across the desk. 'Have a read and tell me what you think.'

Her eyebrows rose at the letterhead, which spelled out the name of one of the top legal firms in Britain, the sort that dealt with members of the Royal Family, zillionaires and temporary inmates of the Priory. Even the paper, crisp and creamy, exuded money and self-importance. The letter was signed personally by Angela Cross, probably the most famous solicitor in England for divorce work, who had inspired the slogan 'Don't get mad, get Cross.' Golly, this really was top league. Her mouth opened in the beginnings of an awed smile. She could hardly believe her luck. Then a name in the typed heading leaped out at her: Jeremy Benson. She skimmed the letter to make sure, but there it was, in black and white. The client was Jez Benson, husband of Cass Carnaby – represented by Fonthill and Rikki.

Her whole body sagged with disappointment.

'No,' she said. 'I can't. I'm so sorry, Angus, but I couldn't work on this case.' She had already slapped the letter down on the desk and was pushing it back to him, out of temptation.

'Why ever not?' he asked, frowning in consternation.

'It's Rikki. He's working with the other side, for Cass Carnaby. Nicholas Fonthill is leading.'

'Oh, I see,' he said, his face clearing. 'How is Rikki, by the way? Doing well, obviously.' Angus McLaren had come to their wedding, and had met Rikki a few times since then, in court or when he came to pick Kate up from chambers. He'd told Kate more than once that she had made an excellent choice of husband.

'*Very* well,' she said with emphasis. If only her old pupil-master had asked her a week ago to work on this case, *she'd* now be the one bounding off to work, bright-eyed and bushy-tailed. It wasn't fair!

'I don't quite understand your reservations, Kate. For the sake of transparency we must of course explain the situation to Mr Benson and ask for his approval, but I can't see why he would object. The barrister world is so small that if husbands and wives – friends, relatives, lovers – didn't oppose one another in court, the judicial system would collapse.'

'I know that. It's just ...' Her voice trailed away. Rikki

was the one who would object. She knew it in her heart. He'd think her disloyal. *But why should he?* Angus McLaren was a bloody QC and *he* thought it was OK. She twisted her hands in frustration. She needed this job. She wanted it. If she turned it down, everyone in chambers would find out, and she'd be scorned as a pathetic female with no balls. *I know I have the body of a weak and feeble woman, but I have the heart and stomach of a king.* Elizabeth I's famous words flashed through her head. Elizabeth had done OK – but then she'd never been married.

She stood up abruptly. 'I'm sorry, but I think it's best if I say no. I'm very grateful indeed for your faith in me, but I'm afraid you're going to have to find somebody else.'

Angus McLaren stood up as well. 'That's a great pity. But of course I respect your feelings.' He escorted her to the door and held it open for her. She could tell he was disappointed. 'And thank you for my sandwich,' he added courteously.

Kate trudged up the stairs feeling utterly defeated. A golden opportunity had been handed to her on a plate, and she'd thrust it away. She'd sunk in the opinion of her friend and mentor. The Benson case would have been meaty and varied – just what she liked. It would have put money and status her way. And she had turned it down, all for Rikki. Would he have done the same for her? Would any man?

As she entered her office, her phone beeped. She read Rikki's hastily thumbed reply to her text: no chance too much work will be late tonite sory. lve you

Kate's mouth twisted. 'And I "lve" you too,' she said to the empty air.

93

Chapter 8

That afternoon Kate found it almost impossible to concentrate. Her office felt stuffy. Banks of charcoal clouds filled the sky and seemed almost to press against her window, screening out the pitiful ration of daylight that remained. Slumped listlessly at her desk, she was scrutinising the initial deposition in an upcoming case of two people who should never have married and had now belatedly realised this.

When he said 'I love you', I think that he really meant this, but I also think that it didn't have any practical implications for him. Perhaps he loved me in his own way, but that didn't mean that he was going to change his habits, or stop working such long hours. He carried on doing what he had always done, and completely ignored my needs. His career came first and I didn't.

Kate hesitated; then struck out 'I didn't' and substituted 'I came last'. She stopped reading and chewed her pencil. This testimony seemed frighteningly familiar. Wasn't what this woman said just what Kate herself felt? Rikki loved her, all right, but did he care about her needs? Was he even aware that she had needs? Now that she had made such a huge sacrifice for the sake of their relationship, self-pity was welling up in her. What had he given up for her? Nothing. Would he ever give up anything for her? Probably not. It was easy to say 'I love you' – but what did love mean if you always put your career first? She struggled with feelings of resentment, clamping her teeth down hard onto the end of the pencil.

There was another thing playing on her mind. One reason why she and Rikki were happy together was because of the equality between them; there was no rivalry in the marriage. Neither had any reason to envy the other. But it might be altogether different if one of them was senior. She remembered Rikki's elation and telling her she'd have to call him 'My Lord' when she'd got all tarted up for him. He had thought that very amusing. Kate gloomily contemplated her future as a jealous, frustrated wife. She pictured Rikki studying a brief, while she made his dinner or watched rubbish on television.

She was still annoyed that he had reacted so calmly to the news of Michael's lecherous behaviour. Kate had a vague notion that a husband ought to go round and punch a man on the nose who had made advances to his wife. She wasn't sure that she *really* wanted him to do something so dramatic, but she was certain that she wanted more reaction than he had shown. At the very least he could *pretend* to be angry with Michael, couldn't he? Was he taking her for granted? Or perhaps he didn't really care. Oh God, it all seemed so familiar from case after case in her experience.

Her mobile rang. She picked it up and looked at the screen: an unfamiliar number. She wondered who it could be. Maybe someone who wanted to give her work? She pressed the green button and lifted the phone to her ear. 'Hello, Kate Pepper speaking.'

'Ah, hello.' The voice at the other end of the line was young, male and probably public school. 'This is Edward Ponsonby from *At the Bar!* magazine.'

'Oh,' said Kate, registering surprise.

'I expect you've seen a copy of the mag hanging about?'

'Oh, yes,' gushed Kate.

'So you know what we do. I hope you don't mind my calling you out of the blue like this.'

'Oh, *no*,' she replied ingratiatingly, before recovering her cool. 'How can I help you?'

'Well,' the man chuckled, 'the thing is, you see, we're doing our annual round-up on the most up-and-coming barristers under thirty-five—'

'I see,' Kate broke in. She flushed. Of course she knew what he was talking about. Every year *At the Bar!* magazine 'celebrated excellence' at the Bar. There were features on outstanding barristers, and awards in various categories, including 'Newcomer of the Year' and 'One to Watch'. The awards were presented in a ceremony hosted by the magazine at a tacky hotel on Park Lane. Kate had been a guest at several of these. The men were all in evening dress and the girls in perfect black suits – so much black and white that from a distance they could be nuns. Poor-quality food and cheap wine were served up by dim waiters at tables hired by legal firms and thrusting sets of chambers across a huge floor area. Onstage, an imported celebrity read out the shortlisted names and then announced the winners, who arrived in succession for their few moments of glory. Each received a trophy, about the size of an Oscar, but coloured silver not gold, scales in one hand, sword of justice in the other. Kate had experimentally picked

up one of these; it was disconcertingly light. The announcement of each winner was accompanied by plenty of clapping,
cheering and wolf-whistling (and sometimes a little booing),
which increased in volume as the evening dragged on. It was
like a school prize-giving day, only much rowdier.

Still, even to be shortlisted for such an award was an ac-
colade to boast about. This prospect changed everything: she
was no longer a humdrum, makeweight barrister, trundling
round the track to finish among the unplaced; she was one
of those tipped for a place on the podium ... Kate Pepper,
'Leading Junior' ... Katherine Pepper, QC ... The Hon. Ms
Justice Pepper ... Judge Pepper ... Her Honour Judge Pepper
... Lady Pepper of Herne Hill ... a glittering career stretched
out in front of her. She could imagine the page now, a challenging interview topped by a serious head-and-shoulders
photograph. 'Kate Pepper, Star of the Bar' ... 'Pepper Spices
Up Family Law' ... 'Kate Will Not Be Tamed' ... What should
she wear for the shot? Something smart but not too revealing
... It might be worth commissioning her own photographic
portrait for PR purposes ... Maybe she could become one
of those media-friendly barristers, presenting television and
radio programmes ... *Pepper Talk* ...

'Ask me anything you like,' she simpered.

'That's very kind of you,' the man from the magazine said.
'I was wondering ...'

What was he going to ask? Where she saw herself in five
years' time? Whom at the Bar she most admired? How she
thought family law was developing? What had attracted her
to the Bar in the first place? How she liked to relax after a
hard day's barristering?

'... so I was wondering whether you would be kind enough
to give me Mr King's mobile number?'

Two minutes later, Kate was in the office kitchen furiously making herself a cup of tea. How could she have been so stupid? Her own simpering voice replayed in her head, making her go hot with shame. How humiliating was it to be rung up not as herself, but as someone's *wife*? Just then Milo Wittering-Coombe put his head round the door.

'Since you're making, what about one for me?'

'Eff off, WC.'

'That's not very nice, Ms Pepper. I thought you might like to congratulate me on my success in *Mitchison* v. *Mitchison*. Didn't you know? Perhaps word hasn't filtered down to you yet. I appeared for your former client in court today. To cut a long story short, Mr Mitchison is going to be working his socks off for the rest of his life to keep his wife in comfort. There won't be any more dirty weekends for him; he'll be lucky if he can afford a cycling holiday in Devon, sleeping in a tent. What a pity you didn't hit it off with Mrs M, eh? My new friend Lexi is delighted. I predict that we'll be doing loads of business together.'

'I'm very pleased for you, WC. It couldn't happen to a bigger shit.'

He leered at her as he disappeared behind the door. 'You just say that because you're jealous.'

It was true, Kate reflected, as she sipped her tea. She was jealous. Not jealous because she wanted to handle the likes of Mrs Mitchison, but jealous that everyone else seemed to be getting on while she was standing still. Her mobile rang again. It was Hayley, back from court, suggesting bunking off for a late-afternoon brownie. 'I can resist everything but temptation,' replied Kate, delighted to have a distraction from her frustrations, and together they escaped to a local sandwich bar, where the waitress behind the counter wore an apron marked BARISTA. They collected their brownies and lattes and found a table. Once Hayley had unloaded the story of her day, Kate griped to her about WC. 'He really is despicable,' Hayley agreed.

'There's something else,' Kate said. She began to explain about Angus's offer.

'Let me get this straight,' said Hayley, her eyes opening wide. 'McLaren's offered you the Benson case, and you've turned him down? Are you out of your fucking mind?'

'You don't understand. I couldn't do that to Rikki.'

'Why the hell not? Do you really think that he would refuse if it were the other way round?'

Kate still wasn't sure about that. 'Well ...'

'Look, forget about being a woman or a wife; you're a barrister. Here is a big case: one that could transform your career. And you're running away from it like a silly school-girl. Get real, Kate! These chances only come along once or twice in a career. You have to grab them when you can, and cling on for dear life.'

They walked back together to the chambers. It was getting dark, and the wind swirled round the edge of the building. 'Angus won't ask you again,' said Hayley. 'Go and tell him that you've made a mistake,' she urged. 'Don't give him time to find someone else.' She gave Kate a parting kiss on the cheek. 'I'll see you later, OK?'

Kate sat in her room, staring out of the window at the lights of boats moving along the river. There was a message on her spike: Lexi had cancelled the lunch they had arranged for the following week. Kate thought about Rikki. She remembered him sitting on the sofa, happily absorbed by the Carnaby files. From a room along the corridor she heard the braying sound of WC's voice. At last she picked up the telephone and dialled a number. 'Angus? I've changed my mind.'

Part Two

Chapter 9

⟨∿⟩ ⟨∿⟩

A shaft of winter sunlight angled through tall sash windows on the first floor of Old Court Chambers, winking off the high chandelier and coaxing rich reds from the opulent Persian carpet. It shone on the elegant marble fireplace (now banned from use by Health and Safety regulations), and gleamed pinkly on the forehead of Angus McLaren as he sat behind his desk, listening to Jeremy Benson with grave attention. Seated alongside Benson – one might almost say, enthroned – on a matching button-backed chair was Benson's solicitor, the formidable Angela Cross of Hinton & Charterhouse, who reminded Kate irresistibly of Camilla Parker-Bowles, though younger, smarter and with a marginally better hairstyle. Kate herself observed the proceedings from a discreet distance, as befitted her junior – and as yet unconfirmed – status, perched on the edge of a leather sofa. She had decided not to tell Rikki about the possibility that she would be joining the Benson team until they'd had his approval and this was definite. No point in upsetting him unnecessarily.

'I've been a judge more times than I care to remember,' Benson was saying, 'but I've never been in the dock before.'

He chuckled at his own joke and waited for the other three to join in – which of course they did. This was not just sycophancy, though all were aware that Benson was their paymaster: the man radiated charisma, from his electric-blue eyes to his Converse-shod feet, which continually shifted and jiggled as if sheer high spirits might impel him into a tap dance at any moment. Kate had never seen a man look less stressed by the break-up of his marriage.

'Now, now, Mr Benson, you mustn't call it the dock.' Angus McLaren wagged his head in genial reproof. 'We shall be in the High Court, not the Old Bailey. However, it is true that you will be under oath. Therefore it is most important to be certain that you have apprised us of all relevant information. You will understand that if our opponents suddenly spring a nasty surprise, that could materially affect the integrity and strength of our submission – and, indeed, the final outcome of the case. There's nothing judges dislike more than muddle. What they want are *facts*, solidly substantiated, and a cogent argument backed up by case law and precedent.'

Benson, who had been nodding and smiling throughout this speech as if he were being interviewed on a chat show, now gestured at his solicitor. 'Tell him, Angie. Is there a single, solitary thing you don't know about me? I tell you, the woman's insatiable! Bank statements, tax returns, work contracts. Pensions, properties, mortgages, cars. I bet she could even tell you my inside-leg measurement.' He grinned at each of them like a cheeky boy, and it seemed to Kate that his gaze lingered for an extra moment on herself. She wished she had not chosen to wear quite such a short skirt, nor to sit on this sofa, since the absence of friction between the leather and her tights meant that she was remorselessly slipping backwards, revealing ever-greater expanses of thigh. Her attempt to wriggle forwards to the edge made the problem even worse, rucking up the back of her skirt practically to her bottom and producing an embarrassingly fart-like squeak from the leather. She placed her notepad over her thighs and held her pen poised.

The flicker of a smile on Angela Cross's face, like that of a headmistress for a wayward but favoured pupil, showed that she had registered her client's comment, but she chose to ignore it. 'The accountancy firm Ringham & Dry have been through the paperwork with a fine toothcomb,' she told Angus. 'I'm satisfied that the Form E is accurate to date. We can always email the judge prior to the hearing if we find that any information has been inadvertently omitted, though I jolly well hope that doesn't happen.'

'No, indeed.' Angus looked alarmed. 'Last-minute submissions are apt to cast a bit of a shadow, I always think. Now, Mr Benson, if we could just go through a few points … I understand that you have already agreed shared care arrangements regarding your children, er, Elvis and Apricot, in the District Court – is that correct? They will live with their mother and visit you from time to time, holiday with you and so forth. Do you foresee any problems there?'

'Nah, the kids are about the only thing we *don't* argue about. I've got no probs with Cass as a mother.'

'And you're still happy with the petition of "unreasonable behaviour"? You don't wish to raise the issue of, ahem, adultery – or fear that she may still wish to bring such a charge against yourself?'

'No point, is there? We've both had affairs, and thanks to the lovely media the entire world knows about them.' Impatient with all these questions, Benson suddenly jumped to his feet and began to prowl around the room. 'Nice bit of art you've got here,' he commented, pausing to examine a Van Gogh self-portrait. 'I'm more a contemporary sort of guy myself – Jopling, Wallinger, that sort of stuff.'

Kate sat up, startled. Could he really be naive enough to think the pictures were originals? Then, with his back to the others, he caught her eye and winked. She flushed and bit her lip, trying to keep a straight face.

Yesterday evening she had decided not to go to the cinema with Hayley and her partner, but spent the evening doing her homework on Benson. She'd read all about his troubled childhood in a deprived Essex family, how he left school at sixteen without any qualifications to work as a runner in the music business, then powered his way upwards until he had set up his own production company. Cass Carnaby had been one of the first artists he signed, and they'd had a tempestuous on-off relationship until finally marrying at Chelsea Register Office, both dressed in Elvis Presley outfits. Benson's company hadn't been successful at first, but his contacts eventually landed him on the judging panel of a musical talent competition, where a combination of outrageous comments, impish grin and tight jeans had got him noticed. The rest was TV-ratings history. Though Kate had never actually watched *Starmaker!*, it was impossible to remain unaware of its grip on a nation currently obsessed with celeb culture and thus mesmerised by examples of ordinary, talentless people like themselves becoming rich and famous overnight. She had assumed Benson would be your average TV sleazebag, and was sick to death of hearing everyone else repeating his silly catchphrases. 'I'll have a little thinky,' was one of them, and when he'd had his little thinky his verdict was either 'You are really ... and truly ... terr ... ible!' or 'You are really ... and truly ... terr ... ific!'

But in the flesh he was not so easy to dismiss. Though Kate had seen countless photographs, they had not prepared her for the charm of his smile or the athleticism of his lean body, outlined by slim black trousers and a V-neck cashmere sweater worn over bare skin. She had scoffed yesterday when Hayley had described him as 'dead sexy'. Surely he was too old, for a start. If she hadn't personally looked up his date of birth, verifying her findings in three separate sources, she'd have put his age in the late thirties, not forty-five. Of course, the Botox injections, which she'd read about in *Femail* online, might explain it. His mid-brown hair, thick and glossy, sprang from his head like that of a cute street-urchin styled by Hollywood. In between Googling, Kate had tried on twelve different outfits (all black) in combination with various accessories, and had had to pretend to a tired and slightly tipsy Rikki, when he finally came home from a 'strategy meeting' at around 10.30 p.m., that she was having a clear-out of her wardrobe. After a great deal of thought and experimentation, she'd decided to wear her hair up in order to appear efficient and not too girly, and was beginning to wish she hadn't. What if Benson thought she was a secretary?

'... obviously an important factor, but even more so is her earning capacity,' Angus was saying. Kate was appalled by her lapse in concentration. There would be no chance of impressing Benson, and certainly not Angela Cross, if she was caught daydreaming.

'Sure, Cass could make a living, but she can't be arsed,' Benson answered, throwing himself back into his chair and crossing an ankle over one knee. 'I set her up with a great career, but she let it slip through her fingers.'

'Perhaps she has been occupied with the children,' Angus suggested.

'Don't make me laugh. I can't think of the number of nannies we've had – and that wasn't good for marital stability, I can tell you. I mean, what's a man to do with a gorgeous twenty-year-old Swedish girl running about in a tiny bath towel? Yeah, that's a good point – write it down. She threw temptation in my way.' He stabbed a finger at Angus, who obligingly made a note on his pad. 'No, I'm the one that's made the money, and she's the one that spent it,' Benson went on. 'It took me years of hard graft to get to that first *Starmaker!* show. I'll never forget it. The winner was a little cracker. What was her name? Annie? Abi?' He snapped his fingers impatiently at Angela Cross, catching her on the hop. Angus looked utterly blank.

'Ally,' supplied Kate from the sofa. 'Ally Dickinson from Sheffield. March 2002.'

Benson's face lit up. 'Hey, I got a fan!' He turned to her, every dazzling tooth on display. 'Like my show, do you?'

Kate could hardly admit that she'd never seen it, but that while wielding her hair straighteners this morning she'd read the whole story of Ally Dickinson's decline from fame and fortune to a council flat in Runcorn and a job in the Co-op. 'Love it,' she told him. 'The best.'

'I *love* this girl!' he announced to the room, before asking Kate, 'So who's your favourite contestant ever?'

Oh shit! Kate crossed her legs and pretended to think, playing for time.

Angela Cross rapped her knuckles briskly on the desk. 'Come along, Jez, there's work to do. 'I've told Angus that you don't want to negotiate, and I must say that would also be my advice at present, since I see no reasonable prospect of a compromise between the five million you've offered, plus family home, and the fifty million she wants. Not to mention her extortionate budget.'

'You're sure that it's a lump-sum settlement that you want?' Angus asked, seeking confirmation from Benson. 'Not periodical payments – that is, what most people call alimony?'

For the first time during the whole conference Benson looked seriously engaged. His face grew sharp. 'No alimony.' He slapped the arm of his chair. 'Absolutely no way. I want to end the whole thing now, once and for all. "Sudden death" we call it on my show.'

Talk turned to practical details: court listing, documents to be photocopied, information to be verified. Kate had a sinking feeling that the meeting was winding down, and no one had yet mentioned her own role.

'Well, I think we're nearly there, Mr Benson,' said Angus. 'Preparing for court is a tedious business, and you've been most patient. Before you go, may I ask if you're happy for my colleague, Kate Pepper, to help with the case?' He gestured at her, still perilously perched on the sofa. 'I believe that Angela has already mentioned to you that Kate's husband, also a barrister, is working in a junior capacity on the opponent's team. Of course, this sort of thing is quite usual, but if you have any doubts about it, we shall naturally respect them.' Kate stifled a qualm at the mention of Rikki. She had nothing to apologise for, had she?

Benson glanced over at Kate. 'You look far too young to be married,' he told her. Finding no acceptable answer to this, she merely smiled, feeling like a fool.

'Kate is an excellent barrister,' Angus said crisply. 'She and I have worked together before, and I have complete faith in her abilities – and in her discretion. Of course, she won't actually appear in court,' he added.

Benson pouted – there was no other word for it. 'Now that's a pity, that is. It's always nice to have a fan when you're in a tight spot.'

Desperate not to appear a silent mouse, Kate spoke up. '"Appear" is a technical term, Mr Benson. I shall be in the courtroom, of course, to help in any way I can. But Mr McLaren will be appearing on your behalf, i.e. presenting your case.'

'Oh, I get it.' He grinned. 'Jez Benson is too big for you to handle, right?'

'Much too big.' If there had been a hint of innuendo in his words, Kate was prepared to play up to it. She wanted this job!

'And you're not, um, experienced enough?' he persisted.

'Not yet, no. However, my services will be available to you night and day – should you be willing to accept them.'

Angus and Angela Cross were observing this exchange with rising interest, their heads swivelling back and forth like spectators at a Wimbledon final.

Kate waited for Benson's verdict, willing him to agree. He gave a teasing smile, which encompassed her secretarial hairstyle, her figure and her legs. 'I'll have a little thinky, shall I?'

Chapter 10

Rikki took the wine out of the freezer, where he'd placed it for emergency cooling on his return from work, unscrewed the cap, poured himself a glass and took an experimental sip. Delicious. Crisp, zingy and chilled to perfection: worth the extra fiver he had splashed out in order to make tonight's supper special, having buggered up Valentine's Day.

Of course that wasn't totally his fault. What red-blooded man wouldn't be excited at the prospect of meeting, let alone representing, Cass Carnaby? Which reminded him: it might be a good idea to take *Cass's Greatest Hits* out of the CD player before Kate got home. He grooved into the living room, pumping his fists in time to the earthy beat, before reluctantly cutting off Cass's throaty growl in the middle of 'Down, boy!' A laugh escaped him. What a flirt that woman was! 'I'm going to put myself entirely in your hands,' she'd purred, as he held the door open for her to leave after the conference on Monday, giving him a final bat of her long lashes. But he was inured to such approaches. Even as a small boy he'd been told endlessly how handsome he was – mainly by his mother, to be truthful. 'Oh, he's going to break so many hearts,' she used to croon rapturously, parading him before clucking friends and aunties. But as he discovered soon enough, hearts had nothing to do with it. By the time he was a teenager, travelling back and forth across London to school, he was already having to fend off approaches from strange women – and strange men – some welcome, many bewildering and some downright unpleasant. He had learned to deal with it. Obviously it sometimes helped that women found him attractive – swiftly he diverted his memory from the times he'd positively exploited this fact – but on the whole he didn't set too much store by his appearance, which was simply the result of a genetic lottery. Moreover, for every stranger who wanted to seduce him there was another who shouted racist abuse – usually 'Paki' when he was a boy, though Nine-Eleven had introduced new variations such as 'Muslim freak' and 'fucking suicide bomber'. 'Listen, guys, I'm a half-Iranian lawyer on my way to work,' he wanted to protest, when he saw the eyes of a fellow-passenger on the Tube flicking warily between his face and the bulging brief-case at his feet. 'I'm a Spurs supporter. I love bacon butties. I've never even been inside a mosque, except as a tourist.' It was always better if he was with Kate. A man speaking fluent, unaccented English to a pretty blonde girl – even if he was darkish-skinned – was OK. It occurred to him for the first time that Kate might be conscious of this, though they had never talked about it – that she deliberately smiled at him and put her hand on his arm as a kind of protection. His face softened at the thought. She was such a sweet girl at heart, so thoughtful and loyal under all that driving ambition.

He flicked through the CD rack for something romantic. That's what girls liked. Things like anniversaries, Valentine's celebrations and candlelit dinners were important to them.

A faint frown of puzzlement furrowed his brow. There had been something odd about Kate on Valentine's Day. Had she been hiding behind the bedroom door when he came back that night? If so, why? And what had happened to the high heels and fishnet stockings, since by the time he returned with the Thai takeaway she was disappointingly swathed from head to toe in a high-necked jumper and jeans, and in a strangely distant mood. Could he, perhaps, have *missed* something ... ?

Rikki dismissed the thought, and slid *Elvis for Lovers* into the player. Whatever had gone wrong that night, he would make up for it now. Returning to the kitchen, he took another glug of wine and looked round complacently at his preparations. The cinnamon rice was already cooked, and keeping warm in a low oven. The prawns were peeled, cleaned and ready to go. Neat piles of chopped coriander, spring onions, peppers and chillies, garlic and ginger lay waiting on a large board. The wok rested on the unlit burner. He'd made a salad – well, emptied it out of a packet into a bowl – and bought a super-expensive bottle of dressing to go with it. Plates were warming. The table was set for two. He had even put new candles in the candlesticks. The perfect husband or what?

Already he could picture her face lighting up when she walked in. He loved the way she could look severe and businesslike one moment, and adorably girlish the next. That was what had attracted him when he'd first seen her – been her opponent, in fact – in some Outer London court. She was pretty, of course, and he had a weakness for long-legged blondes in particular. But there were plenty of pretty girls. What had caught his attention was her formidable concentration on the matter in hand, coupled with a vulnerability that made her blush when she mispronounced a word and was corrected by the judge. She had absolutely trounced him, too. He wasn't sure he liked that, but he definitely liked her. Afterwards, they'd chatted in the robing room, while they packed their paperwork, gowns and wigs into wheelie bags. His was a mess, with a couple of stray tennis balls and a half-eaten sandwich still in its supermarket packet. Hers was immaculate: he'd watched with amusement while she expertly folded her gown and zipped it into a plastic clothes-bag. There was a containment about her which he found intriguing – even exciting.

'Wow. Miss Organisation. No wonder you won. Want to fold mine up, too?'

'No.' She'd given him a stern look.

'Sure?' He teased, waggling his eyebrows. Unexpectedly, her expression had melted into a reluctant, shy smile and then a gorgeous laugh. He'd felt strangely rewarded.

Until then he'd taken girls as they came – and went. He liked women. With five older sisters, how could he not? He liked their openness, their chatter, their infectious collapse into giggles, the knick-knackery of their bedrooms, even their bossiness. There was hardly a time when he hadn't had a girlfriend. He'd loved them all, and usually regretted the end of the affair. Quite a few had survived the transition from lover to friend. But Kate was different. It was hard to say exactly why. Perhaps it was because neither of them was a fully paid-up member of the privileged class in which they moved – she because she was not privileged, and he because he was not quite English. This slight dislocation from the (often smug) norm was something that bonded them. He liked her company. He enjoyed her quick brain, and admired her grit. She was tough and capable, and yet ... his overwhelming impulse had been to protect her, to make her happy, to dispel for ever the dark cloud of her childhood. It had been a delight to take her to Italy and witness the spontaneous joy of her reaction. The force of his love had shocked him. *This is the one.* Having never seriously thought about marriage, suddenly he wanted to grab this wonderful girl while he had the chance.

Damn, the olives! Thinking of Italy reminded him that they were still in the fridge. He decanted them into a bowl and popped one into his mouth. He was starving. Kate had better come home soon or he might collapse from hunger. He hoped that she wasn't still feeling down about losing that client – what was her name? Mitchell? It was a bit embarrassing that he'd got a big job just now, but, hey, that's the way it went. Rikki enjoyed a pleasant reverie as he contemplated his new brief. His career was hotting up. He'd even been interviewed over the phone by some guy from *At the Bar!* It was mainly straightforward stuff. Where had he been to school? (St Paul's.) What about university? (A history degree from Corpus, Oxford.) How did he feel about acting as a junior for Cass Carnaby? (Honoured and delighted.) What did he feel was the most important new development in family law? (Some guff he could no longer remember.) He hoped he hadn't sounded like a prat. Should he have asked for copy approval, he wondered, or was that too pompous?

He heard the front door slam. 'Honey, I'm home,' Kate called. A moment later she joined him in the kitchen. 'Mmmm ... this looks exciting.' She kissed him on the ear. 'I'm a lucky woman.'

'You're right, as usual.' He lit the burner underneath the wok and dribbled in some oil.

'Do I have time to change?' she asked.

'No.' Secretly he found her rather sexy in the austere outfits she wore to work. 'Pour yourself a glass of wine. There's some open in the fridge. Then sit down and relax.'

'Whatever you say, boss.' She grabbed an olive, took the wine from the fridge over to the table and poured some into the waiting glass. She carried it through to the living room and leafed through today's post, stacked on the table, but didn't seem to open or read anything. Then she came back in again and gave him a brief, reflexive smile. It struck him that she was wound up about something. Well, all the more reason to give her a delicious meal.

The oil was beginning to smoke now. Rikki swept everything from his chopping board except the coriander into the wok, where it sizzled and spat viciously. He jumped back as a spray of hot oil landed on his hand. 'Christ!' he yelped. 'Quick, Kate! I've burned my hand!'

She ran across and took stock of the situation. 'Put it under cold water,' she told him calmly, already turning on the tap.

'Jesus! That hurts.' He winced. 'Can't you get a bandage or something? Or some ointment?' Now she was removing the hot pan from the stove and giving the vegetables a stir before they burned. It didn't seem to him that she was taking his injury as seriously as she should. And he didn't like her interfering in his cooking.

He removed his hand from the water and inspected the red mark. 'Do you think we should go to hospital? Will it leave a scar?'

To his irritation, she smothered a laugh. 'I think it will be OK.'

'Well, I don't know,' he said doubtfully, examining his wound again. It might *look* small, but Kate didn't seem to understand how painful it was. 'I'm feeling a bit faint,' he told her. 'I might have to sit down for a bit.'

'OK. If you want to.' A smile still twitched at the corners of her mouth. 'Shall I finish off the cooking?'

'No, I'll do it,' he said in a martyred tone. 'Though it's probably ruined now.'

Actually, it looked and smelled delicious, once he'd brought the vegetables back up to temperature and tossed in the raw prawns, chasing them about the wok with a wooden spoon until they turned pink. His hand still stung, but nobly he refrained from mentioning it.

'All right, I think we're there,' he announced. 'Sit down.'

'Can't I help?'

'No, Ms Pepper, you cannot. This is my show.' Taking the rice out of the oven, he heaped a mound onto each plate, arranged the prawns on top, and chucked on a generous sprinkling of coriander. Then he carried the plates triumphantly to the table and set one down in front of Kate.

'Thanks, Rikki. This looks lovely.'

'All part of the service,' he called, as he went back to the kitchen to retrieve his glass and the bottle, and to take off his apron. Finally he sat down opposite her and spread a napkin on his knees. Then he raised his glass and clinked it with hers. 'To us.'

'To us,' she echoed.

'Well, go on,' he urged. 'Eat it while it's hot.'

She raised her fork, then hesitated. 'I have something to tell you.'

'That sounds ominous.'

'You mustn't take it the wrong way.'

'That *does* sound ominous.' He stabbed a prawn, and paused.

'It's good news, really. In fact, very good. I've been given a big-money job.'

'Really! That's fantastic.'

'That's what I think.' Kate still hadn't touched her food. What was the matter? 'I mean, we both want each other to succeed, don't we? You wouldn't want to stand in my way?'

'Of course not.' But he was beginning to get a bad feeling. 'Who's the client?' he asked.

She stared into her wineglass, then raised her eyes to his. Her beautiful blue eyes, which he loved, and in which he read a mixture of anxiety and defiance. 'My chambers is going to be representing Jeremy Benson. Angus McLaren has taken the brief. He's asked me to act as his junior.'

Rikki dropped his fork onto his plate with a clang. 'You're joking.'

'No, I'm not. It's a great honour.'

'I don't understand. Surely you can explain that in the circumstances, you can't take the brief? McLaren will understand, won't he?'

'It's you who doesn't understand, Rikki. I *want* this job. It's important for me. I'm a barrister too, remember? Or had you forgotten that?'

'Of course I hadn't bloody forgotten!'

'Well, then, what's the problem? You're acting for your client, I'm acting for mine.'

Her coolness enraged him. He ripped his napkin from his lap and threw it on the table. 'For God's sake, Kate! You must see. We'll be fighting *each other*. You know how destructive divorce cases are – how they leak poison into everything they touch. I don't want that to happen to us.'

'Why should it? This is just work, Rikki. It's not personal.'

'Of course it's personal!' He stood up, shoving back his chair. How could he explain the dread that he felt? Why couldn't she understand how it would hurt him – hurt them both – to be locked in an antagonistic struggle? Kate was his wife, the most special person on earth. Their relationship was precious. Private.

Frustration boiled up inside him. He pointed an accusing finger. 'You know what? I think you engineered this whole thing, because you're jealous.'

'I am not. Calm down, Rikki.'

'You can't stand me getting ahead of you, even for a moment. Kate – I love you,' he said beseechingly. 'You don't need to compete with me. It's not a fight either of us can win.'

'It's not a fight, it's a court case. And somebody will win. I'm sorry, but I just can't see it the way you do.'

Rikki was prowling up and down and round the table. How could she just sit there, straight-backed and controlled? Did she feel nothing? He was so upset and angry he couldn't think straight.

'I'm going out,' he told her, suddenly grabbing his coat from the back of the sofa.

'Out where?' She came over and held on to his sleeve. 'Please don't go, Rikki.'

'I need to think.' He stalked to the door and flung it open. 'Don't wait up.'

Elvis's voice followed him as he stormed down the corridor.

Chapter 11

෧෨ ෧෨

Beep, beep, beep, beep ...

Kate groaned. Without opening her eyes, she groped around on the bedside table for the alarm clock. With a flick of her thumb she silenced it, and lay prone for a while, her hand still stretched out and her face crushed against the pillow. Her body cried out for more sleep. She snuggled down underneath the duvet to escape the sunlight streaming in through a gap between the curtains. But it was no good. The sounds of traffic outside reminded her of work. Her busybody conscience told her that she must get up and make herself ready. She forced her eyes open. And then she suddenly remembered what had happened the night before.

'Rikki?' Kate sat up and swung her feet out of the bed. Was he sleeping on the sofa? She pulled on her silk dressing gown and padded through into the sitting room. There was no sign of him. When she had gone to bed last night he had still not come back. Probably just working off steam, she had concluded. She was now wondering if he might have come back late and then left early. But no, his briefcase was still here.

Oh well, let him sulk. He was liable to fly off the handle at the slightest provocation. Rikki had been spoiled, as a result of being the only male child with an indulgent mother and five adoring sisters. I hate him, I hate him, I hate him. I love him, I love him, I love him.

Kate drew back the curtain. It was a bright, windy day, with trees bending in the breeze and clouds scudding across the sky. She wandered into the kitchen and switched on the kettle. There were the plates from last night's supper, still on the drainer where she had left them. When Rikki had stalked out last night she had at first been too upset to eat, but the aroma from the plate in front of her had been too mouth-watering to resist. She had speared a prawn with her fork and popped it into her mouth. Delicious. Then she had taken a forkful of the rice, which had absorbed some of the yummy juices. She had washed this down with a swig of wine. After a while she had taken another bite, and then another. It had seemed a shame to let it go to waste. A girl had to eat, after all. By the time she had finished her plate was clear and the wine bottle was half-empty.

The water boiled, and the kettle switched itself off. Kate dropped a tea bag into a mug and covered it in water. She teased it with a spoon for a while and then fished it out, dropping it in the bin. She topped up the mug with milk. Kate picked up her mug and sauntered back to the table. Seated there, she noticed a lever-arch folder on the desk in the corner of the room. That must contain Rikki's case-notes. Kate was suddenly curious. Rikki was obviously rather taken with Cass Carnaby: what had they said to each other? She wanted very much to know what was in that folder.

For several long minutes she sat staring out of the window at the passing clouds. Then a nasty thought struck her. She had assumed that Rikki had crashed the night at a friend's house, or perhaps gone home to 'Mama'. But supposing that he hadn't? What if he had been in an accident? She imagined him lying in a coma, or feebly calling out her name from a hospital bed. Or worse ... supposing he had been more upset than she had thought? What if he had done something to himself?

She tried his mobile, but it went straight to voicemail. Where could he be? The practice managers would know what he was supposed to be doing today, but it was too early to call his chambers. She picked up his hefty briefcase, plonked it on the table, and opened it, but there was nothing inside. He must have his diary with him. Unless ... She glanced across at the folder. There was no reason to hesitate any longer – surely there would be something in there about where he'd be today. Suddenly decisive, Kate walked over to the desk and began reading.

Ten minutes later she heard the doorbell ring. With a guilty start, she closed the folder and sprang to her feet. Striding across the room, she picked up Rikki's briefcase and placed it back on the floor where she had found it. A moment later she opened the front door, and with a flood of relief found her husband standing there, unshaven and a little dishevelled. Kate felt embarrassment at her earlier stupidity. Of course Rikki hadn't done anything to himself! She had been a fool to think any such thing.

'Rough night?' she enquired.

'I slept in the car,' Rikki explained, unsmiling. 'I, er, went out without my house keys.'

'You must have been in a hurry.' She wasn't going to make this too easy for him.

'I need some coffee,' he said, and walked past her, a little stiffly, towards the kitchen. Kate decided to get dressed for work. She didn't have time to hang around talking.

A quarter of an hour later she was in the shower, washing her hair, when she heard a knock on the bathroom door. She stepped aside from the jet of water, pulling her hair back from her ears. 'What is it?' she shouted.

'Are you going to be in there for ever?'

It was absolutely typical of a man, thought Kate, to start badgering you to come out only a few minutes after you'd entered the bathroom. Didn't they understand about hair? 'I'll come out when I'm ready,' she bellowed.

'But I have to get ready for work,' she heard him shout.

'So do I.'

A short while later she emerged from the bathroom, a towel wrapped around her. 'At last!' he exclaimed, pushing past her. Kate heard him showering as she dressed. When she was ready to go out she picked up her bag, walked through to the kitchen and helped herself to some coffee from the pot. A moment later Rikki appeared, now shaved and respectable, and, like her, wearing his coat. He looked so handsome that she had to restrain herself from rushing over to embrace him. They had not touched since his return, she realised. He did not seem to be in a good mood, and Kate had the impression that he had been rehearsing what to say to her. She stiffened, preparing to defend herself.

'Well,' he said flatly. 'Have you got anything to say to me?'

Kate could tell that he was hurt. She wanted to say, 'Please don't look so unhappy. I love you: we can work this out.' Instead she said: 'Like what?'

'I know that I should try not to let this affect us,' he continued, 'but I can't help feeling betrayed.'

'Betrayed?' she snorted. 'Don't be ridiculous.'

'You must know how important this is to me,' he went on, 'but you seem willing to sabotage it nevertheless.'

'You're being absurd. Anyway, I can't waste half the morning psychoanalysing you,' she breezed, picking up her bag. 'Some of us have to get to work.' Even before the words were out of her mouth she realised that this sounded harsh, but it was too late.

Rikki looked crushed. He opened his mouth to speak, and then shut it again. 'I have to get to work too,' he said, grabbing the folder and stuffing it into his briefcase. He followed Kate into the hall and out onto the landing, slamming the door behind him. 'We'll talk about this later,' he announced, as they descended the stairs.

Outside the front door, Kate looked him in the eye. 'There is nothing to talk about,' she declared, then turned on her heel and started walking.

Rikki took a few steps after her, protesting, then changed his mind. He spun round and marched off in the other direction.

Chapter 12

Rikki stood with knees slightly bent, feet apart, sideways on to the court, front foot pointed towards his opponent. *Concentrate!* He'd been playing badly for almost an hour. It was all Kate's fault, of course. He gripped the racket in his right hand against the ball in his left. Fixing his eyes on the target, he sucked in a deep breath, and rocked his weight onto his heels, as he swung his right arm back and tossed the ball high in the air, stretching his left arm straight above his head. Then he swung his right arm forward, arching onto his toes, catching the ball at its highest point, as it hung motionless before it began to drop. The satisfying *thwack* told him that this was a good serve. At last!

'Long, I'm afraid.' His opponent, his sister Yasmin, did not look very sorry. In fact she was grinning.

'What!'

'Long. At least six inches outside the box.'

'I can't believe it.'

'Would I lie to you?' she challenged him. Though far from convinced, Rikki grunted in acquiescence, and fumbled in his pocket for another ball. He could never stand up to his sisters, who were all much older, and who had established an unassailable moral advantage over him while he was still a small boy. Though she was the next youngest in the family, there was more than a decade separating him from Yasmin. He had been still at school when she married. 'You were a mistake, of course,' his mother had confirmed, when he was old enough to understand, 'but a *lovely* mistake.'

His sister must be in her forties now, Rikki realised, though her body showed no sign of ageing; on the contrary, she could out-run him and hit the ball frighteningly hard. She usually emerged victorious from their regular Thursday-lunchtime games. Yasmin was a fitness fanatic, spending several hours a week at the gym. Looking at her lithe figure on the other side of the net, it was hard to believe that she was a middle-aged woman with two teenage sons. Rikki was reasonably lithe himself, but then he was only thirty. Whether he would be in such good shape ten years on was another matter. He didn't have the dedication to spend hour after sweaty hour working out.

Now he needed to concentrate again. The problem was that his second serves were the weakest aspect of his game. He had never found a happy medium: either he sent down thunderbolts, which often resulted in a double fault, or what he sent over the net was accurate, but so feeble that it was easily despatched. Lacking confidence in his thunderbolts, he decided to try one of his girly-but-safe second serves. He lobbed the ball in the air and tapped it over the net. Advancing towards the net like a shark sensing blood, Yasmin took the ball on the rise and smashed it back over the net straight towards him. Rikki contrived to put his racket in its path, but without any control, and the ball soared up into the air before clattering against the wire netting that enclosed the court.

'Game and set to me, I think,' announced Yasmin smugly. 'Shall we take a break? You look as if you could do with one.'

They bought a couple of hot drinks at the little café in the square, only a few metres from the courts. It was just warm enough to sit outside in the winter sun, even in shorts, providing that you had been warmed by vigorous exercise beforehand. They sat at a little metal table.

'So, bro, tell me, why are you looking so tired?' Yasmin began. She leaned across and ruffled his hair. 'You haven't been working too hard, have you?' She glanced disapprovingly in the direction of Rikki's chambers, on the west side of the square. Just then the sky darkened as a cloud crossed the sun. Looking up, he could see a bank of menacing grey approaching from the west.

Rikki hesitated. 'Come on, Rikki,' she cajoled him. 'You know that you'll feel better if you open up to Big Sister.'

She was right, of course. He needed to talk to someone, and Yasmin had always been the sibling to whom he felt closest. 'If I tell you, can you keep it to yourself? And not tell anyone in the family, especially not Mama?'

'Mum's the word.'

Rikki acknowledged the quip with a grin. Like all Persian mothers, Mama fussed over her only son. They both knew that the safest way to stop her from fretting was to keep her in the dark. Their father was quite different, never seeming unduly concerned whatever they did. But then Papa was English, and the quintessential absent-minded academic. His parents had met in the early 1960s, when Papa had been supervising a dig at an Achaemenid site near Persepolis, and Mama had been a young graduate student who came along to help. They sometimes joked that Papa had been too preoccupied

127

to look for a wife, so he grabbed the nearest woman to hand.

'OK,' Rikki said. 'Well, you know this big case I told you about?'

'So you *are* working too hard?'

'No, that's not the problem. The problem is Kate. We had a big row last night and I ended up sleeping in the car. Or rather, not sleeping.'

Yasmin made a face. 'What was the row about?'

'Well, it's the case. Kate is appearing for the other side.'

'And that is a problem because …?'

Rikki felt frustrated. Surely Yasmin, of all people, would understand?

'Are you saying that it's not permitted for husbands and wives to appear on opposite sides in court?' Yasmin asked.

'No, no, it's not that,' he corrected her hurriedly. 'It's just that this case is so important to my career, and I don't want to make a mess of it.'

Yasmin frowned. 'So you feel that you might make a mess of it because Kate is involved?'

'Well … yes, I suppose that I do.'

'Can you explain why?'

'It's hard to explain. For me, court is like the stage, and when I'm appearing in court I'm like an actor, and I identify utterly with the part I'm playing. The fact that it's a contest makes it all the more dramatic. I'm anxious that I won't be at my best if I appear against Kate … Though it may not come to that,' he finished lamely.

'I thought as juniors you wouldn't have to speak in court. And anyway, isn't it just as difficult for her?'

'Apparently not. So far as I can tell, Kate doesn't have the same difficulty. Of course, she's so single-minded.' He paused, aware that Kate and Yasmin were very different people. 'I don't know, maybe it's an English thing. I just can't divorce the two sides of my life ... so to speak,' he added, smiling.

'Does she know that you feel like this?'

'I've told her, but I don't think she takes it seriously.'

Yasmin took a sip of her coffee, looking thoughtful. 'In that case, Little Brother, I think that you have a problem.'

ᏩᏒ

'Come in, King.' Fonthill gestured towards a chair. 'Sit down, please.' Rikki obediently complied. Fonthill swivelled round in his high-backed chair to face him. 'What was it that you wanted to see me about?'

Rikki swallowed. He'd been dreading this interview. 'I'm afraid that there has been an unfortunate development.'

'Oh?'

'You see, it's my wife—'

'Oh God, she isn't pregnant, is she? I suppose you'll be wanting paternity leave. How very tiresome!'

'No, no, it's nothing like that,' Rikki cut in hastily. 'It's just that ... I suppose you know that she's a barrister?'

'I had heard a rumour to that effect.' Fonthill was looking dangerously bored.

'Well, she's been asked to appear – as a junior, you understand, to Angus McLaren in *Benson* v. *Carnaby*.'

Fonthill sat up abruptly, a look of horror on his face. 'But that's our case!' he spluttered.

'Yes. I know that it's very unfortunate. I have tried to persuade her not to take it.'

'But it's all agreed! Surely Jenkins hasn't done the dirty on us?'

'Er, no, you misunderstand me. My wife is appearing for Mr Benson.'

Fonthill let out a sigh of relief and sat back in his chair, which spun slowly away from Rikki. 'Is that all?' he asked. 'You had me worried there for a moment. I thought I'd lost my brief.'

'No, no, nothing like that.'

'Well, you did the right thing in letting me know.'

'Do you want to ask someone else to take over from me?' Rikki asked timidly.

'No, it's too late for that. Though of course we'll need to ensure that the client doesn't object. You'd better leave that to me. But now I come to think of it, there is something else about which I want to speak to you.'

'Please go ahead.'

'Now, you understand, don't you, that the Bar isn't all glamour and big money?'

Rikki nodded. Strangely enough, he was aware of that.

'Sometimes one has to take on tedious cases which will never be lucrative.' Fonthill sighed theatrically. 'Such is the cross we bear.'

Rikki was already pretty sure that if anyone was going to be bearing a cross, it wouldn't be Nicholas Fonthill, QC.

'I'm afraid that it's another of these fathers whingeing about not having access to his offspring. You think he'd be grateful not to have the little monsters hanging around his neck, wouldn't you? Some people don't know their luck.'

Divorced fathers demanding greater access to their children were increasingly common, though not very popular with barristers, as there was little prestige and not much money to be made out of them.

'I don't know why he has to bother *me* about this,' Fonthill expostulated. 'Why doesn't he just dress up as Batman or something and jump off a high building?'

Rikki was used to Fonthill's fulminations, which formed part of his carefully cultivated persona.

'I wouldn't normally consider a case such as this,' Fonthill continued, 'except that the man in question happens to be a client of Justin Jenkins. Justin has asked me to see him as a favour.' Fonthill spat out this last word as if it had an unpleasant taste. 'We do want to keep Justin happy, don't we?' He cracked his knuckles.

We certainly do, thought Rikki, though he simply said, 'Yes.'

'Good. Now, I'm in court tomorrow morning and unfortunately I've been called away from chambers afterwards on urgent business out of town.' Rikki knew that this was code for riding to hounds, Fonthill's only known passion. He assumed this meant too that the weekend's weather forecast was good.

'So, sadly, I won't be able to see Mr – er – Amis. I *thought* that I *might* hand this plum over to you. Though I'm concerned about being accused of *favouritism*. I've been so *generous* to you lately.'

Rikki marvelled at how this 'cross' had become a 'plum' in a matter of minutes. But however tedious it was, he knew that he had no choice other than to take it.

'I'm very grateful to you, Mr Fonthill.'

'Mr Fonthill, *sir*.'

'Mr Fonthill, sir.'

෧෨

'My wife insists that our son has violin lessons,' the man said gloomily. 'In my view it's a complete waste of time. He's tone deaf and has no interest in that kind of music. I think that it's just snobbery. Why should I be expected to contribute to the cost when I don't see the point of it?'

Kate took a deep breath. 'The thing is, Mr Tompkins, we need to concentrate on the big picture. In the scheme of things violin lessons don't count for very much. What we want to do is to achieve an overall financial resolution with Mrs Tompkins. Try to look at this as a whole, and not the detail.' They were sitting in a small ante-room of a local county court. It was a modern building, bleak and anonymous. Outside, a grey sky threatened rain.

'That's all very well for you to say,' continued Tompkins, 'but you don't know her mother. She's always looked down on me, and thought that I wasn't good enough for her daughter.' He snorted. 'Not good enough, just because I don't see the point in violin lessons. Honestly, if you heard him practising—'

'We mustn't get bogged down,' Kate cut in. 'We only have an hour to reach a resolution before the hearing. It will be much cheaper for both parties if we can agree a clean-break settlement before then. You have in front of you the statement of assets which your solicitor prepared on your instructions. I have weighed up the possibilities and prepared a summary of a proposed agreement. Would you mind taking a look at it?' She handed him the document.

Tompkins gave it a cursory inspection. 'Here's another thing,' he said almost instantaneously. 'She's claiming that mountain bike is worth a thousand pounds. I had a search on eBay last night and found one almost identical selling for four hundred and ten pounds! That's less than half what she's claiming it's worth. How can you trust a woman who exaggerates like that?' He held up both hands and shrugged his shoulders in a gesture of appeal. 'Mind you, it didn't have the heavy-duty tyres, which adds another hundred and twenty-five quid, but even so ...'

Kate sighed. At times like this she wanted to lean across the table and give her client a good shake. 'Mr Tompkins,' she said seriously, 'it's my duty to warn you that if we can't reach a resolution with Mrs Tompkins's representative in the next' – she checked her watch – 'forty-eight minutes, you will be liable for court fees, amounting to enough to buy a whole fleet of mountain bikes. I strongly advise you to study the proposals I've put forward and tell me what is the maximum figure you will allow me to offer the other side.'

'Salsa classes,' said Tompkins, unperturbed. 'What does she need them for? She's forty-three years old! I ask you, why does a forty-three-year-old woman go to salsa classes?' He stared at her quizzically. 'Unless,' he added, his face brightening like a detective who scents that he's on to something, 'she's up to no good.' He shot Kate a knowing smile. 'Salsa classes!'

This was the kind of dreary case that Kate dreaded. It provided no stimulus to her mind and no opportunity to exercise her skills. The best she could hope for was to persuade clients like Mr Tompkins to avoid shooting themselves in the foot, which right now he was doing with both barrels. She needed to escape from this world of petty squabbling, to join the elite of those barristers who handled the most interesting and most lucrative cases. Why couldn't Rikki understand that? Just then her mobile announced that she had a message.

'Oh, er, excuse me a moment.'

'You carry on, don't mind me. Salsa classes!'

Kate opened the message. Great to have you on the team x J. For a moment she wondered who on earth 'J' could be. Then her heart swelled. Jez Benson had sent her a text! She closed her eyes and smiled. One day soon, all this would be far behind her.

∽

It was raining when Kate emerged from the court, so she sheltered under her umbrella on the long walk back to the underground station. Sad suburban villas lined the long, featureless road. She picked her way carefully along the pavement, trying to avoid the puddles. 'I can stand any kind of torture,' Angus always said, 'except wet feet.' She smiled. Dear Angus was a bit of a wag.

As the rain drummed down her thoughts turned once again to Rikki. Really, he was behaving in the most childish manner! And he seemed to be thinking only of himself. He didn't seem capable of appreciating that if this case was significant for him, it was significant for her too. Her career was equally important, wasn't it? Some women seemed happy to play second fiddle to a high-achieving husband, but not Kate Pepper. Oh, no.

Her mobile was ringing. Holding her umbrella in one hand, Kate fished in her bag for the phone and peered at the display, wondering whether to take the call. It was Angela Cross. Angela was the kind of practical, no-nonsense professional woman that Kate admired, and Kate hoped to impress on her that she was a professional too. She flipped open the phone and answered. 'Kate Pepper speaking.'

Angela explained that she had been trying to reach Angus and had been told that he was in court all day. 'I need some assistance,' she said. 'I have the strong impression that even at this late stage my client is not being completely honest with me about his assets. The rich are different, you know. I've found this to be true again and again. They imagine that the law doesn't apply to them. Can you help me persuade Mr Benson that he must come clean? I don't think that he quite appreciates the dangers of non-disclosure.'

'Hmm,' said Kate. 'It's interesting that you should say that.' She thought guiltily about the files she had leafed through this morning. 'Of course I fully agree that we must make it clear to him what a risk he is running.'

'And of course now it's become very urgent, given that we're in the High Court next week,' said Angela. 'The problem is that I can't get hold of him by telephone. According to his PA, he's gone abroad. She won't even tell me where he is.'

'Have you tried his mobile number?'

'Would you believe that he won't give it to me? Some absurd excuse about "needing head space".'

'What do you recommend?'

'The PA has said that if I send him an email, she will forward it to him. Apparently that's the best she can offer.' Angela's exasperation was obvious. 'God only knows how one is supposed to represent a client in such circumstances. Anyway, I thought that if you could send me an email as soon as possible, making it clear how seriously the courts take such matters, that would add strength to my argument. Would you mind doing that?'

'No problem. I'm on my way back to chambers at the moment and I'll tackle it as soon as I get there. Give me a couple of hours or so and I'll wing it over to you.'

Chapter 13

ⓈⓈⓈ

This is so not me, thought Rikki, as he descended the dark steps into the basement club, while a pounding rhythm attacked him out of the gloom. It would be stupid to back out now, though, having parted with £50 for his 'annual membership fee' at the door. At the foot of the steps a neon sign glowed with the word GIRLS. Rikki paused, still uncertain whether to go in. Michael took his arm and propelled him forward. 'Come on, old chap,' Michael bellowed in his ear, 'they don't bite, you know … well, actually they do, ha ha.' He chuckled knowingly, with the air of a man of the world, and pointed to a red mark on his neck. Rikki groaned. How did he get into this?

The answer was depressingly simple: he was being carried along by events, like a piece of flotsam being swept out to sea by the ebb tide. This morning he was still hoping that he could persuade Kate not to take the Benson brief. But she hadn't even been willing to hear him out. He was still reeling from her decision. How could she have pressed ahead, knowing how upset he would be? Because she was a selfish cow, he told himself bitterly. What mattered most to her was

Kate Pepper, not her husband. Of course he knew that wasn't wholly fair – but there was a grain of truth in it, nonetheless. Rikki felt as if he had been handed a beautiful present, which had almost immediately been snatched away. If Cass Carnaby objected, he would be off the case altogether.

He didn't know how to speak to Kate when she was in this implacable frame of mind. The only thing he was sure of was that he couldn't stay around her while they were both involved in this case. Aside from anything else, there were ethical considerations. For a case like this he would inevitably have to bring work home. Yet he couldn't take the risk of compromising confidential client information. That could be enough to have him debarred – to have them both debarred. Didn't she realise what a risk she was taking? Being Kate, she must have done: she was no fool. She was putting their entire future in jeopardy. How could she do this to him – to them both? Was her career more important to her than her marriage?

So he had to go somewhere, and it didn't really matter where. Fortunately he kept a change of clothes in chambers, so he didn't have to go back to the flat immediately. But what was he going to do that evening? He couldn't sleep in the car again. Somehow he didn't want to go and stay with a friend – or, even worse, his parents. They would want to know why he was there, and start trying to interfere. His sisters were absorbed in their families. The situation was delicate enough without anyone else getting involved, however well meaning. Rikki was a private person who didn't easily share his problems with other people. He knew that was a failing; women were always telling him so.

But he had made one decision. It wouldn't do anything to solve his problems, but it might make him feel a little better.

He had decided to tell that lecherous twit Michael to leave well alone. He steeled himself for a stern conversation. But even that had gone wrong. Michael had not seemed surprised when he telephoned: on the contrary.

'Aha, I know why you're calling,' he'd said, in a surprisingly genial tone.

'You do?' Rikki was so taken aback that all his reprimands died on his lips.

'Of course. You've had a tiff with the wife, haven't you? I should imagine that she's a very fierce lady. So I suppose you're looking for a place to lie low?'

'Well ... actually, I am. But—'

'No probs, Rikki, my lad. You can have the spare room, for a short while anyway. I call it the spare room, though it's really a large cupboard. Still, I suppose you won't mind that for a few days until the little lady calms down, eh?'

'Er ... I suppose not.'

'Twenty-eight Lincoln House, Percy Street, N1, five minutes' walk from Liverpool Street station. Key's with the porter. I'll give him a ring now and tell him to expect you.'

'Um ... thank you.'

So that's how he'd found himself as Michael's guest, making it difficult for him to reproach Michael for his behaviour towards Kate. And of course, being a guest, he felt obliged to pass some time with his host in the evening. Which is how he'd ended up here, in the 'Acapulco Club', in a dingy Hoxton side street. It was a large basement room, warm and humid. He could see no windows. A number of tables, most of them empty, littered the floor. There was hardly anyone else here: perhaps a dozen people in all. Most of them were men in suits, but a number of young women moved between them, dressed in what appeared to be skimpy bikinis and strappy high heels. They emerged and disappeared through a doorway shielded by thin plastic strips, above which was another neon sign: PRIVATE. A moving pattern of lights swept the walls and shone lurid colours over their naked flesh. Along one wall was a bar, with a large man in attendance. Another sign above his head read EROT-IQUE DANCING, a phrase Rikki remembered from the exterior. In the centre of a room was a raised dais, and on this a dancer was performing unlikely contortions round a vertical stainless-steel pole. The music was monotonous and very loud.

'Fantastic, isn't it?' Michael leaned over and shouted in his ear. Fortunately there was no need to make any more response than to smile weakly at him. Michael steered Rikki towards the table near the girl on the dais. She was a scrawny blonde, with slim hips, long legs, mid-length hair and thin, Slavic features. Her lips were spread in a permanent pout, while she stared into the middle distance, as if dreaming of the endless Steppe. He noticed that she had very small breasts. The music was just beginning again, and she leaned her head back, gripping the pole with one hand and twisting herself slowly round three hundred and sixty degrees, scanning the room. She began gyrating her hips in a slow, easy motion. Several times she flicked her head, so that her immaculately groomed hair flew out sideways before dropping again with a pleasing bounce. Rikki was happy to note that he felt no feelings of arousal whatsoever. Gloomily he contemplated lapsing into a squalid bachelor existence with Michael, staying up late, conducting inane conversations with bored girls with whom he had nothing in common, drinking too much, eating bad food, and even smoking the odd cigarette.

A nearly naked waitress bent over to ask Michael something, and he whispered something in her ear as he reached for his wallet. The girl on the dais climbed the pole and slid slowly down, her legs wrapped tightly round. Then she spread her legs wide, a gymnast who'd fallen on hard times. Rikki found himself inspecting her thong from an uncomfortably close distance. Michael smirked at him. The waitress brought them a bottle and two champagne glasses, which she filled. Michael slyly offered her a note; she reacted with apparent astonishment at his generosity. Rikki took a sip of the 'champagne', which was lukewarm and tasted nasty.

Meanwhile, the girl was now lying on the floor of the dais, performing some kind of sensual press-ups. Rikki tried to avoid Michael's eye. As though suddenly inspired, the girl leaped to her feet and skipped carelessly forward, like a ballerina who'd forgotten to get dressed. In a gesture of submission she stretched her leg up the pole and began to pull herself up feet first, so that her long hair brushed the floor. Rikki stole a glance at Michael, whose face was now flushed. He wondered how long he would have to endure this before he could decently leave.

The music stopped, and the girl on the dais made a tour of the tables to receive the appreciation of the patrons. Michael whispered in her ear and tucked a note into her thong. Rikki got to his feet and made his way to sign marked TOILETS. When he returned to the table a few minutes later he found that two scantily clad young women had joined them, accompanied by two more champagne glasses. He was introduced to 'Svetlana', who appeared to find him most amusing, though conversation was inaudible above the thumping beat of the music. The other young woman was laughing too, as Michael confided something in her ear. Svetlana leaned forward and raised her glass in the gesture of a toast, resting her hand gently on Rikki's knee. Another girl was now on the dais, one hand gripping the pole while she strutted in a circle, lifting her feet high. Rikki noticed that Svetlana was now stroking his knee. He withdrew her hand slowly, and gave her a rueful grin. Then he turned back to look at the stage, where the dancer appeared to be scratching her back against the pole while she writhed as if in ecstasy. Rikki wondered, not for the first time that evening, what Kate was doing.

Chapter 14

❦ ❦ ❦

Kate returned home that night energised by her discussions with Angela Cross. She didn't know whether to be disappointed or relieved when, looking up from the street at the living-room windows of their flat, she saw that they were dark. Either Rikki was still sulking, or he was working late. She set her jaw, determined to carry on behaving normally. There was plenty of work to do, now that Jez Benson had had his 'little thinky' and she was definitely on the case.

A parcel was propped up outside the door to the flat. She stooped to pick it up, noticing in the semi-gloom of the landing light that it was much battered and covered with foreign stamps and Customs stickers, some in oriental script. There was more post inside, which swooshed back along the floor as she pushed open the door. Though it was wholly illogical to think that Rikki might have written her a note and dropped it through the letter box, she couldn't help feeling a prickle of hope that he might have done. His moods were unpredictable. Stormy as he had seemed this morning, he could well have changed his mind and impulsively bought a 'Sorry' card as a prelude to coming home later tonight for a reconciliation.

But there were only the usual bills and unsolicited letters concerning double-glazing and pet insurance. She chucked the latter in the bin and put the former on the long desk she normally shared with Rikki, in the 'Bills' section of her four-storey in-tray. (The other sections were labelled 'Personal', 'Work' and 'For Filing'.) Then she hung up her coat and turned her attention to the parcel, addressed to 'Mr and Mrs King'. Generally, it was only banks and utility companies that insisted on calling her Mrs King – when they didn't address Rikki as Mr Pepper. Fetching scissors from a kitchen drawer, she cut through the thick paper wrapping, revealing a long, slim box with a small card with silver wedding bells printed in one corner and a typed message: 'To Kate and Richard, with best wishes from David and Mai.' Her expression tightened. 'David' – not even Dad, or Daddy as she had called him long ago. Mai was his Vietnamese wife. They lived in Saigon with their two children, now teenagers. Inside the box was a pair of salad servers made of clear plastic, tinted a pale aquamarine on the handles. *Gee, thanks, Dad. Only about eighteen months late. And he isn't called Richard. Otherwise, ten out of ten.* Looking more closely at the packaging, she saw that one of the stickers read, 'By Sea Mail.'

Well, what did she expect? Not much, any more. Her father had left her mother when Kate was seven. No one had explained to her what was happening and, oddly, she couldn't remember overhearing any quarrels. If anything, the atmosphere at home had been one of sullen silence. Generally her mother was on the sofa watching mindless television, and her father in the garden, tinkering with a bit of machinery. And then one day he was gone. She knew that her parents had met while working for the local Water Board, her mother in customer services and her father in surveying. The nature of his work meant that he was usually out and about in his van, which, she later decided, might have contributed to the problem between her parents, though as she grew older Kate suspected that he had simply outgrown his pretty but unadventurous wife, since he now seemed to have a rather high-powered job to do with water resources in Vietnam. That was about all she knew. He had written a few letters to her – more often postcards – after he first left home, which she still possessed, though they told her little. *Dear Katy, How are you? I am fine. Thank you for the drawing you sent me. Is it a circus? I hope you are working hard at school. Love, Daddy.* Apparently he also sent maintenance cheques to her mother, though she complained that they were never large enough.

Kate was never sure if her mother's drinking was the cause or the effect of her father's departure. Either way, she had fallen apart once he had gone. Kate started finding her in bed when she returned from school, and after an embarrassing conversation with a boy in her class, whose mother worked in the same office as Kate's, she realised that her mother had lost her job. The house grew messy and dusty, the small back lawn rank with weeds. Tea became an increasingly late and eccentric meal: toast and tinned pineapple, for example, or frozen peas and a Crunchie bar. Her mother was no longer so pretty. Her hair went unbrushed and her eyes became wandering and vacant. Often she smelled funny. Once, Kate had found her asleep on the tiled kitchen floor. At first she had been terrified that her mother was dying – or perhaps had been put under an evil spell, like a character from her children's books. Remarks from neighbours, some kindly and many not, plus the bottles she found in the dustbin, plus a poster she'd perused in the doctor's surgery, gradually enabled her to put two and two together – even before Social Services came calling. She had written a desperate letter to her father, begging him to come home and look after Mummy, but after two months it had come back again, marked 'Not Known at This Address'. Later she learned that he had moved all over the country, taking temporary posts before moving to Australia, then Vietnam. Cheques still came from the bank, but she heard nothing from him. When she was eleven he had got in touch with her mother to ask for a divorce so that he could marry Mai. Despite everything, Kate was convinced that he longed to know all about her, and had sent him a detailed letter about her achievements at school, enclosing the latest photo of herself in uniform, hair scraped back into a ponytail and an eager smile that revealed her new big teeth. When he didn't reply she told herself that the letter must have got lost. She wrote again, whenever there was something she had achieved of note – a school prize, her O-level results, her A-level results, her first from Birmingham. Occasionally, he wrote back, sometimes after an interval of several months or even years. *Dear Kate, Thank you for your interesting letter. I'm sorry it's taken so long to reply. I should tell you that we moved a while ago, and are now living at ...* Slowly and painfully, it dawned on Kate that he simply wasn't interested in her, and never would be, not even if she became Prime Minister, or won an Oscar, or flew to the moon. He didn't dislike her or disapprove of her; he just didn't care.

Kate was still holding the salad servers tightly in one hand. Might as well keep them, she thought. They were quite attractive, and when they broke, as such plastic items did sooner or later, she would be able to bin them without a pang. She carried them into the kitchen, washed and dried them, and stowed them in a drawer. Then she opened the fridge door and stared at its contents for several long moments before shutting it again. She wasn't hungry. Anyway, there were all those documents to read through, which Nexus were submitting to the judge on behalf of Cass Carnaby. On her first perusal it had seemed to her that some items were missing – perfectly possible, given Rikki's occasionally slapdash methods. His easy-going approach to life sometimes irritated her.

Kate decided to change out of her work clothes and tackle the contents of her briefcase. In some ways it would be quite pleasing if she were able to point out to him an omission or a mistake.

She was sitting on the bed in her bra and pants, peeling off her tights, when the house phone rang. Rikki! Kate jumped up and lolloped into the living room, trailing the tights that were still attached to one foot. Her hand hovered over the receiver while she composed herself. Cool but not unfriendly: that was the tone.

'Hello, Kate speaking.'

'Oh – Kate.' The familiar voice rose in surprise, as if Kate were the last person Rikki's mother might expect to find living with her darling son. 'I hope that you are well.'

'I'm *fine*, thanks,' Kate answered with unnecessary emphasis. 'And how are you, Banu?'

'Thank you, I am as well as can be expected,' came the queenly reply. In Persian, Kate had learned, Banu meant 'lady', or sometimes 'princess'. 'I wonder if I might speak with my son, please?' she continued.

'I'm afraid he's not here. Er, not home yet, I mean,' Kate gabbled.

'So late?' There was a sharp intake of breath. 'Poor Rikki, he works so hard.'

'Well, it's all go, you know, being a barrister. As a matter of fact, I'm just about to sit down myself and—'

'You see, Kate, I am worrying about his hand.'

'His hand?' Kate frowned in puzzlement. 'What hand?'

'The one he burned so badly when he was cooking your dinner.'

'Oh, that.' Kate made the mistake of laughing.

'It's important to take care of these things, you know, Kate.' Banu's voice was reproving. 'We don't want Rikki to be *scarred for life*.'

'Honestly, it was nothing, just a tiny little—'

'I must say I don't really know why Rikki was cooking at all, when he's so busy. In any case, he told me that you don't have any bandages or ointments. Can that be true?'

Kate rolled her eyes. 'Really, Banu, all he needed was to run it under the cold tap. He's fine.'

'That's not what I hear. Yasmin told me that it was bothering him yesterday, when they played tennis. He showed her the mark.'

Huh – with a magnifying glass? Kate wanted to say, but didn't. It drove her crazy the way Rikki's family seemed to ring each other every five seconds to report on some minor detail. Say Yasmin's hoover broke down: Yasmin told Nazneen, who told Farida, who told Lilya, who phoned back Yasmin to ask if it was mended yet, while their mother wittered and twittered about it to Kate and Rikki, if she got the chance.

'Now, Kate, I am going to give you the name of a special cream. It must be put on morning and night. Maybe you can find a chemist that stays open late. Have you got a pen?'

'Yes,' Kate lied, flaring her nostrils. She bent down and yanked the tights free of her foot while Banu painstakingly spelled out a long word with lots of 'y's and 'z's in it.

'Twice a day, remember. And tell Rikki to give his poor old mama a ring before I forget I ever had a son.'

'Will do.'

'Well, I must let you get back to your preparations for supper. Goodbye, Kate.' As always, she put down the phone before waiting for a reply.

Shaking her head in bemusement, Kate replaced her own receiver and sat for a moment in her underwear, thinking. Tennis, eh? It didn't sound as if Rikki was exactly pining for her. Why not? And what, she wondered, had he said to his sister? Probably nothing, she acknowledged. Whatever his faults, Rikki was loyal. And he was proud – too proud to admit that he had stomped off in a sulk and had spent the night in his car. She pictured him as she had seen him this morning, tired and tousled, and wished he'd just come home and say sorry so that they could get back to normal.

In the bedroom she tossed her tights and today's shirt into the laundry bin, which was close to overflowing. Rikki claimed not to be able to understand precisely how the washing machine worked – or the central-heating controls, DVD recorder or the car radio. It was funny the way men were so keen on gadgets but needed a woman to operate them. With a sigh Kate sorted out the lights and darks and put on a wash in the kitchen. It was tempting to pull on some old pyjama bottoms and a T-shirt, but she decided instead on a short, flouncy skirt and a skinny top that Rikki always said matched her eyes. She brushed her hair and put on some lip-gloss, then placed her laptop on the desk and switched it on. When Rikki returned he would find her attractively poised over her work, so absorbed that she hadn't even noticed how late he was. With an expert finger she revolved and tapped the mouse-pad of her computer, automatically checking for new emails while she bent down to pull a bundle of documents from the briefcase at her feet. Refocusing on the screen, she was startled to see 'Rikki King' in bold black letters. She hesitated, caught between hope and foreboding, then took a stiffening breath and opened the message.

Dear Ms Pepper,

Mr Nicholas Fonthill, QC has asked me to apprise your side of the fact that we intend to submit as evidence the contents of Bundle 3(b) as detailed on the attached summary. We trust that your side will make no objection, but should you wish to do so, kindly inform us by return.

Yours faithfully,

Rustom King

Nexus Chambers

There was a PS at the bottom:

Kate – I'm going to stay with a friend for the next couple of days. You have placed us in an impossible position by insisting on opposing me in *Benson* v. *Carnaby*, and I don't have the energy to argue at present since I have so much work to do. Maybe we can talk at the weekend.

Rikki

I hope you are OK.

Of all the pig-headed, high-handed, self-righteous, self-pitying, cold, unfeeling … Running out of adjectives, Kate vented her annoyance by stabbing the Delete key, and then had to go into her Deleted Messages box so she could read it again. What 'friend', exactly? 'So much work' that he had time to play tennis and gossip to his sister – hah! Kate folded her arms and glared at the screen, but however many times she read the message it got no friendlier. Yes, she was OK; in fact, she was absolutely fine. Tossing back her hair, she clicked out of her emails and brought up her notes on Cass Carnaby's ridiculously extravagant 'budget'. She would show Rikki what hard work really meant. She would *win* this case – well, with Angus, of course. *At the Bar!* would realise that it had, after all, chosen the wrong rising star to profile.

Such was her determination that she did, in fact, manage an hour's work. But it was hard to keep her concentration from straying. Rikki's things were beside hers on the desk – the carved cedarwood box in which he kept important documents, a old Post-it note in his familiar handwriting, reminding him of a dentist's appointment (long past), the slate paperweight she'd given him in the shape of a tennis ball. His grey jumper was slung over the chair next to hers. When the washing machine beeped to indicate that its cycle was finished, she jumped up eagerly to transfer its contents to the dryer, and decided to wind down by watching a movie. Bending down to the shelf beneath the television, she rifled through the jumbled DVDs and videos. *Indecent Proposal, Love Actually, The Matrix, All About My Mother*, 'Federer v. Nadal/Wimbledon' … 'Rikki and Kate's wedding'. Kate hesitated, then drew out the box and opened it.

She couldn't help smiling as the first arty shots of sun-glinting-through-leaves and pretty-flowers-bedecked-with-dewdrops rolled across the screen, accompanied by a triumphal trumpet concert – Mozart, she thought. It had been risky to choose an outdoor venue for the reception, but the gods had smiled on them, producing a day of warm, blue-skied perfection, so warm for early September that she hadn't even needed the little jacket that matched her dress. The Physic Garden was Rikki's idea. She hadn't even heard of it – Chelsea wasn't exactly her stomping ground – and was a little embarrassed by her ignorance when she learned that it had nothing to do with physics but was an old and famous garden originally established to grow medicinal plants. Apparently, lots of famous people had parties here, not famous as in celebs but arty, bohemian types like playwrights and musicians.

Oh! There was her mother, looking pretty if slightly over-dressed in a green silk suit with gold buttons and a large hat sprouting matching green feathers. Inevitably, her arm was tightly linked with that of a stocky, bald man who looked down at her fondly. Thank God for Greg, who had entered their lives when Kate was a teenager and set them back on track. He had met her mother in a bar, of all places. Both were alcoholics, both divorced, both depressed. But a spark had kindled between them, and together they had started going to AA. He was a taciturn, matter-of-fact man, hard to get to know, and initially Kate had felt almost jealous to be ousted from her position as Controller of the Household. But the benefits of his presence were soon apparent. He adored her mother, and she turned to him gratefully like a flower to the sun. Over long months her drinking diminished, and finally stopped. They all moved into a new house, not much bigger but a lot nicer. In due course Kate went off to university. Greg and her mother were so wrapped up in each other that she sometimes wondered if they even noticed her departure. She watched now as her mother looked at a prof-fered tray of champagne flutes, glanced enquiringly at Greg and, reassured, accepted a glass that Kate knew contained elderflower cordial mixed with sparkling water. Phew. Her family and Rikki's were an uneasy mix, but weddings always scattered a little stardust on their guests. With good will and politeness on both sides, the event had passed off better than she might have expected.

The camera panned round to linger on an exuberant knot

of Rikki's sisters, gossiping on a bench; then Yasmin, in a full-length embroidered silk dress, inclining her head to listen to Sam, who had clearly been at the champagne and was recounting some anecdote with whirling hand gestures. And here she was herself, smiling impishly as she stepped out of the pavilion, where she remembered she'd been snogging Rikki in a hidden corner. He was behind her, holding her hand. She could see the flamboyant waistcoat he'd worn under sober grey, then the dazzling white of his shirt, finally his face, ridiculously handsome and alight with happiness.

Abruptly, Kate pressed the Stop button and switched off the screen. She checked the time by her watch: 11.15 p.m. Time for bed. She wondered where Rikki was now and what he was doing.

Chapter 15

'Taxi!' yelled Rikki, jamming the bulky folders into his side to free an arm. He waved frantically as the cab drove steadily past, oblivious to his signal. Sighing, he took the folders in both hands once more. At least it wasn't raining. He was on his way to a meeting with Justin Jenkins and Cass Carnaby, and for at least a couple of reasons he didn't want to look like a drowned rat.

Rikki stood on the kerb on the south side of Fleet Street, shivery in the cold morning air. Fonthill had summoned him first thing. The QC was already dressed for court, and obviously impatient. He had thrust the folders towards Rikki. 'Jenkins is seeing his client this morning. Take these over to him and make sure that both of them approve the changes I've marked. He must initial the pages where I've indicated. I want these folders back here by lunchtime. Got that?' Fonthill extracted his wig from its box and plonked it on his head. Then he glared impatiently at Rikki. 'Well, what are you waiting for?'

'So Ms Carnaby has no objection to my acting for her as junior, though my wife is acting for her husband?'

Fonthill had rolled his eyes. '*Of course not.* Why would she?'

A taxi pulled up beside him, its kerbside window lowered. Rikki craned his neck to speak to the driver. 'Are you free?'

'That's why I stopped, isn't it?' replied the driver huffily. 'Hop in.'

Rikki gave him directions and then leaned back in his seat as the cab pulled away from the kerb. He wondered what Kate was doing at this moment. Being organised and efficient, no doubt. Did she ever stop to think about him?

'You a lawyer, then?' asked the driver.

Rikki's heart sank. Evidently the cabbie had recognised the address. 'Yes,' he admitted cautiously.

'Mind if I ask you a question? The thing is,' he continued without waiting for an answer, 'I've got this garden wall, see. And what do you think my neighbour's gone and done ...?'

This sort of thing happened all the time. No doubt it was the same for all professions. Investment bankers were asked why the local cashpoint machine never worked; publishers were sent thousand-page manuscripts by a friend of a friend of a friend, requesting their expert editorial comments; doctors were lured into corners at parties and shown strange, hideous growths.

Rikki allowed his thoughts to wander. It was a bit demeaning to be acting as Snape's messenger-boy, though on the other hand he had to admit that he was excited about the prospect of seeing Cass Carnaby again. She was so ... what was she so? Glamorous, he supposed. But since when was he interested in glamour?

Rikki checked his reflection in the cabbie's rear-view mirror and smoothed his hair. He hoped he didn't look too dissolute. He felt weary after a couple of nights in a row without adequate sleep. They hadn't left the pole-dancing club until it closed at two o'clock last night ... no, this morning. By then they were the only two remaining customers. Michael had spent most of the last hour with a girl sitting on his lap, feeding her a succession of notes to keep her happy. Meanwhile Rikki had struggled to make conversation with Svetlana. Eventually the music stopped. A large man with a thick accent had approached the table to warn them that the club was closing. Michael had insisted that it was his duty as a 'gentleman' to see the girls into a taxi, and while they were waiting in the cold outside he had tried to persuade them to come back to the flat. There had been a lot of giggling and hair-tossing on the pavement. When their taxi arrived Michael had 'helped' the girls to climb aboard, promising to come back to the club very soon.

The cab pulled up outside a tall office building in the City, emblazoned with the logo 'HSM': Hill Stone McFarlane, where Justin Jenkins was one of the senior partners.

'So what do you think?' asked the cabbie. 'Should I remove that trellis, or could he have me for damage to property?'

'Not my speciality, sorry,' Rikki replied, reaching for his wallet.

The driver looked aggrieved. 'So what is your speciality?' he demanded.

'Family law,' he answered, counting out a tip.

'Ah. Now, that's interesting, that is, because my auntie ...'

Shaking his head, Rikki made for the swing doors and approached a set of security barriers, guarded by a uniformed man behind a desk. Following instructions, Rikki typed his name into a keyboard, which generated out a credit-card-sized pass. The guard slid the pass into a plastic wallet on a chain and handed it to Rikki. The security barrier swung open to admit him.

A few minutes later the lift disgorged him on the fifth floor, where he had been instructed to report to reception, though in fact Jenkins's office was on the floor above. From the lobby Rikki chose the door marked 'HSM Reception', leading into a sitting area of sofas and low tables scattered with newspapers and magazines. A huge logo dominated one wall, while the opposite wall listed the range of the firm's activities in a fashionable lower-case typeface. From behind a long desk a severe middle-aged woman scrutinised him critically. 'I'm here to see Mr Jenkins,' Rikki announced. 'He's expecting me,' he added helpfully. The receptionist gestured for him to sit. A few moments later a smartly dressed young woman emerged from behind a smoked-glass screen, and introduced herself as Jenkins's assistant. Mr Jenkins was in conference with his client, she explained. If he would hand over the documents, she would ensure that Mr Jenkins saw them to him straight away. She made it obvious that Rikki's presence at this meeting was not required. Mr Jenkins would be grateful if Mr King could wait while he checked their contents. It should not be more than an hour at most ...

Rikki felt a surge of disappointment. Fetching and carrying ... this was the less glamorous side of a big-money case. But there was no point in complaining. He handed over the folders, explaining what Mr Fonthill wanted done. Once the smart young woman had disappeared, Rikki picked up a newspaper and settled down to read it on one of the sofas. After a while he put it down again and idly picked up a magazine. Inside was yet another article about Cass Carnaby – 'My Secret Heartache'. Ordinarily, of course, he wouldn't read this sort of thing, but now he felt professionally obliged to do so. The article focused on her husband's infidelities and the pain this had caused her. Rikki struggled to reconcile this with the impression given by Cassandra Carnaby herself. There were a number of beguiling photographs. It was frustrating to think that at this very moment she was somewhere in the building.

Half an hour later the young woman reappeared with the folders. Mr Jenkins had initialled the pages as indicated by Mr Fonthill. He also had some notes, which he would send over by email later in the day. Would Mr King please alert Mr Fonthill?

Rikki said he would. Obediently he gathered up the folders and returned to the lobby, where he pressed the call button and waited. After a minute or so there was a beep and the lift doors opened. Inside was a queenly figure – Cass Carnaby! Rikki was stunned into temporary paralysis. 'Mr King,' she said, raising an eyebrow, 'what a nice surprise.' For a moment he hesitated, flummoxed. She looked at him quizzically, and asked: 'Going down?'

He flushed and stumbled into the lift. 'I didn't expect to see you,' he stammered. 'That is to say, I had expected to join you in the conference, but when I arrived I was told that you and Mr Jenkins wouldn't need me.'

'That mean old Justin wanted me to himself. He's very protective, you know. Thinks I need to be guarded from predatory barristers.' She gave him an alarming smile.

The lift doors closed, and they began to descend. 'I, um, I was so glad to hear that you didn't want me to resign, given that my wife is now acting for the other side.'

'Oh, I still want to have you.'

Rikki blushed. Was everything this woman said an innuendo, or was he being over-sensitive?

Outside, a limousine was waiting for her. 'Perhaps I can drop you?' she suggested, as they hovered on the pavement.

'Oh, really, no, it's too kind of you.'

'Nonsense,' she said commandingly, 'get in.'

She went first. Rikki tried to look away as she bent over and climbed in, expertly smoothing down her tight skirt before reclining onto the soft leather bench seat. He followed and sank down beside her. The chauffeur took the folders from him and closed the door behind him with a satisfying thud. Tinted windows protected their privacy. The limousine began to cruise forward. It was snug and surprisingly quiet here in the back, almost like being in bed. Rikki exchanged a glance with Cass, who raised an eyebrow at him. He smiled nervously.

'It's Rikki, isn't it? I don't think that I can call you Mr King any longer.'

'Rikki is fine.' He was beginning to relax with her.

'And you'll call me Cass? I shan't feel easy with you otherwise.'

'If that's what you'd like.'

'Well, Rikki, you know, I shall need you to be on top form in court next week. And if you don't mind my saying so, you're looking a little peaky. I hope that terrifying Mr Fonthill hasn't been working you too hard?'

Rikki laughed. 'Oh, no, that's not it. I'm just not sleeping very well at the moment.'

'Mind if I ask why?'

'Well ... you see, I've moved out of my flat and I'm staying with a friend for a while – and, er, it's not very relaxing.'

'When you say "I", you don't mean "we"?'

'Er, no, I don't.'

There was an awkward silence before Cass asked: 'Why don't you go somewhere else?'

'There isn't really anywhere else I can go, just at the moment.'

Cass frowned. 'I see.' She looked pensive. 'Perhaps I can help? I've just had a thought. There's a flat I know that is vacant at the moment. It's in Holland Park, near me. It has only one bedroom, but it's quite comfortable for a single person. Why don't you stay there for a while?'

'Oh, I couldn't possibly.'

'Why on earth not?'

'Professional code of conduct. There are strict rules against barristers accepting hospitality from their solicitor's clients.'

'It's not mine, you silly boy.' She placed her hand on his arm. He felt his resistance weakening. 'It belongs to a friend. She's gone to Morocco for the indefinite future. A *man*, of course,' she murmured confidingly. 'She left me her keys. I know she'd love to lend it to you.'

'I – I really shouldn't.' He thought of Michael's cramped little flat, his hideously uncomfortable Z-bed, and more ghastly evenings at the pole-dancing club. The prospect of even one more night at that place filled him with gloom. He gazed at her irresolutely.

She squeezed his knee. 'Don't be so stuffy.'

Chapter 16

For the past few days Kate had been working frantically to clear the decks for the opening of the Benson case in the High Court next Monday, and on Friday evening was still at her desk, bashing out emails, when most of her colleagues were sloping off for the weekend. It was all very well wanting a big case, but the extra workload was punishing. Angela Cross ('Call me Angela, now that you're on the team') sent through a constant stream of queries and requests, drastically compressing the time Kate could spend on other clients. The Hildebrand article was still unfinished, and needed to done by Monday. A constant, gnawing anxiety about Rikki troubled her sleep. And by late afternoon she still hadn't decided what to do about Michael, with whom she had an assignation at the Ritz early that evening.

In response to his invitation she had, after much inner debate, texted back – Sounds fun! – intending to wind him up and then stand him up. But the quarrel with Rikki had changed her perspective. Men shouldn't be allowed to get away with selfish, shoddy behaviour. She'd a good mind to go after all, and tell Michael to his face that he needed to shape up or she'd spill the beans to Sam. Besides, she'd never been inside the Ritz, and she could do with a stiff drink.

Damn! Her internal line was ringing. Devoted though she was to Angus, the thought of yet another discussion about the minutiae of the Benson case made her heart sink. She snatched up the receiver. 'Hello. Kate Pepper.'

'Ah, Miss Pepper, I'm sorry to disturb you' – it was the Head Clerk speaking – 'but I have a Mrs Bunyan here, who would very much like to speak with you. And, ahem, a baby.'

Kate's eyes opened wide. Sam! And Milton! What was going on?

'Thank you. I'll be right down.'

Swiftly, Kate completed her email, skimmed through for errors, and clicked Send. Snatching up her handbag, she hurried along the corridor and clattered down five flights of stairs. Sure enough, as she turned the final corner, there was Sam, looking extremely out of place in her shearling coat and Ugg boots, festooned with miscellaneous bags and gripping the handle of a pushchair in which Milton lay slumped in sleep. Her face was a picture of anguish.

'What on earth's happened?' Kate demanded, taking Sam by the shoulders and scanning her huge, tragic eyes.

Sam threw herself onto Kate's chest and began to sob un-inhibitedly. Kate rubbed her back, feeling self-conscious as a dapper pair of barristers strode past, averting their eyes from this unseemly display of female hysteria. One of the young Mr Hair Gels sidled out of the clerks' room to gawp.

'The small conference room is free, miss, should you wish to avail yourself of it,' offered the Head Clerk, apparently addressing his words to the ceiling.

'Good idea.' With some difficulty Kate managed to extricate

herself from Sam's clinging embrace and steer her down the corridor towards the room in question. They were doing quite well until Sam stopped dead, and in a voice vibrating with panic said, 'Where's Milty?'

'Who? Oh, yes. I'll, er, fetch him.'

Eventually she got the three of them inside, shut the door, parked the pushchair in a corner, and sat Sam down at the conference table, placing the inevitable box of tissues in front of her. Sam took a tissue and blew her nose. Pulling herself together, she announced, 'Michael has been cheating on me.'

'The bastard!' exclaimed Kate, feeling obscurely guilty.

'I've suspected that he was unfaithful for some time. I put a private detective on to him. I have all the evidence I need for a divorce ... The thing is' – her voice began to shake – 'I still love him.' Sam dissolved into tears.

'My poor darling ...' Kate put an arm around her friend, who sobbed uncontrollably for several minutes, while Milton slept on unperturbed.

'And then I thought of you, my best and cleverest friend in the world.' Sam looked up trustingly into Kate's face. 'The thing is, I've got nowhere else to go.'

'You don't mean ...'

'It'll only be a few days. I wouldn't ask, only I know that Rikki's staying with Michael at the moment.'

'What?' Kate's head was spinning.

'I thought you knew.'

'I ... you ... Of course you can stay as long as you like.'

Sam's relief was obvious. In her confusion, Kate was suddenly inspired. She pictured Michael lounging against a bar in anticipation of some hanky-panky with herself, and instead catching sight of his wife marching towards him in her present get-up while pushing his son and heir in a pram.

'I have an idea,' she suggested. 'Do you know the Ritz?'

☾☽

'Look, Milton, an apple! A lovely big green apple.'

Held gingerly on Kate's knee, Milton patted the cardboard picture book with a fat hand, bounced up and down enthusiastically, and let out a crow of delight, along with a long thread of drool. Kate watched it heading straight for her cream-upholstered sofa, and tipped Milton sideways so that it landed instead on the already damp front of his babygro – a ridiculous word, in her opinion.

Being landed with Milty-wilty to bring home to the sanctuary of her own flat, while Sam swanned off to the Ritz unencumbered, was not at all what she'd had in mind. She'd felt a complete laughing-stock on the Tube, with Milton under one arm and her briefcase and Milton's bags in the other, and hated being an object of sympathetic kindness. Strangers had offered her their seat, or at least a sympathetic smile. One old granny-type had asked how old Milton was, reacting with visible alarm when Kate answered, 'Oh ... a few months or so.' Hastily she'd explained that it was a friend's baby, though the woman had looked unconvinced and might even now be phoning Social Services.

Milton made a wild lunge for the book and started to chew it, though he didn't seem to have many teeth. Kate thought it was rather clever of him to recognise the picture of an apple as food. 'Yes, apple,' she crooned encouragingly. 'Can you say that, Milton? A-pull.' Could babies talk at six months? She had no idea. Oh God, her mobile was ringing. She reached

163

down to pull it out of her handbag, hoping that the call was from Sam, on her way back to reclaim Milton.

No such luck. 'Hello, Angela,' she said brightly. 'How can I help?'

'I need to get hold of Angus asap. I've tried his home number and his mobile, but he seems to have gone awol. Any ideas?'

'No, sorry ... He and his wife are big opera fans. I suppose it's possible that they're at Covent Garden and he's switched off his phone.'

'Hell's bells! Ring me if you have any other ideas. Top priority. Must dash.'

The call rang off, and simultaneously Milton began to whinge fretfully. Kate tried to tempt him with the book but he batted it out of her hand with epic scorn. In moments the whingeing had escalated to howls. His legs went rigid with fury. Oh God! What was she supposed to do?

Milk! That was it. Kate carried Milton into the kitchen, opened the fridge and found the bottle of expressed breast milk (ew) that Sam had given her in a cool bag. Milton was now emitting enough energy to power their entire flat – if only she could find somewhere to plug him in. *Warm the milk*, Sam had said. But how? She dumped the bottle in the sink and began to fill it with hot water. The bloody thing floated, so she weighted it down with an iron casserole dish, not that easy to do one-handed, while Milton's howls skewered her brain. And was that her mobile again?

'Hello, Angela.'

'Can you believe it? The little toerag has swanned off to his blasted island in the blasted Caribbean!'

'... er, McLaren?'

'Do keep up. Jez Benson, our esteemed client. I know he's

up to something, and I jolly well intend to find out what it is. I say, have you got a baby there?'

'As a matter of fact, I have. But it's not mine.'

'Thank God for that! Stand by for my call.'

Finding that she'd been shut off, Kate put down the phone and picked up the bottle. Was the milk too hot? She tested it on her arm, the way people did on TV. She'd soon find out. Oops, top off first. She aimed it in the general direction of Milton's mouth, and he homed in on it with the rapacity of a shark in a feeding frenzy. As the milk filled his stomach, his little body trembled with relief and slowly stilled to contentment. Kate carried him back to the sofa and sat herself in the corner, with the baby lying across her lap, his head in the crook of her arm. Blissful silence. This was almost pleasant. How fine babies' hair was! And how tiny their noses! Even though Milton was so small, he was very expressive. His feet rubbed against each other in ecstasy, while his eyes studied her so intently that she began to think he really might have a brain. Halfway through drinking, he stopped sucking and she withdrew the bottle cautiously, wondering what would happen. His face dissolved into an enormous, enchanting, transforming smile. Milton liked her! Kate felt indefinably stirred. She realised that she was beaming back at him, and on impulse bent to kiss him on the forehead. Milton seized the opportunity to grab his bottle back, and continued to suck contentedly while Kate watched his eyelids droop, flutter and peacefully close. The bottle slipped from his mouth. Milton was asleep.

She carried him carefully into the bedroom and stopped, undecided. Had Sam told her that Milton absolutely must sleep on a bed, or that he absolutely must not?

೧೨

Shortly before ten o'clock that same evening, Kate was working on her article, laptop on her knee, when the entryphone buzzer sounded. Checking the video, she made out the substantial figure of Sam leaning her full weight against the front door, and buzzed her in. She opened the door to the flat and left it ajar, then returned to her computer to save what she had written. She saw with horror that she'd typed 'Mr Justice Wart' instead of Ward – that would never do – and sat down to correct the typo.

The next thing she knew, there was a terrific crash as the front door flew back against the wall. Sam show-stepped into the room, one fist raised defiantly in the air, belting out a song from *Chicago*.

'"He had it coming, He had it coming, He only had himself to blame..."' She grinned at Kate, swaying gently. 'Done it! All shorted out. No more nonce ... nonces ... nonsense ... es.'

Kate stared at her, aghast. 'Sam, you're drunk!'

'So what? I had five cocktails and they were all d'licious. I *love* the Ritz.'

'Here, come and sit down. I'll fetch you a glass of water.' Sam collapsed on the sofa. 'So, what happened?'

'I've got him by the balls.' Sam grinned. 'He's very apolo-apolo ... sorry.'

'You're letting him off awfully lightly,' Kate suggested.

'Zat what you think?' Sam kicked off her shoes. 'I put him right. No more messing around with other women or I chop his balls off. Milty and me is coming back to London.'

'You're not serious?'

'Bored with the country anyway. Going to sell the house, sell the pyade-a-bloody-tare ... Buy a nice house in Fulham. Why is the room spinning round?'

'Have a glass of water.'

'No more drink, thanks all the same ... I'll just shut my eyes for a minute ...' She was asleep.

Kate returned to her laptop. Half an hour later she was just putting the finishing touches to her article when the phone rang again. The noise woke up Milton, who started crying.

'It's Angela again. You're going to have to go out there pdq.'

'Go out where?'

'The West Indies, of course. I've booked you business class on a flight to Antigua tomorrow morning. A private plane will collect you from there to take you to the island where Benson is hiding.'

'What? No ... I can't possibly!'

'No such word as can't. Didn't they teach you that at school?'

'I'd have to ask Angus.'

'I've told you, he's not answering any of his numbers. Anyway, I'm the one instructing and that's my instruction. Haven't you got rid of that baby yet?'

'Can't you go?'

'No can do. It's Nigella's eighteenth this weekend. You fly out at ten tomorrow morning from Gatwick, arrive mid-afternoon, and fly back on Sunday night, arriving on Monday morning. You can sleep on the flight, go straight to work when you land and be at your desk by nine, ready for the High Court at ten. You won't have time to feel jet lag.'

Sam entered the room, carrying a now-screaming Milton.

'But this goes against the Code of Conduct! Seeing a client without a solicitor present! What about the Bar Standards Board?'

'Don't you worry about that. Barty Wittering-Coombe and I are cousins. I know where his toys are buried.'

167

'But I can't!'

'Oh, do buck up, for heaven's sake, girl.'

'No, really, I couldn't.'

'Give me one good reason.' Angela's voice assumed a flinty edge.

'*Waaaaaaaah!*' cried Milton.

'Shut up, shut up, shut up!' Sam responded, clutching her head.

Kate looked around her flat, now covered in baby paraphernalia. She contemplated a weekend of chaos, disruption and no Rikki.

'Gatwick, did you say?'

Chapter 17

It was ten o'clock on Saturday morning. Rikki stood outside his own block of flats, tapping in the entry code. He was carrying a bunch of daffodils and felt distinctly nervous at the prospect of seeing Kate. But he was fed up with not sleeping in his own flat, in his own bed, with Kate in it. She was his wife, and they ought to be together, come what may. If he put this proposition to her calmly, without losing his temper, she would surely come round to his view and drop the Benson case for the sake of marital harmony. What was it Winston Churchill had said? 'All I require is compliance with my wishes, following reasonable discussion.'

And if she was not compliant? Or reasonable? Well, there was always the Holland Park flat as a last resort. Yesterday afternoon a motorcycle messenger had delivered a package to him at chambers, containing a key and a handwritten note from Cass giving the address of the flat. She had signed it 'Love, Cass XX'. Both the familiarity of the note and the offer itself made him queasy. Still, anything would be better than Michael's place. What was that guy up to? Rikki felt intensely embarrassed to be made a party to his philandering, particularly when he had a great wife like Sam. Before leaving for work yesterday Michael had announced that he would be out for the evening – maybe not coming back at all that night. From his knowing wink Rikki had guessed that he was meeting 'someone special': another Eastern European bimbo on the make, no doubt. So it was a surprise when Michael returned to the flat not only early, but alone, while Rikki was morosely eating cereal in his pyjamas in front of the ten o'clock news. Even more surprisingly, Michael had seemed curiously subdued, and had slunk straight to bed, without even a final nightcap or one of his boastful maunderings about the 'killing' to be made in China or the idiocy of people who kept their savings in a building society.

On his way up the stairs, the woman who lived in the flat above theirs passed him in running clothes. 'A bit late for Valentine's Day, isn't it?' she laughed, checking out his flowers. 'Or is that a peace offering?' She continued cackling as she jogged off round the landing. Very funny. It would be good, though, if he and Kate could make peace, now that his mother had taken to ringing him up on a regular basis and asking pointedly if everything was all right. He loved her, of course, but if he gave her the tiniest chink of an opening she would be in with all guns blazing, aimed squarely at Kate. He must at least protect her from that. His father and Kate got along fine, but Kate and Mama were like oil and water. This had little to do with Kate herself, he knew. No daughter-in-law on earth could be good enough for Mama. Rikki was her darling: embarrassing but true. He had reaped the benefits throughout his childhood, and now he was paying the penalty. She had a nose like a bloodhound for trouble, and he wanted to keep her at bay for as long as he could.

He took the last flight of stairs two at a time and paused

outside the flat to rummage in his pocket for the key. For a moment he hesitated. It was strange to be back. He felt almost like a visitor and wondered if he should perhaps ring the bell first. No, that was nonsense. Squaring his shoulders and grasping the flowers tightly, he unlocked the door, stepped inside and immediately tripped over a folded pushchair.

A figure sprang to her feet from the sofa, holding a baby to her shoulder.

'Sam!' he exclaimed.

'Rikki!'

'I was expecting to see Kate.'

'I was expecting Michael.'

A silence fell. Rikki moved the pushchair from its booby-trap position, piling it next to a mound of bags and coats. Then he gave a low laugh. 'I suppose it's quite funny, really. I mean, you staying with my wife and me staying with your husband.'

'Not *very* funny,' Sam said sternly.

'No. Of course not.' There was another silence. 'I just meant that husbands and wives normally live with each other, not the husbands in one place and the wives, you know, somewhere else. Er, together,' he floundered.

'That is so. *Normally.*'

He couldn't tell if Sam was cross with him or with Michael. Both, probably. That seemed to be the general state of relations between the sexes these days: women on the offensive, men on the defensive. Soon there would be nothing a man might do to win a woman's approval beyond unscrewing a particularly obstinate lid from a jar. Even then she'd probably complain that he'd spilled the contents, or put the lid down in the wrong place, or looked too smug about his own prowess.

'So Michael's coming here, is he?' he asked conversation-ally.

'Yes. Any minute. We're all driving back to Somerset to-gether.'

'Good, good. Excellent.'

Though he felt it was impolite, Rikki couldn't help his gaze straying away from Sam to flick round to the room, taking in the empty galley kitchen and the open bedroom door.

'Has Kate gone out?' he asked.

Sam hesitated. 'Yes.'

'Oh, come on, Sam.' Rikki gave her a smile. 'We've always been friends. Don't let's quarrel just because everyone else is. Sit down. Relax.' Her round brown eyes looked slightly wary, he thought, but when he dropped onto the sofa, plac-ing his flowers on the coffee-table, she sat down at the other end, with Milton on her knee.

'Hey, Milt, give me a high-five.' Rikki held out his palm, and after staring at it for some moments Milton made an uncoordinated lunge with his open, three-toothed mouth and tried to chew Rikki's fingers. Sam couldn't help smiling indulgently, and offered Milton the beads round her neck to play with instead.

'I know it's not any of my business,' she said to Rikki, 'but try not to be too hard on Kate. Whatever she's done – or whatever you think she's done. Look at me. I've forgiven Michael, even though he's been a total arsehole. At least, I haven't forgiven him, exactly – not yet, anyway – but I'm not letting him just slip away from me. It can happen so easily.'

'We'll be fine,' Rikki said breezily, feeling that it was a bit much to compare either himself or Kate to a wandering willy like Michael.

'Michael's been under a lot of strain, you know. I might

as well tell you that the bank is closing down his department and he'll be out of a job by the end of the month.'

'I'm sorry to hear that,' Rikki said dutifully.

'No, you're not,' Sam retorted. 'But never mind. I know you think Michael's a bit of a buffoon, but he's not. He's clever, and rather sensitive. All he needs is a bit of ... direction.'

Rikki nodded.

'And even if he is a buffoon, I love him,' she concluded defiantly. 'And so does Milty. So we're going to sell up and come back to London, and if necessary *I'll* find a job. Frankly, I think I'll turn into a cow if I stay in the country. The fantasy is great, but the reality is dull, dull, dull.'

'My feelings exactly. So, er, what about Kate?' he asked, after a decent interval.

'What about her?' Sam looked flustered.

'I thought you were trying to tell me something about her.'

'No, no. Well, yes.' She grinned appealingly. 'I just wanted to say that maybe you should cut her some slack. Sure, she's a bit uptight sometimes, but you've got to remember that she held herself together through sheer willpower when she was a kid – not just herself, but her mother and everything else – and it frightens her to let go. You should have seen her when she first turned up at university. If she got a 2.1 on an essay instead of a first, she didn't cry, or even look disappointed; she just went straight to the library and rewrote it. God, she was terrifying! But then, underneath, there's that silly kid she was never allowed to be. I think that's why she loves you, Rikki.'

'Because I'm silly?'

'Because you're fun. You relax her. You make her feel

safe. Look at how quickly you guys decided to get married. I couldn't believe it when I heard. If I had to choose the least impulsive person on the planet, Kate would come top of the list. So you two *must* belong together,' she concluded incoherently, her cheeks flushed with conviction. 'Only a genuine thunderbolt could get through that armour. You know how normally she likes to think everything through, and make her little lists, and plan and prepare, and how the unexpected freaks her out.' Sam chuckled fondly. 'I wish you could have been here last night when she heard she had to fly out to the West Indies *this morning* and—'

Rikki's spine stiffened as if he'd been shot in the back. 'The West Indies?' he said incredulously.

Sam's hand flew to her mouth. Her eyes stretched wide. 'Oops.'

Chapter 18

'Another rum punch, miss?'

Startled, Kate opened her eyes and put up a hand to shade them from the sun. Jeremy Benson's butler was standing a respectful distance from her in his white tunic and black trousers, dangling a silver tray at his side.

'No, thanks, Solomon. But the one I had was delicious. Here, let me give you the glass.'

'Thank you, miss. Is there anything else I can get you? Some sliced mango? Or pineapple?'

'No, really, I'm fine. And please call me Kate.'

'OK, Kate.' He grinned, and headed back towards the house at a laid-back pace, singing under his breath.

Kate's gaze lingered on the dazzling white villa with its red roof and deep wraparound veranda, panned across the kidney-shaped swimming pool where she'd already spent a very pleasant half-hour on the lilo, and swept out to the wide turquoise sea, dotted with yachts. She settled back on her padded sun lounger, adjusted her bikini, and closed her eyes again, feeling the sun warm her skin and melt deep into her bones. This was paradise. She knew she should be doing something

– making phone calls, checking her emails, casing the joint, plying Solomon with questions – but she couldn't move. It was jet lag, she told herself, though in truth the business-class flight, with free champagne and the latest magazines on offer, had not been exactly arduous. In fact, she'd been so absorbed in reading about the bust-up of one of Hollywood's golden couples that when the captain announced that they would be landing in ten minutes, she'd barely had time to nip into the cramped loo and change from trousers, ankle boots and a jumper into sandals and a sundress, before strapping herself in for landing. Having never been to the Caribbean before, she peered out of the window in eager anticipation, but could see nothing but water flecked with white foam. She was beginning to worry that they might actually land in the sea when the wheels engaged on tarmac with a bump, and a line of palm trees flashed past, fronds whipping in the wind.

It was a shock to step out of the plane into steamy, enveloping heat. By the time she'd passed through Immigration and Customs controls, which operated at a maddening snail's pace, she felt limp and disoriented, and was relieved to spot a friendly-looking West Indian man of about fifty in the airport lounge, holding up a placard bearing her name. Introducing himself as Solomon, he carried her bag to a Mercedes parked outside, stowed it in the boot, and opened the door to its luxurious, air-conditioned interior. Mr Benson had business 'in town', he explained, but Kate was to make herself at home and he'd meet her for drinks by the pool at around six thirty. According to Kate's watch it was long past six thirty already, so she adjusted it backwards by five hours to local time, which was mid-afternoon.

For a mile or so they drove along a modern highway lined with the usual tourist hotels, shops and restaurants, which

Solomon pointed out proudly, though Kate found the landscape much more interesting once they turned onto a narrow, pot-holed road and began climbing into the interior of the island. Lush greenery of every shade, from olive to emerald, pressed in on both sides. She saw the flick of a lizard darting for cover behind a giant, spiky plant, and a jungly tree bearing a bunch of bananas at least three foot long. Bougainvillea cascaded in a brilliant magenta tide across the corrugated-iron roofs of tiny cottages wedged into the hillside. They passed a small boy carrying a crudely woven cage with two live chickens inside, and a woman wearing a Sunday-best-type dress, shielding herself from the sun with a black umbrella. Groups of men loitered outside roadside shacks with CARIB BEER painted on the wooden walls in sizzling yellow and blazing blue. For the first time in her life she felt conspicuous as a white person, and she couldn't help thinking of Rikki, and how he sometimes suffered from the opposite experience.

What had happened to him? Where was the boyish, laughing, loving man she had married? Who was this new person who slammed doors and ignored her feelings – who resented her achievements and wanted to keep her down? Who went to *sex clubs*! She could hardly believe it when Sam told her that the private detective had seen Rikki emerging from an 'erotic dancing' club in the small hours of the morning. How could Rikki want to watch some bimbo with fake boobs and a fake smile, writhing round a pole for money? It was so tacky! Yet apparently preferable to coming home to his wife. A lump rose in her throat and she bent her head, blinking away tears. She caught sight of her wedding ring and felt an impulse to tear it off and hurl it into the bushes. No. That would be silly. She simply wouldn't think about him. At present she had more important things on her mind, like Jeremy Benson.

'It's all down to you,' Angela had said, when Kate took her final call in the Gatwick departure lounge before boarding the plane. 'I don't care how you do it, but find out what he's not telling us or Angus McLaren will find himself trussed like a Christmas turkey before he's even made his opening statement. Keep me briefed.'

The thought of Benson now made Kate sit up smartly on her lounger. It was time to get going. She'd been idle for far too long. Besides, the sun was very strong here, and a red nose would hardly add to her persuasive powers with Benson. Gathering together her towel and sun cream, she stood up and pushed her feet into the pair of flip-flops she'd found in the guest suite. (A suite! She could get used to this life.) She climbed the steps onto the veranda and walked along to the sliding glass doors that opened onto her bedroom – a vast temple of luxury with acres of stone flooring, a high vaulted ceiling supported by wooden rafters, and a super-king-size four-poster bed with white muslin curtains and a coronet affair from which, at the pull of a ribbon, you could release an all-enveloping mosquito-net. But that was for later. Right now she had business to do: shower, hair, a subtle touch of make-up, the knock-out dress she'd bought for a party last summer. There might even be time to fast-forward through a couple of the videos of *Starmaker!* – she'd noticed that box sets had been thought-fully provided – in case she was questioned again about the show. She picked out one of the DVDs at random, turned on the equipment and pushed in the disc. Now, where was her sponge bag? The *Starmaker!* signature tune suddenly blared out at top volume. Kate grabbed the remote and pointed it at the TV to lower the volume, just as Jeremy Benson's now familiar face filled the screen. His laughing eyes seem to look straight into hers. She couldn't help smiling back.

The headland seemed almost to float on the molten sea, like a black dragon shooting flames of orange and yellow across the sky. They flared fiery red and then vaporised in clouds of deep, smoky purple. A gathering darkness blurred the sharp outlines of palm trees, then swallowed them up. Crickets began their rhythmic chorus.

'The daily show,' said Benson, with a proprietorial sweep of his hand.

'Spectacular,' breathed Kate, who had never seen such a sunset. 'In fact, almost as good as your own show.'

'Flatterer.'

They were sitting in deep wicker chairs on the veranda, drinking rum punches. The gentlest of warm breezes rose from the sea and whispered among the trees. Kate glowed with sunshine and contentment. Jet lag made her feel slightly spacey, as if she were floating in a bubble, but that was pleasant, too. She had to keep reminding herself that she was *not* here to enjoy herself. The court action was scheduled to begin in only two days' time! Tomorrow she would be flying back to London, and Benson had already told her that he was leaving early in the morning. She dared not return to Angela empty-handed. If she was to get anything out of him, it would have to be tonight.

She had heard Benson return in his jeep at around six, but he did not appear on the terrace, where she was pretending to read a book, for another half-hour. She wore her hair down this time, falling to her bare shoulders in smooth, slithery layers, and the lilac dress with string straps that crossed over at the back. Her legs were bare – well, apart from a smidgen of bronzing cream – and ended in sparkly silver shoes. At last she heard him approaching, and rose to her feet to greet him.

'So, Mr Benson,' she began, stretching out an arm.

'So, Ms Pepper,' he echoed teasingly, gripping her hand and looking her straight in the eye. He looked trim and handsome in short-sleeved shirt, chinos and slip-on shoes.

'You can call me Kate.'

'And you can call me Jez.'

She drew herself up primly, inadvertently sticking out her chest. 'I don't think that would be very professional.'

He shrugged. 'Have it your own way, Ms Pepper.'

'Oh, all right then. So tell me, *Jez*, how did your business go today?'

'What business?' he asked blandly.

'That's what I'm wondering. Solomon said you had some business in town. I don't believe we have a note of any business ventures outside of the UK.'

He shook his head, chuckling. 'What a Miss Nosey Parker you are – though a very pretty one, I gotta admit. If you must know, I was making arrangements for our dinner tonight. Lobster has to be ordered in advance, you know ... You do like lobster, don't you?'

'Well, yes.' Kate adored it. 'But, Mr Benson, I mean Jez, I have not flown all this way to eat lobster! We need to have a serious talk.'

'Old Iron Knickers breathing down your neck, is she?'

Kate tried not to smile. 'You may think this is some sort of game, Jez, but I assure you that it is not. On the contrary, it is a very serious matter. You may be putting yourself in jeopardy. Angela has asked me to come all this way at the very last moment to ensure that you understand how important it is that you divulge *all* your assets to the High Court on Monday morning.'

'We've been through this before,' he said impatiently. 'I've already made a sworn statement, haven't I?'

'Hear me out, if you will, Jez. The first thing you should realise is that if the other side can show that you have been less than frank, then even Angus's formidable courtroom skills will not be able to retrieve the situation. You will be sending him in to fight for you defenceless and unarmed. The judgment is certain to go against you, and you will be liable for all the costs. If it can be shown afterwards that you have not divulged all your assets, this could result in whatever agreement is reached being set aside. But that's not the worst of it. If either party is found to have lied to the court under oath, he or she could be convicted of perjury. This is a very serious charge, carrying a statutory prison sentence. Remember what happened to Jeffrey Archer and Jonathan Aitken.'

'Are you suggesting that I'm a liar?'

Kate had rehearsed this speech several times, and she could see that what she said was getting through to him. 'What you must appreciate is that it is not too late to shift your position. We can stand up in court on Monday morning and say that it has come to our attention that there are assets which you have failed to previously disclose. There will be no penalties at this stage; on the contrary, such a disclosure could be to your credit. But after that, it will be too late.'

Jez stopped her flow with a raised palm, then aimed his finger at her like a gun. 'Enough already! I'm sorry, Kate, but you've given me plenty to think about, and a man can't think on an empty stomach. What say you and I make a deal? Eat first, talk later.'

What could she do? Kate gave him a brilliant smile. 'Sounds good to me.'

She'd expected that Solomon would drive them to their

destination in the Merc. Instead, Jez led her to the far side of the pool and down a series of steep steps cut into the hillside, lit by sensor lamps that flashed into action at their approach. 'Better take off those girly shoes,' he warned. 'I don't want you suing me if you take a tumble.' Mildly irritated that she'd got all dolled up just to go for a hike, she nevertheless did as he suggested, hoping she wouldn't tread on something squishy or poisonous. At the bottom of the stairs her feet sank into fine, velvet-soft sand still warm from the sun.

'Ooh, we're on the beach!' she exclaimed, and couldn't resist running down to the lacy frill of water, kicking up spurts of sand. The sea was so warm that she closed her eyes with pleasure at the sensation of it gently lapping her ankles.

'Over here, you crazy girl,' called Jez.

She saw that he was standing on a wooden pier with a string of lights looped along its edge. At the end of the pier was a large, sleek motorboat. Kate took a deep breath. This was going to be a night to remember.

◦◦

'... and then there are the barristers who do commercial law,' Kate was saying, waving a lobster claw. 'The Testosterone Terrors – I'm afraid they're nearly always male. Enormous fees, super-enormous egos. The Chancery lot are more nerdy: they swoon over small print; and Human Rights are fanatical – you can spot them by the mad gleam of certainty in their eye. What else? Well, the ambulance-chasers are pretty low: that's Personal Injury. You wouldn't believe the scams they run, with their tame doctors signing so-called "medical reports" when they haven't even seen the patient. Then right at the bottom are the Criminal barristers – they're the utter dregs. Apart from solicitors, of course. Is there any more of that delicious sauce?'

Jez, who had been listening with amusement, passed it across the table. 'And you need some more wine, too.' He pulled the bottle out of an ice bucket that stood on high legs stuck into the sand, and filled her glass.

'Mmm, lovely. This is a fab place, Jez.' Her sweeping gesture encompassed the whole outdoor restaurant area, surrounded by coconut palms and lit by flaming torches and flickering candles, the attentive waiters, the steel band playing at an unobtrusive distance. Beyond was the sea, black except for the occasional light of a passing boat, and above the dark sky. A warm breeze massaged her bare shoulders, and tousled his unruly, brown-blond hair. Large insects flew in and out of the light. 'And weren't we lucky to get this table? I love it being practically *in* the sea, with nothing and no one to interrupt the view.'

He chuckled at her naivety. 'They always keep this table reserved for me when they know I'm on the island. Great boys, all of them. Love my show.'

It was the word 'boys' that gave Kate pause. She knew that there was something unusual about this place, and it wasn't just its exotic location. Every single dinner guest was white and every single member of the staff was black. It made her uncomfortable. She dipped her fingers in the water bowl and wiped them dry on a napkin, then pushed away her plate. In a moment it was whisked from sight.

Jez leaned forward to rest his elbow on the table, and propped his chin in his hand, studying her face. 'And you're a Divorce barrister, is that right?' he asked.

'We prefer the word "Family" – oh, bitter irony! I'm not sure exactly where we are in the hierarchy at present. There have always been a lot of women and gays in family law, which obviously lowers its status. In fact, the Family Division in the High Court used to be known as the Farmyard Division because of the noise of sobbing and squabbling. But now that one in two marriages ends in divorce, I'm afraid we're doing rather well – oh, sorry, Jez, that wasn't very tactful.'

'But it's true. Look at the two of us. My marriage has broken up ... and yours?'

'... is fine. Absolutely great.' She felt no compunction about lying. Where was Rikki tonight? In a tacky club? With another woman? She didn't care. He could not possibly be having as much fun as she was.

'He doesn't have a problem with you taking the opposite side to him in court?'

'Oh, no. He understands that I'm my own woman. I do as I please.'

'I bet you do,' he said admiringly.

They fell silent for a moment. The band had stopped playing, and now Kate could hear the quiet murmur of conversation, the bustle of the waiters, the chirruping of the crickets and the soft sound of the surf. A waiter cleared away their plates, and returned with tropical fruits. Kate took a spoonful of mango, and could not suppress a purr of pleasure; it was the most delicious she had ever tasted. Jez beamed at her.

'I've been thinking about what you said earlier. It's not really about the money, you know. I've plenty of that now. No, it's not the money, it's the principle of the thing. What I resent is all those years of grafting, while Cass sat around on her arse painting her nails and belly-aching about things not being quite perfect. I worked damn hard for my money, and now she wants to take half of it away from me. I don't mind paying her off, even meeting her ludicrous demands – but why should I hand her half of everything I've created?'

Kate gazed at him ruefully, dangling her wineglass from one hand. 'I don't make the law,' she said. 'I just *do* it.'

Jez rose to his feet. 'Come on,' he urged. 'Let's go before I become bitter and boring.' He reached inside his pocket and dropped a handful of notes on the table. The waiter gratefully wished them goodnight. Jez led Kate away from the lights and down onto the beach towards another wooden pier, where the tethered speedboat was bobbing gently against the side. He held her hand as she stepped down into the boat. It was not easy to keep her balance and she quickly sat down near the back, though Jez had frowned when she referred to it earlier as such. He untied and coiled the moorings with professional expertise, and stepped down into the boat in one easy movement, taking the rocking in his stride, and pushing them away from the pier with his foot. Leaning over the powerful outboard, he started the motor with one deft movement. The engine began to emit a deep gurgling sound. Jez sat down on the other side of the outboard, near enough to Kate for their legs to be touching. The boat edged slowly away from the pier. Once they were clear, Jez opened up the throttle and the boat surged forward, the bow angling upwards as they picked up speed. Tiny droplets of salty spray spattered Kate; the breeze tossed her hair, and brought up goose pimples on her bare skin, though the air was still warm. She looked back at the beachside restaurant, already receding into the distance. Behind them the wake glittered and slowly faded. Around was nothing but dark water, while above the sky shone with stars.

She looked at him happily, and he smiled back at her. 'I feel completely alive,' she bellowed, as he leaned across to hear. It was too noisy for conversation. The wind tugged at the sleeves of his shirt, and blew his hair into his face, so that he was forced to use his spare hand to brush it out of his eyes.

As they approached his house, Jez cut the motor, so that the boat glided forward and gently bumped the pier. Picking up the painter, he stepped out gracefully and with practised ease wrapped the rope round a wooden bollard. Once both ends of the boat were secured, he reached down and took Kate's hand, and she skipped lightly onto the pier, carrying her shoes. He pointed the way towards the house. The sand was cool underfoot. Kate was reluctant to spoil the moment, but she had to make the effort. 'Jez, is it time for that talk?'

He made a face, like a naughty boy facing his punishment. They had reached the pool, now enticingly illuminated. 'I think a swim first, don't you?'

It was impossible to resist the lure of that rippling water. Kate made an unconvincing show of reluctance. 'All right, then. Just for a few minutes.'

When she emerged from the changing hut in her bikini a few minutes later, he was already in the pool, and beckoned to her from the shallow end. She laughed with delight. Without hesitation she dived in, and swam underwater almost the whole length of the pool until she reached the place where he was standing, surfacing in front of him. As she swept her hair back, wiping the water from her eyes, she was acutely aware of his physical presence. He was gazing at her intently. Very slowly he reached his arms round her waist, and drew her towards him. She felt her body weakening. Their lips met in a long, slow kiss. She found that he had undone the top of her bikini. With one last effort of resistance she leaned back, adopting what she hoped was an expression of disapproval. 'I'm not much good at talk,' he said, and kissed her again.

Chapter 19

An icy wind knifed into Rikki as he came out of Holland Park Tube station and turned down the avenue, lugging a heavy bag behind him. The key to Cass's friend's flat was in his pocket, and he was bloody well going to stay there, foolish or no. In theory he could have slept in his own flat tonight, but the thought sickened him. He didn't want to be reminded of Kate. He couldn't bear to see her dressing gown hanging in the bathroom, the girly clutter spread across her chest of drawers, the dent of her head in the pillow.

It was bad enough that she had accepted the Benson brief in the first place. But to cohabit (there was no other word for it) with her client in a Caribbean hideaway was beyond endurance. Sam had been distressingly vague about where exactly Kate had gone. 'The thing is, I was very ... tired last night,' she had told him apologetically. 'I think it might have been "St Something".' Since practically every island in the Caribbean was 'St Something', this was not helpful. Of course, he could probably find a reference to it on the Net, but Rikki refused to stoop so low. Anyway, he could already picture it: opulently vulgar, with fake colonial columns clashing horribly with plate-glass windows, an infinity pool – a carport! – obsequious black servants. And at the centre of it all Jeremy Benson, with his dazzling white teeth, his inane catchphrases and his brain the size of a peanut. Rikki tormented himself with images of the two of them strolling along a white beach.

He knew only too well that the man was a lothario, who would attempt to get inside the knickers of any attractive woman. Didn't Kate realise that she was putting herself in a very vulnerable position? He tried to telephone her, but it went straight to answer phone. Perhaps there was no reception wherever she was. In a jealous rage he imagined her at a beachside restaurant, warmed by the night breeze from the sea, eating dinner *à deux* with that man, while he plied her with drink. But of course it would be early afternoon there. He conjured up another image of Kate in her bikini, stretched out by a swimming pool while Benson massaged her shoulders. *Damnit!*

Or perhaps she hadn't gone at all. Maybe Sam was right that she had set out for the airport, but the long slog to Gatwick would have given Kate plenty of time for reflection. Staying in a client's home was unprofessional to the point of lunacy. Surely she would have realised that she could be putting her whole career in jeopardy. Anyway, what was so urgent that she had to fly out there at the very last minute before the case came to court? Could this have something to do with Benson's attempts to conceal assets from his wife, in particular the megadeal that he had failed to hide from Cass? But Kate didn't know about that. Rikki shook his head, trying to clear it. The woman he knew and loved – the careful, conscientious girl Sam had described only this morning – would never have got on that plane. Apart from anything else, she would have remembered that she was married – to *him*. Even now, she could be back at the flat, perhaps wondering where he was. Perhaps even ready to apologise and make up.

Half convinced, Rikki turned into Campden Hill Road. Cass's friend's flat had turned out to be the basement of a vast stuccoed Georgian house: as she had told him, perfect for one person, with generous-sized rooms, opulent furnishings and, best of all, a very large comfortable-looking bed. He had moved in this morning. On his arrival he had found a note from Cass, explaining that she had laid in some supplies to get him started ... exploring, he had found some delicious food in the fridge, as well as several half-bottles of excellent champagne. The discovery had made him slightly uneasy, but he told himself that it was harmless, and that anyway nobody would know about it.

Keen to escape from the chill wind, Rikki clattered down the stone steps to the door of the flat, and fumbled in his pocket for the key. He opened the front door and stepped inside. He reached for the hall light, but paused before flicking it on. There was something in the air: the faintest scent, perhaps, that made him feel he was not alone. A burglar? He put down his bag and stood still, listening intently. A faint sound, almost like a stifled giggle, came from the bedroom. His brow cleared and an incredulous smile tugged at the corners of his mouth.

There was a game he and Kate liked to play, when one of them (usually him) came home and found the flat in darkness and the other one (usually her) apparently out, though in fact hiding naked in their bed. They always provided a clue to their presence. If, for example, Rikki saw Kate's briefcase plonked right in the middle of the living-room floor, or a pair of shoes kicked off by the bedroom door, that was his cue to say in a loud, stagey voice, 'Hmmm, Kate doesn't seem to be home. I wonder where she can be?' He would pretend to search the flat, looking for her. 'Is she in the kitchen? ... In the bathroom?' Then he'd sigh elaborately. 'Oh well, I guess I'll just take a little nap while I wait for her to come home.' Next, he'd go into the bedroom and take off all his clothes, resolutely ignoring the obvious body-shaped mound under the duvet until he lay down and 'discovered' a gorgeous, naked girl in his bed.

Now a low sigh of pleasure came distinctly from the bedroom. Rikki unbuttoned his coat with trembling fingers and flung it over a chair. Joy and relief surged through him. Kate had not gone to the West Indies. She'd tracked him down to this flat and blagged her way inside in order to stage a surprise reconciliation. A grin spread across his face as he undressed hastily, dropping his clothes on the floor. Of course he would forgive her everything. He pictured her waiting for him next door and started to plan their erotic little pantomime. He wouldn't turn on the light in the bedroom, but would feel his way to the bed and sit down. 'This bed's awfully lumpy,' he'd complain, and start patting the duvet experimentally, like a large squashy parcel whose contents he was trying to guess. 'Is it Goldilocks? ... Julia Roberts? .... Could it be the Queen? Will she stick her head out in a minute and say, "Ay em a postage stemp"? Rikki chortled to himself as he yanked off a sock. Then he imagined how he'd slide his hands under the duvet and feel his way slowly up her bare body. Thoroughly excited now, he extricated himself from his boxer shorts, padded across to the bedroom door and pushed it open.

Hmm, new perfume. Sexy. He liked it. He shuffled forward in the darkness, not quite sure where the bed was. *Ouch*, he'd found one edge of it with his bare knee. Bending over, he groped across the bedclothes and encountered warm, smooth skin. His hands identified the curve of a hip and slid across her stomach and up towards her breasts. A hand reached out and stroked him. *Oh God* ... Instantly his prepared dialogue deserted him. That wasn't fair! Kate didn't usually...

Something was not quite right. His brain and his body were sending him conflicting signals. Now her arms were around his neck, drawing him close. But at the last moment he pulled away.

'Cass...?'

Part Three

Chapter 20

Kate paid off the taxi and strode into the Temple, suitcase trundling behind her. The magnificent ironwork gates stood wide open, as if to welcome her back. There was a nip of morning frost in the air. The sky was a clear, rain-washed blue. Under the trees in Old Court, early daffodils poked their heads out of the dull winter grass.

Today was the day. As she stepped into chambers and automatically paused in the entrance hall to check her pigeon-hole, she felt a charge of excitement.

'Ah, there you are, miss.' The Head Clerk materialised Jeeves-like at her side. 'Mr McLaren says, would you care to step into his office at the earliest opportunity? I'll get one of the lads to take that up for you, shall I?' He gestured at her suitcase, and in a moment had despatched it upstairs in the grip of one of the juniors. 'Big day for us,' he continued, rubbing his hands with satisfaction. 'I've already had the media on, asking a silly load of questions. Will Mr Benson be in court today? Can they interview him? Might they be allowed into the courtroom – just as a special favour?' He blew disparagingly through his teeth. 'The British public's ignorance of the legal system is shocking. *Shocking*, it is. Still, I mustn't keep you. Your first big case, I believe?' He held out his hand. 'May I be permitted to wish you all the best?'

'You absolutely may.' She shook it warmly.

Swelling with gratification, she marched up the stairs. Her first big case, indeed: the culmination of thirteen years of study and hard work. It hadn't been easy – many hopefuls stumbled by the wayside – but she'd done it. *Benson* v. *Carnaby* was her route to the top, and nothing was going to stop her. She pictured herself in the special silk QC's robe addressing a judge in the High Court, perhaps even putting him right on an obscure point in the Matrimonial Causes Act 1973. Or the Appeal Court – even better – since the public was admitted to appeal hearings and there would be an audience to appreciate her eloquence.

'Oh, sorry.' Carried away by this vision of herself as a latter-day Portia, Kate had not been looking where she'd been going, and at the turn of the stairs had cannoned into someone coming down. She saw that it was WC, who drew aside to let her pass. Although he said nothing, she thought that he looked at her with new respect. Word had no doubt got round of her crucial role in what was bound to be the most high-profile divorce case of the year – if not the decade. This was a pleasant thought. Kate could afford a moment of sympathy for poor WC, stuck with the Mrs Mitchisons of this world, before reaching her office and unlocking the door. Her suitcase had already been deposited outside. She wheeled it in, and dumped her bag and briefcase, extracting the items she would need in court. The Head Clerk would have told Angus of her arrival in chambers, so she must be quick, but first things first. How did she look?

In the corner of her office was one of those old-fashioned,

built-in closets, just deep enough to hold a few hangers, with a single shelf above. Kate opened the door and examined herself in the mirror hanging on the back. Despite the long flight, her face showed no sign of jet lag. If she said so herself, the effect of lightly tanned skin, blue eyes, blonde hair and – she leaned forward to double-check – white teeth, was rather glamorous. How fortunate it was that she caught the sun easily, without burning, considering the short time she'd been in the Caribbean. The image of white sand lapped by pale aquamarine water filled her mind. Only twenty-four hours ago she'd woken up to a fabulous day of clear skies and brilliant sunshine. It had taken a moment to remember where she was, then she'd grabbed one of the dressing gowns provided, opened the doors, and padded barefoot along the veranda. The air was warm and impossibly fresh. She could smell the sea, and the sweet fragrance that wafted from a tree festooned with violet-blue blossom – and coffee. Breakfast had been laid out for her on a shady terrace that looked over the green headland and across a bay to a harbour town topped by a square stone fort. Within moments of her flopping down to admire the view, Solomon arrived to wish her good morning and ask what she'd like for breakfast. She'd decided on brown toast, yoghurt and fresh pawpaw with lime juice squeezed, Solomon informed her, from the fruits of Mr Benson's very own trees.

Jez had told her last night that she probably wouldn't see him today, as he was due to leave early for a business meeting. But he'd promised to answer her questions.

'Has Mr Benson already left?' Kate enquired.

'Oh, yes. He caught the early flight to New York.'

'*New York?*' She nearly had a heart attack. 'He's supposed to be going to London.'

'New York first, he said, then London.'

Kate had given an exasperated sigh. The man was incorrigible. She'd told him a million times that his case was listed to begin on Monday morning. Was he so used to fawning and flattery that he thought a High Court judge would sit twiddling his thumbs until Jez chose to show up?

Solomon set off to fetch her breakfast, then turned back. 'Mr Benson said to use the mask and fins, if you would like. There's a stretch of coral reef right off our beach here. Oh, and he left an envelope addressed to you. Shall I bring it?'

Kate had studied the envelope's contents as she sat on the veranda eating her breakfast, and the rest of the morning had passed in frenetic activity as she relayed them back to London. Her mobile phone was in danger of overheating from all the phone calls back and forth between her and Angela, and her and Angus. It was too distracting, as well as too hot, to work outside, and, besides, she needed access to a fax machine as well as her laptop and phone, so she was confined to the house while the sun rose higher in the sky and the rest of the world played. In between phone calls and emails she composed the driest of dry reports of her 'conference' with Jez, sticking to essentials. By the time it was finished to her satisfaction and emailed off, she felt radioactive from too much staring at her computer screen, and stepped outside to lean on the veranda rail, marvelling again at the beauty around her. She could hear the faint put-put of motorboats as they plied their way around steep rocks from one sandy cove to the next, and high-spirited screams of children having fun on a distant beach. She checked her watch. If she packed right now, she might just have time to fit in some snorkelling before the private plane ferried her back to Antigua airport.

Solomon had said that the richest reefs were further

out, only accessible by boat, but for Kate, who had never snorkelled before, the abundance of life that teemed in the shallows only a few yards offshore was a revelation. Most of the fish were small, but they made up for it by their stunning colours: scarlet, magenta, jade green, banana yellow; striped black and white like zebras; spotted pink on primrose, like the most flamboyant polka-dot tie. She loved the way the tiny turquoise ones dodged in and out of their knobbly coral landscape in shoals, changing direction in a split second to shoot through the water like an electric flash. Best of all was the large luminous-blue fish with a black-rimmed eye and yellow tail, which Solomon said might have been a Queen Angelfish …

… Angelfish – Angela! – Angus! – the case! Kate's eyes snapped back into focus. She tore off her coat, and changed quickly into the spare set of court clothes that she always kept in the office: black skirt, black tights and her court shirt, plain white and collarless. Then she lifted down several black leather cases of different sizes from the cupboard shelf and placed them on her desk. One was not much bigger than a ring-box. The catch snapped open at her touch to reveal two pearl collar studs with gold fastenings. A bigger one held the two strips of white material known as 'bands', which some believed symbolised Moses' tablets of stone. Next, she opened the medium-sized oval box, whose black suede interior held a stiff, white wing collar. Barristers were permitted to wear various styles of shirt and collar, including what was called a 'ladies' collarette' – a white bib with a vicar's collar at-tached – but Kate thought it made her look like a nun and preferred to stick to the traditional wing collar. After all, that's what the men wore. She went back to the mirror and fixed the collar to her satisfaction, then tied on the bands, which hung down below her collarbone in an upside-down V-shape. Returning with it to her desk, she opened the largest box and took out her barrister's wig, which was made of white horsehair, with a frizzed crown and five rows of curls ending in two tails, looped and tied at the bottom. In many ways it was a ridiculous thing to stick on your head, and was a few hundred years out of date, having evolved from the eighteenth-century fashion for powdered wigs. Wigs were hot and itchy, and ruined your hairstyle. There had been countless moves to abolish them. As a family lawyer she wasn't always required to wear one, since they were thought to intimidate stressed parents and children. Their virtue was to minimise the individual lawyer and emphasise the law itself. Also, dressing up was fun. Nobody became a barrister unless they liked showing off.

If she was travelling to a distant court Kate carried her wig and robes in her barrister bag, so as not to look an utter idiot, but since the High Court was so close and she'd be walking up there with others dressed the same, it would be OK to put them on now. But she took the bag anyway, from a hook in the cupboard, as it might be useful later. A dark blue drawstring affair, rather like a large and superior shoe-bag, it was embroidered with her initials in gold-coloured thread. The letters were large, and elegantly scrolled. Into it she stored last-minute items from a typed checklist: mobile phone, wallet, hair grips, lipstick, a comb and a tiny bottle of perfume. Everything else she needed – documents, notepad, pens, etc. – was already downstairs in a wheelie bag, which she'd providently packed herself on Friday.

Time to go. On went the wig, and finally the wide-sleeved black gown, which stretched unflatteringly below her knees and was even more old-fashioned than the wig, being modelled on a garment worn by those mourning the death of Charles II in sixteen-something: no one had ever explained exactly why. She took a final, approving look at Ms Pepper, junior barrister on the rise, then closed the cupboard door.

৩৩

Even before reaching Angus's office she could hear that he was in fine fettle. 'O Sole Mio' wafted down the corridor in deep, warbling tones. Singing lubricated the vocal chords, he claimed.

'In!' he called, in response to her knock. His face lit up when he saw her. 'Kate! Splendid girl! Come in, come in. Can you tie this blasted thing for me?'

He had got as far as his shirt, waistcoat and collar, but couldn't manage the bands, which were indeed fiddly to tie unless you were used to fastening necklaces by feel alone and had, like Kate, spent many hours in girlhood contriving intricate plaits down the back of her head. She tied on the bands and helped him into his court coat.

'Even got the Dragon to starch my shirt!' he marvelled. 'Mustn't let down chambers, especially not when the eyes of the world are upon us. I must say you're look very bright-eyed and bushy-tailed for someone who flew in at some unearthly hour this morning.'

'I conked out on the plane and slept like a baby. Anyway, I'm far too excited for jet lag.' She bubbled with laughter. 'This is my first experience of being led in a really big case. It's a milestone.'

She could tell that he was excited, too, like a warhorse hearing the trumpet call to battle. His step seemed quicker, his movements more precise, as he put on his gown, similar

201

to hers but made of silk, and opened his wig box, which was the old-fashioned kind made of black-lacquered steel. The gold detailing had faded with the years, as had his initials, A.H.M., and the box was scratched and dented with use. She thought of all the times he must have stood up to face a judge; the quick intelligence and sheer doggedness that had impelled him from a junior like herself to a silk of the highest respect; the moments of triumph, and of bitter failure; and was assailed by a wave of affection.

'I wanted to say ...' she began and trailed off. Angus looked up from rummaging for something in one of his desk drawers and peered at her quizzically. 'What I mean is ... well, thank you for your faith in me. I won't let you down.'

'My dear girl!' He came over to her and put his hands lightly on her shoulders, looking into her face. 'You deserve it. Look how you've saved our bacon with this Benson chap. I'm proud of you, and you have every right to feel proud of yourself.' He smiled and gave her a little shake. 'Right. Time to see what God has in store for us. Why don't you be the one to look it up today?'

Kate walked over to a lectern in the corner of the room that held a large Bible, which it was Angus's habit to consult at random before an important case. She closed her eyes, opened the Bible and stabbed a finger onto the page. Opening her eyes again, she read aloud, 'And they shall smite the heathen in the low places and in the high, and righteousness shall be on their side.' She looked up at Angus with an awed expression.

His face was gleeful as a schoolboy's. 'Always a good thing to have the Almighty on one's side. Shall we go?'

☙

Kate felt like one of the Magnificent Seven as she marched through the Temple, shoulder to shoulder with Angus, with a retinue of junior clerks and pupils pulling wheelie bags full of documents in their wake. Other barristers were pouring out of handsome red-brick buildings and emerging from stone cloisters, scattering pigeons before them with loud chatter and flapping black robes. They gathered from Pump Court and Garden Court, from Essex Court, once the home of the diarist John Evelyn, and Brick Court, spared by a whisker from a Luftwaffe bomb. An outsider stumbling on the scene might almost mistake it for the film set of a high-budget period drama – until they spotted the number of barristers talking purposefully into their mobile phones. Superficially it was a glamorous spectacle, lent added gloss by today's sunshine gleaming on the mottled trunks of plane trees and catching the iridescent wing of a duck bobbing on the pond in Fountain Court. But this was business, not entertainment.

Reaching the top of Middle Temple Lane, they passed through an archway into the bustle of normal street life. Here, the wide thoroughfare of the Strand cut across their path, bearing the usual noisy traffic of cars and lorries, black cabs and red buses. On the opposite side of the street, dwarfing vehicles and pedestrians alike, rose the Royal Courts of Justice. Kate had spent countless hours in this building, dating right back to her pupillage, but today the sight of its cathedral-like façade of pale stone, with elaborate arches and stained-glass windows and a steeple affair on top, made her heart skip a beat. *Benson* v. *Carnaby* was no ordinary case, as was evident from the scrum of reporters and cameramen hanging around the entrance. Parked on a traffic island that separated the two lanes of contra-flowing traffic were several TV vans, bristling with antennae.

With Angus she joined the procession that now funnelled over the zebra crossing, quickening her pace as one taxi driver lost patience and pressed forward with a blare of his horn, scattering barristers like magpies. Though the main public entrance was via an ornate Gothic porch, they were heading for one of the side gateways, which led directly to the courtrooms, robing rooms, consultation rooms and other areas reserved for those on legal business. They were just about to step inside when a sudden commotion made them turn back. The media pack were stampeding towards a long, black car with tinted windows that had drawn up to the kerb. Two heavily built men jumped out and stood protectively on either side of the rear door. Reporters jostled for position. Photographers shoved their camera lenses through the crowd, trying to force a clear view; the emerging lenses looked like pig snouts converging on a trough. There was even a man on a camera crane, firing off shots from his perilous vantage point above the crowd. As the car door opened the decibel level rose even higher. Angela stepped out first, looking formidable in an elegant black suit and a single string of pearls, with her hair positively glued in place. Next came Jez, in a well-judged suit of mourning grey, teamed with a white shirt and sober tie – very different to the outfit in which Kate had last seen him.

'Is it true that Cass wants fifty million?' a voice shouted.

'Where'd you get the suntan, Jez?' demanded another. Angela raised her palm in a queenly gesture, refusing to comment. Jez looked serious, his head bent and eyes lowered, for once not courting the camera. The two bruisers forced a passage through the baying crowd, sheltering Angela and Jez between them as they dashed for sanctuary.

'Come on, Kate.' Angus sounded disgusted. 'Let's get out of the way before we're trampled to death.'

'More water, anyone?' asked Angela.

Kate longed for another glass, though she daren't say yes in case she got desperate for the loo in the middle of the proceedings. Judges did not look kindly on bathroom breaks. But her mouth was dry. Now that she was actually here, ready to go into court, her nerves were beginning to tighten. There was a tense mood in the small side room that had been allocated to Benson and his team for reasons of privacy. Normally Kate, like other barristers, sat with her clients and their solicitors at a table in one of the vast, echoing hallways outside the courtrooms. In some provincial courts, the lack of space meant sitting virtually cheek by jowl with her opponent, or even scrounging a single plastic chair for her client. This wood-panelled room, with its large table and padded seating, was luxurious by comparison. Why wasn't she enjoying it?

Maybe it was the fact that Jez had hardly spoken to her. Instead he kept cracking bad jokes with Angela and checking his hair in the mirror provided, as if he was about to go on set for one of his TV shows. The wig was doing its trick: she was no longer Kate, but a lawyer. Or perhaps it was be-cause Angus had withdrawn from her, as he read with sober concentration through his opening statement, glasses on nose and pencil in hand. Or perhaps the Victorian Gothic gloom of this place was getting to her. She must 'buck up', as Angela would say. But deep down she knew perfectly well what was bothering her. In a few moments she would see Rikki for the first time since their chilly exchange in the flat, after he'd slept in the car: four days ago, but it felt like a month. How would he look? What had he been doing? Was he still angry with her? Hands in her lap, back straight, she stared down at the floor, as if its intricate patterning of coloured tiles might yield an answer.

A knock on the door made her jump. It was the judge's usher, indicating with a nod that the judge was ready for them.

'Right.' Angus squared his papers on the table and tucked a hand into his waistcoat. Withdrawing his pocket-watch, he opened the lid. 'Mr Benson, the moment has come for us to go into court. I don't expect you to be required to do anything this morning, other than to comport yourself as a sober citizen and look as if you are listening. I would remind you that you may not under any circumstances interrupt the proceedings, no matter what our opponent may say. If you wish to raise a point, you may write it down and pass me a note. There will be a chance for you to speak later, when I lead you through your testimony. And don't forget to bow to the judge.'

'Aye, aye, Captain,' said Jez.

Angus was not amused. He closed his watch with a snap, and rose to his full height. 'Everyone ready?'

Kate scrambled to her feet. adrenalin pumping through her veins.

'Come along, Jez.' Angela addressed him as if he were a naughty pony. He stood up obediently.

Angus gathered them one by one. After his keen eye had scrutinised them one last time, he nodded sharply. 'We're going in.'

Chapter 21

‘Ah, King, I was wondering if you might show up.’ Fonthill was his usual sarcastic self. Back turned, he was peering into a mirror to tie his bands. ‘I trust all the horrible documents are prepared and waiting downstairs …? *So* kind. No doubt you’ve been *hard at it* all weekend, have you?’

Rikki reddened, but Fonthill was too busy preening himself to notice.

‘Gown!’ he commanded, clicking his fingers. Feeling like a butler, Rikki fetched the gown from where it lay draped over the back of a leather chair and helped Fonthill into it.

‘Wig!’ Rikki retrieved it from its box, and watched Fonthill place the absurd object on his head and smooth the stiff grey ringlets that hung down below his shoulders like the ears of a bloodhound. His own wig was already beginning to itch.

‘Do we know yet who we’re up before?’ Fonthill was turning his head this way and that, admiring each profile. ‘I hope it’s not a *woman*. They are always *so* unsympathetic to the wives.’

‘Yes, I double-checked this morning online. It’s Mr Justice Overend.’ Rikki kept his face straight and his voice steady.

Humphrey Overend was widely known as 'Judge Over and Out', due to his increasing deafness.

Fonthill's features contorted into a grimace of horror. 'I do so hate *shouting*,' he shouted. 'Make sure I have plenty of water. And buy me some throat lozenges. I must be at *peak* performance.'

Rikki nodded. Fonthill was revelling in the attention that *Benson* v. *Carnaby* brought him, losing no opportunity to cavort in the spotlight of publicity. Only this weekend he had been profiled in a national newspaper as 'A Star at the Bar'. The profile had even referred to his nickname, Snape – 'always used affectionately, of course'. By contrast, Rikki was feeling increasingly nervous, not just about appearing in court but about seeing Kate – moreover, Kate in the same room as Cass.

'So.' Fonthill spun round, obviously satisfied with his own appearance. 'Are we ready for battle? I have to confess that I am feeling *rather confident* today,' he revealed gleefully. 'By telling porkies about his assets, Benson has delivered himself into our hands. I predict a very satisfactory outcome.' He cracked his fingers together, and without more ado strode to the door and flung it open. '*Do* keep up,' his voice boomed from the corridor as Rikki scurried after him.

Downstairs they collected a retinue of excited pupils and clerks, charged with ferrying the paperwork to court, and stepped out into Lincoln's Inn Square. Fonthill clasped a hand to his wig as a skittish breeze swirled around the empty space. To Rikki's surprise, he did not follow the normal route to the back entrance of the law courts, but took the long way round to the Strand. The reason was soon evident. As the buzzing throng of pressmen came into sight, Fonthill's gait turned almost into a swagger. '*So* gratifying,' he murmured to Rikki, though he refrained from answering any questions but swept straight inside, robe billowing. Rikki looked about nervously for Kate as they made their way up a grand stone staircase and through the hallways, but all barristers looked alike in their wigs and enveloping black. An usher showed them into one of the empty consultation rooms, and Rikki supervised the unpacking and arrangement of the bundles and files while Fonthill paced back and forth, gesturing widely and muttering under his breath like an actor waiting to go onstage.

A few moments later Rikki sprang to his feet as Jenkins entered, followed by Cass, whose dark eyes widened as she caught his glance. Her hair was now tied back, and she wore a smart suit. The overall impression her appearance conveyed was unusually demure, almost prim – rather different from what she had been wearing last time they met, Rikki recalled. Fonthill exuded bonhomie. 'Justi-i-in. *Delighted* to see you. And Cass. May I say that you look *radiant* this morning?' From behind Fonthill's back, Rikki rolled his eyes.

They sat down, and Fonthill took them through what was going to happen in court that day. He assured Cass that she would not be required to submit herself to cross-examination until later in the proceedings. Both sides would go in before the hearing started. 'May I advise you not to acknowledge the opposition in any way, Mrs Ben— sorry, Cass? Much safer just to ignore them, however irritating they might be.' He explained that everyone should rise and bow when the judge entered. 'A dip of the head will do; you won't have to *genuflect*,' he told them. 'It's merely a gesture of respect. Judges are not deities – though some of them may behave as if they were.' Once the judge had opened proceedings, Counsel for the Petitioner – 'That's Mr McLaren, acting for Mr Benson, of course' – would make his opening case. 'He'll probably *drag on* until lunchtime.' He licked his lips. 'The afternoon will be *mine*.'

An usher arrived and told them that they could go in now. 'Shall we?' asked Fonthill. They followed the usher into the courtroom. Benson's team had arrived before them. As he entered, Rikki stared at Kate, who sat stony-faced, avoiding his eye. She was seated behind Angus McLaren, who gave him a distant smile. Rikki had heard enough about McLaren over the years not to be deceived by his kindly demeanour into underestimating him. Sitting behind Kate was a woman whom Rikki identified as the solicitor, Angela Cross, and a bored-looking man with a face familiar from television: that must be Benson. Just then he leaned forward and whispered something to Kate which made her smile. Rikki felt a stab of jealous fury.

'All rise for the Honourable Mr Justice Overend.'

There was a scraping of chairs as everybody stood. A tubby man, dressed in red robes and a full wig, shambled in and sat down behind the lectern that dominated the courtroom. His eyes scanned those present over the top of his half-moon spectacles, before inviting them to be seated. Here we go, thought Rikki.

The judge leaned forward and hunched his shoulders. 'For the benefit of those new to the High Court', he explained that this was not a trial, but a hearing. 'There is no jury,' he continued. 'I shall consider all the evidence myself and come to a judgment as soon as possible after the hearing closes. In doing so I shall have to determine certain issues of fact.' Just then he was interrupted by a tinny version of 'My Way'. The judge paused and fiddled with his hearing aid, confused about where the tune was coming from. Jez Benson was fumbling with a phone. 'Sorry, Your Honour, I forgot to switch it off.'

Mr Justice Overend frowned, but made no further comment. He asked both sides to be brief and to keep to the point. 'I shall not hesitate to intervene if I feel that either side is departing from these simple rules and leading us into territory foreign to the matter in hand.' The judge identified the husband as 'the Petitioner' and his wife as 'the Respondent'. Over the next few minutes he succinctly and carefully summarised the position set out by each of them in their written submissions, and identified the issues that would need to be determined. Then he looked up. 'I now call upon Mr McLaren to present the case for the husband.'

McLaren rose to his feet. 'Before I begin, My Lord, we wish to draw your attention to a voluntary disclosure by the husband. He now recognises that his original Form E statement of assets was incomplete. Formerly he had believed that the further assets detailed in this supplementary schedule were irrelevant to these proceedings, and he now acknowledges that he was mistaken.'

'Hell,' muttered Fonthill.

'My Lord, I think you will agree that this disclosure reflects to the credit of the husband.'

'One moment,' interrupted the judge. 'Have I received a copy of this document?'

'I regret not, My Lord. May we now distribute copies to you and to My Learned Friend and My Friend opposite?' He gestured towards Fonthill and Jenkins. Rikki saw that Fonthill seemed ready to protest, and then thought better of it. He could scarcely object to a disclosure likely to benefit his own client.

'Very well, Mr McLaren, I will allow it.'

'Shit,' grumbled Fonthill under his breath, and then spoke up, 'Thank you *so* much', as he received two copies of the document from McLaren. Without even glancing at it he passed them back to Rikki, who passed one on to Jenkins and scanned the other. It was as Cass had indicated: Benson was on the brink of signing a major new business venture in Las Vegas. Though the contract had yet to be signed, the deal had been agreed in principle.

McLaren then resumed his submission to the court. He outlined the story of the marriage from the moment the two had met, eighteen years earlier. At that time, he said pointedly, 'the wife' had been receiving treatment at a well-known health farm for a condition described as 'sex addiction'. Mr Justice Overend appeared startled at this revelation. Rikki was acutely aware of Cass sitting with Jenkins behind him. She leaned forward and whispered in his ear, 'Don't pretend to be surprised, big boy.' A little later Cass leaned forward again to whisper something, provoking a stern glare from the judge. After that she passed him the first of several scribbled notes: *What do you think the Old Boy wears under that robe? Y-fronts and sock suspenders?*

It felt very unnatural to Rikki to be so close to Kate without speaking to or even looking directly at her. He wondered if she felt the same. He tried to read her expression, but she remained self-possessed and apparently impassive. He tried to concentrate on the other side's submission, looking for holes in the argument. From time to time he made a note on the pad in front of him.

McLaren was now describing Benson as 'a hugely successful music and television producer, responsible for a string of successes, most notably *Starmaker!*, a format adapted for television audiences around the world'.

'Enlighten me,' interrupted the judge. 'Is this a talent contest?'

'It is indeed, My Lord, and an extremely popular one.' Rikki struggled to suppress a smile.

'Very good. Proceed.'

McLaren explained that Benson was now a very wealthy man. 'The wife' had shared in this wealth and enjoyed a style of life available only to the very rich. They owned homes in London and New York, in Gloucestershire and the Caribbean, and employed staff to supply every conceivable need. McLaren asserted that the wife had made no significant financial contribution during almost twenty years of marriage.

He then detailed the 'unreasonable behaviour' on which the petition for divorce was founded. 'This included refusing to watch his television programme, and referring to it as *Star*— I'm sorry, My Lord, may I pass you a note of the term she used?' There was a pause while McLaren handed a folded-up sheet of paper to the judge, who unfolded it and then looked very shocked.

'Then, of course, there was the notorious incident in which the wife emptied a glass of champagne over her husband's head during a live television awards ceremony ...' he paused to emphasise the enormity of the crime, '*in the presence of members of the Royal Family.*'

Another note was passed over Rikki's shoulder: *It was cheap fizz*. Privately he allowed that Cass's behaviour had been 'unreasonable' according to the legal definition: 'the Respondent has behaved in such a way that the Petitioner cannot reasonably be expected to live with the Respondent.' A thought occurred to him for the first time: was that true of Kate?

McLaren turned to the financial settlement. 'We submit that this is a straightforward case. The husband's wealth is a result of his own energy and talent alone. Because of this the wife's claim should be determined by reference to the principle of need alone. Her needs should be fairly assessed, not predominantly by reference to the standard of living during the latter years of the marriage.' He described her own assessment of her needs as 'exorbitant'. He referred to 'the wife's post-separation misconduct', as instanced in the 'Conduct Note'. This was among the many documents that Rikki had scrutinised in the past few days. He remembered one incident singled out in the Note: on a late-night television chat show Cass had described her husband as 'not well endowed'.

As Fonthill had predicted, McLaren's submission lasted all morning. Rikki was forced to concede that he had made a strong case. From time to time he stole a glance at Kate, who looked increasingly smug as the argument developed. When McLaren concluded, the judge adjourned proceedings for lunch. Everyone present stood and bowed as he left the courtroom.

'That *was* a surprise,' snapped Fonthill as soon as they were back in the meeting room. Because of the media gauntlet outside, it had been decided that they would remain here for lunch, supplied by outside caterers. 'We had them by the goolies until this last-minute disclosure. I wonder ... Do you suppose they somehow got wind of the fact that we knew Benson was withholding something?'

'I was turning over the same point in my mind,' replied Jenkins. 'I wondered whether there was anything in our submission to raise their suspicions. But having reviewed the matter, I really don't think that there was.'

Just then Cass rejoined them, after a visit to 'the bog'. Jenkins was at his most solicitous. 'My dear Cass, I hope that you haven't been upset by anything that was said in court this morning?'

'Oh, no, I've heard much worse. I sound a right cow, though, don't I? I wouldn't want to be married to me.'

All three men chuckled. 'My dear, if I were available, I should be down on one knee,' quipped Jenkins.

∾

In the afternoon it was Fonthill's turn. 'My Lord, what we have heard this morning is a *travesty*,' he began. 'When Cassandra Carnaby married Jeremy Benson she was a star and he was, frankly, a nobody. She had released a number-one hit …' he paused, to consult his notes, '"You Can Have Me Any Way You Want Me, Baby".'

'Mr Fonthill,' interrupted the judge, 'have you taken leave of your senses?'

'I was merely referring to the title of the song, My Lord.'

'Am I to understand that Mrs Benson was a performer?'

'A singer, My Lord, and a very successful one.'

The judge made a note on his pad. 'Would I have heard any of her songs?'

'I doubt it, My Lord. But many people not only heard but bought them. She was therefore independently wealthy …' Fonthill portrayed Cass as a talented, beautiful woman, who had forsaken a lucrative and successful career in order to marry and raise a family. 'Instead she has dedicated her life to her husband and her children.' When she met 'the husband', she had already reached the pinnacle of her profession, adored by millions: 'Who knows where she might have gone from there?' Sadly, he had insisted that she abandon her calling when they married. Fonthill's voice wavered, as he painted a picture of an artist whose creativity had been stifled by a tyrannical husband. While he jetted around the

215

world attending glamorous functions, she had remained at home, cooking for the children, packing them off to school, and sewing buttons onto her husband's shirts … What an old ham, thought Rikki.

The husband had vetoed all of the many promising opportunities which had come her way, Fonthill maintained. The wife had several times been asked to present programmes on television, which was anathema to him. In contrast, she had encouraged and inspired the husband from the very beginning. Indeed, without her input and support it was unlikely that he would have been successful at all.

'Load of bollocks,' commented Jez, loud enough to halt Fonthill in mid-flow.

His interjection caused consternation in the courtroom. McLaren looked round in obvious disapproval; Kate stared at him in horror. Rikki saw Benson's solicitor tug hard at his sleeve. The judge banged his gavel on the lectern. 'Silence in court!' he ordered. 'Mr Benson, you will not speak unless asked to do so by a member of this court. Is that understood?'

'Sorry, Your Honour, I didn't like what he was suggesting.'

'Nevertheless you will keep quiet. I warn you that if there are any further interruptions I will halt this hearing and have the person responsible ejected from the court.' Benson made a face.

Fonthill resumed his submission. Contrary to what they had been told earlier, the wife had made and continued to make a significant contribution to her husband's career. Her creative suggestions were recognised by the production team as being 'of the utmost value'. Mr Benson's most successful television programme was called *Starmaker!* It had been said before that the biggest star created by the programme was

Benson himself. 'We submit that it was his wife who enabled Benson to become a star.'

It was therefore quite wrong for the wife's claim to be decided on the basis of need alone. She had lost significant income when she was obliged to give up her career as a successful singer. Following her marriage she had been denied opportunities to other career avenues that would undoubtedly have brought rich rewards. Furthermore, she was entitled to a significant share of the wealth that had accrued and continued to accrue from her husband's business activities. Following the separation from her husband, she had been the victim of a cruel campaign of vilification that had damaged her earning capacity within the media. For all these reasons, concluded Fonthill, 'We submit that her claim of fifty million pounds, far from being exorbitant, is comparatively modest. Indeed, given the substantial new assets revealed *only this morning*,' he sneered, 'we submit that she deserves more.' Fonthill paused, holding his pose dramatically as if milking the applause from an imaginary audience, before returning to his seat.

'Thank you, Mr Fonthill.' Since it was now late afternoon, the judge adjourned the hearings for the day. 'We will resume tomorrow at ten o'clock.'

෧෨

'You were marvellous, sir,' gushed one of the more impressionable juniors.

Fonthill smirked. 'You are too kind. Though I do think that we were on good form this afternoon, don't you, King?'

'Oh, indisputably.' By now they had parted from Justin and Cass for the day, and were leaving the law courts by the main entrance. It was cold and dark, but most of the journalists, photographers and television crews were still gathered outside, though the stars had already left. As the barristers reached them, one cried out, 'It's Snape! Tell us what happened, Mr Fonthill.'

Fonthill halted, beaming. A large, shaggy microphone was thrust in his face. Several flashbulbs went off, temporarily blinding him. The television camera attached to a crane began wheeling round. Questions were fired at him from all sides. 'Are you going to win?' ... 'Is Cass being too greedy?' ... 'Will Jez cough up?'

Fonthill waited for the questions to subside. Then he cleared his throat. 'In essence, this is a case of a husband refusing to fulfil his obligations,' he said. 'We will ensure that justice is done.' He paused while a further volley of questions was discharged. There was a creaking sound, and then a loud crack, as the hood shielding the camera on the crane snapped off and fell. It hit Fonthill a glancing blow and knocked him to the ground, where he lay still. The cameraman swore. Somebody screamed. Rikki bent over him, 'Mr Fonthill, are you all right?'

Fonthill slowly opened his eyes. His wig was askew. With great dignity he opened his lips and spoke: 'My Lord, I beg to request an adjournment.'

'I'm sorry?'

'The owl and the pussycat went to sea ...'

'Mr Fonthill?'

''E's gone potty,' said someone in the crowd. 'Voldemort's got to him at last.'

'... some honey and *plenty* of money ...'

Rikki looked over his shoulder at one of the clerks, who was peering down at the stricken silk with puzzlement and concern. 'Mr Fonthill's had a knock on the head,' Rikki explained. 'I think that he needs to be taken home. Will you help me get him into a cab?'

Together they helped a reluctant Fonthill to his feet and dragged him away from the cameras and the microphones. As they were helping him into the back of the taxi, Fonthill turned round and declaimed to the curious press: '... which they ate with a runcible *spoon*.'

Chapter 22

By the time Kate reached home that evening, she was feeling weary. Two transatlantic flights in two days had messed
with her body clock. The euphoria that had kept her afloat in
court had now evaporated, leaving her as limp as a deflated
balloon. Stumbling into the dark flat with both hands full,
she dropped her bags right where she stood, and listened to
the silence. *Honey, I'm home …*

Even when she switched on the lights and drew the curtains,
the flat still had a stale, untenanted air. No one had been
here since Saturday, when Sam and Milton had presumably
departed back to the country. Sam must have fiddled with the
hot-water system, since when Kate went to take a shower the
water ran lukewarm, then icy. Shivering with cold, she pulled
on jeans, a toasty angora jumper with a deep fold-over collar
and an old pair of battered sheepskin boots, then went to
look for something to eat.

Opening the fridge, the first item she spotted was a small,
unfamiliar jar: examining the label, she learned that it was
potato and cauliflower purée (yuk!) labelled 'Down the Little
Red Lane – organic baby food – from 4 months'. Now that

she thought about it, there was a distinct whiff of *eau de Milton* about the place, which she traced to sacks of dirty nappies stuffed into the kitchen bin. Kate removed the bin bag from its stylish steel enclosure and carried it downstairs at arm's length, nose averted, then dropped it into one of the large wheelie bins that were stashed down the side of her block of flats. Folding her arms against the cold, she ran back inside. What now? First, she decided to wash out the bin thoroughly, and turned on a music radio station to keep her company. In the process of cleaning the bin she managed to dribble dirty water on the floor, which now needed mopping. Having cleaned the dirty patch, she realised that it was now visibly cleaner than the rest of the floor and thought she might as well mop the whole thing.

The truth was that she didn't know what to do with herself. She longed to tell somebody about her trip to the West Indies and her first day of *Benson* v. *Carnaby*. Relating the dramas of life to another person doubled the fun of having them. 'Snorkelling? ... How amazing ... The judge said *what*? ... Oh, Kate, you didn't!' Several times her hand hovered over the phone, but at the last minute she shied away from ringing home or talking to her friends, who might pick up signals that all was not well between herself and Rikki.

She hadn't known what to expect in the courtroom this morning. Would he look tired and drawn? Might he appear slovenly and debauched, after his pole-dancing expedition? Or penitent? But he was none of these; he just seemed distant. He hadn't even acknowledged her – not that she'd have responded if he had done. She had certainly imagined that he would at least look at her. Well, he could go on sulking if he wanted to. It was very juvenile in her opinion. Altogether he was behaving like a silly schoolboy. That whispering and note-passing with Cassandra Carnaby had been most unpro-fessional.

Nevertheless, when the phone rang, startling her out of her thoughts, she hoped it might be him. Perhaps he was ringing to make things up with her. She let it ring five times while she collected herself. Also, she must not give him the impression that she had nothing to do but sit by the phone waiting for him to call.

'Hello?' she said, in a cool, casual voice. There was silence at the other end. 'Hello?' she repeated more sharply.

She heard a series of indistinct noises. It sounded as if someone was crying. Kate was suddenly alarmed. 'Rikki, is that you?'

Then a wavering voice said, 'Kate?'

'Angus?' She pressed the phone to her ear, to listen more intently. He sounded odd. 'Are you all right?'

'It's Mary. She's gone.' His voice broke on the last word.

Who was Mary? Kate didn't know what to say. Angus sounded utterly desolate. Was Mary perhaps the real name of the Dragon? Had she left him?

'I'm so sorry, Angus,' she told him. 'What can I do? How can I help?'

'The case ... You see, I don't think I ...' He stopped again, overcome. The weakness in his voice was shocking. Was this the same man who had marched up to the court with her this morning on tip-top form?

'What about the case?' she pressed. 'Is there something you need?'

'Not sure I can manage, you see ... Arrangements ... tele-phone ... funeral. All that.'

Funeral! 'Angus, has somebody died?'

'Found her on the floor. Gone. Just … gone. ' He began to sob.

Kate couldn't bear it. 'Listen, Angus, I'm coming round. Don't worry about the case. I'll deal with it. Have you got anyone there with you?'

'They've taken her away. She's *gone*.' His voice rose in desolate disbelief.

'OK. I'll be there in the next hour. Make yourself a cup of tea with lots of sugar and, er, keep warm.'

He didn't answer. She pictured him wandering into the street, disoriented, without a proper coat on. 'Wait for me, all right? Find something to read. Listen to some music … Promise me that you'll stay in the house until I get there.'

The phone clicked as he hung up without replying. Kate replaced her own receiver and dashed for her coat. God! Where did he live? She had never been to his house. Angus was a very private man. She was on the brink of telephoning chambers to see if the clerk on evening duty would give her the address when she remembered the Christmas-card list. Of course! She switched on her laptop and waited while it loaded with agonising slowness. At last it was ready, and with a few swift keystrokes she searched 'My Documents/ Personal/Christmas-card list', and scrolled down through the document: 166 Strand-on-the Green. Where the hell was that? *Stay calm, Kate.* Money, credit card, phone, *London A–Z.* She wound a scarf round her neck and ran out of the door.

൭

Angus's house was right on the Thames, an imposing eighteenth-century brick building guarded from the tow path by a low wrought-iron gate. Kate unlatched it, strode across a narrow strip of garden and banged the heavy brass door-knocker. Lights blazed from the uncurtained windows, but she couldn't see Angus inside. She waited anxiously, and after no response banged the knocker again. A chill mist rose from the river and stole about her feet.

At last she heard movement, and approaching footsteps. The door opened. Angus stared at her vaguely, as if surprised to see her. He was still wearing the clothes he'd gone home in from chambers, though his jacket was unbuttoned and he'd taken off his tie. His hair was dishevelled, as if he'd been rubbing his hands over it. She stepped inside, shut the door behind her, and took his arm, leading him down the corridor and into the first room she came to. It was a dining room, charming rather than formal, with wooden panelling painted a soft grey and blue cushions on the window seats. The table was covered with papers, half-empty mugs, a telephone tethered to the wall, Angus's tie – still knotted in a wide loop, as if he'd wrenched it off in distress – and a scattering of sugar that had spilled from the bowl. She guided him to the chair in which he'd evidently been sitting, and he slumped heavily onto the seat with his arms hanging loose. She pulled another chair close.

'Found her in the kitchen,' he murmured. 'Must have been preparing the supper. Hope she didn't suffer.' His face twisted with pain at the thought.

'Angus, I'm so, so sorry.' Kate was shocked by the change in him. His voice was low and lifeless. The light had gone out of his eyes. He looked shrunken, defeated.

She touched his shoulder. 'Have you eaten anything?' He stared at her blankly. 'Right. This is what we'll do. You go upstairs and have a hot bath, and I'll cook us something. I

224

haven't eaten yet, and I'm starving,' she added, hoping that his innate politeness would make him agree, for her sake if not for his. The trick seemed to work, for with a little more coaxing he struggled to his feet and went obediently out of the room. A few moments later she heard his effortful tread on the stairs. Kate blew out her breath. Poor Angus. He was in no condition to appear in court the next day. What should she do? Was it too late to get hold of one of the clerks? Should she ring Angela? Her eye fell on the messy table. First, she'd tidy up and make supper.

Among the papers she couldn't help noticing a doctor's certificate. 'Mary Alexandra McLaren, *née* Peterhouse. Age: sixty-five. Cause of death: spontaneous myocardial infarction.' Was that a heart attack? Carefully she sorted the papers as best she could into piles, and ranged them along the top of the sideboard. She unknotted Angus's tie, coiled it neatly and placed it beside the papers. Then she picked up the mugs and sugar bowl and went looking for the kitchen, which was at the back of the house overlooking the garden. It was a bit spooky to see the preparations that had been so abruptly interrupted. On the draining board was a saucepan of peeled potatoes sitting in water. The peelings were still in the sink. There were some mushrooms in a brown paper bag, and a chopping board and knife already laid out to slice them. Kate opened the fridge, wondering what else had been on the menu, and found two unwrapped steaks on a plate. She hesitated, wondering if steak wasn't too robust for someone whose wife had just died. But no. Angus was a man. Men always felt better after a good meal. Also in the fridge she found mustard and horseradish sauce, which she took out in case Angus liked them with beef, a packet of salad leaves and some home-made dressing in a jar. Eventually she tracked down a couple of wedges of cheese on a special plate with a lid, biscuits to go with them and a bottle of red wine in a rack, which she opened and set by the stove. She'd already spotted a fruit bowl on the sideboard in the dining room. That would have to do.

As she set about her preparations she couldn't help thinking about the dead woman. Mary. Her image of a hatchet-faced tyrant – the Dragon – ticking off Angus if he wasn't home on time, issuing commands to him by telephone in the office, scowling over household chores – began to change as she took note of her surroundings. The kitchen had a cosy feel. Even in February there were cheerful red geraniums in flower on the window sill. A row of beautiful handmade plates in vivid blues hung over the cooker, and on the wall next to the door was a lovely watercolour of boats on the river, with some kind of water bird in the foreground and an island behind – perhaps the view from this house? In one corner was a comfortable-looking small armchair, the chintz covering worn from use, and a law journal balanced on one arm. She pictured Angus sitting here, feet outstretched, eyes alight, chatting to his wife. She found she was smiling at the thought, before she remembered the reality of his distraught, crumpled condition. *Don't worry, Mary, I'll look after him.*

∞

'And here she is again – do you see, by that rock?' Angus pointed to another photograph. A tender smile animated his face. 'That was a grand holiday. Two weeks on Mull with hardly a day of rain – and the most marvellous birds.'

'Did Mary paint them?' Kate asked. 'I was just wondering because I saw a—'

'Oh, yes,' he interrupted. 'She's a very fine painter. Had an exhibition in a gallery in Chiswick last summer, and sold a fair few of them. Loves birds, just like me ... I mean, she did.'

'What about this photo?' Kate hurried him on. 'Was that in Scotland, too?'

Angus had come down to dinner in corduroy trousers and a thick jumper, looking somewhat better after his bath, though she had found it difficult to get him to concentrate on anything, including eating. It did not seem right to talk about *Benson* v. *Carnaby*. He hunched in his seat at the table exuding silent despair, not even hearing her banal remarks about the food or noticing when she proffered the pepper grinder or the mustard pot. Only one thing was on his mind – one person, to be exact – and finally, hoping that she wasn't overstepping the mark, she decided to prompt him. 'Tell me about your wife, Angus,' she said gently, and the floodgates had opened.

He had met Mary after knocking her off her bike in Merton Lane, when she was on her way to a tutorial and he was running into Christ Church Meadow, late for rowing practice. Yes, yes, of course that was in Oxford. They were both undergraduates there. She'd been terribly cross – shouted at him, actually. But she was the most beautiful girl he'd ever seen. He'd managed to get the name of her college out of her, and after that had besieged her until she finally agreed to go out to the cinema with him. 'She liked to say it was out of sheer pity, but that was a joke, to keep me on my toes. Which she certainly did! Lord, the hoops I had to jump through.' Angus chuckled at the memory, forgetting the present. 'She refused to marry me until she finished her degree, then swanned off to Africa for a year, teaching English and riding mules about the place, while I sweated over my Bar exams. Then she wanted to train to be a teacher. Very clever woman, you know, much cleverer than me. But I played a long game, and in the end she said yes.'

Kate listened and prompted, and was pleased to see some colour returning to his cheeks as he automatically ate the food in front of him and sipped his wine. Her picture of a battleaxe waiting at the door with frying pan poised vanished as he told her about Mary's career as a history teacher, and eventually headmistress, at one of the finest girls' schools in London. On retirement, she became a magistrate and a prison visitor. He'd worried that this might be too hard on her, what with her dicky heart. 'But I couldn't stop her. Didn't want to, really, if it made her happy. That's all I ever wanted, you see: to make her happy.' He leaned forward intently, placing a hand on Kate's arm, willing her to understand; and she nodded because the lump in her throat would not allow her to speak.

Over the cheese he raised the subject of *Benson* v. *Carnaby* himself. 'I don't think I'm going to be up to it, Kate. I've never liked missing a day in court, but one must be realistic. Any client I am representing deserves my full attention, and I'm simply not able to offer that just at present. I need twenty-four hours at least to sort myself out.' He took a sip of wine, adding, 'But you'll manage.'

'*Me?*'

'Well, of course.' His raised eyebrows suggested surprise that she might think there was any other possibility.

Kate felt the panic rising. Tomorrow, the cross-examinations would begin, requiring a mastery of detail and a commanding presence. She would be battling with Snape! A single mistake – one sign of weakness – and he would demolish her with his sneers and side-swipes. Her heart began to thud. It was one thing to help Angus prepare his cross-examination, discussing strategy and offering bright suggestions; quite another to carry out the task on her own. Here it was, the opportunity she had longed for, to show off her talent for advocacy and knowledge of the law – and she was terrified.

'Odd to think that Mary will never iron my court shirt again,' Angus said broodingly. 'Never tell me about her day ... Never ...' He bowed his head, fighting against tears.

Kate saw that she couldn't ask for his advice on the case. It was too cruel, and too selfish. She could worry about it later. Her immediate priority was to calm Angus down again, so that she'd feel able to leave him alone. That's when she'd had the lucky inspiration of asking to see a photo of Mary.

He'd brought her upstairs to this delightful sitting room, lined with bookshelves, where a large sofa and comfortable chairs were drawn up to face a television. 'We were going to watch *University Challenge* tonight,' he explained. 'It's one of our favourite programmes.' While she fastened the shutters and drew the curtains to shut out the gloomy night, he brought out an old-fashioned album with stiff black pages and stick-on corners to hold the photographs. They sat side by side on the sofa, and he showed her Mary as she had looked in the early 1960s, when he had first met her: a slight girl with long brown hair and an attractive strong-boned face. In one photo she was laughing up into the face of a tall young man, thin as a beanpole with a halo of unruly blond hair, who held her protectively with one arm, looking proud as punch. Kate didn't at first recognise the man, but she recognised the expression. 'Angus, that's you!'

He'd fetched one album after another, unfolding a record of life together: holidays, new cars, new houses; Angus with his leg in a cast in some ski resort, Mary on the top of the Empire State Building wearing an 'I love NY' cap; the pair of them pulling a Christmas cracker, surrounded by friends.

'Why did you call her the Dragon?' Kate asked curiously. 'She looks lovely.'

'Oh, I don't know. It started as a joke. Then – well, it was a kind of protection, I suppose. Marriage is a private thing. I wanted to keep it to myself. And it stopped people expecting her to turn up to dreary law dinners, which she wouldn't have liked – though I would.' He sighed, and shook his head. 'But one can't have everything. Marriage is give and take – a partnership. One has to adjust. It's painful sometimes. But it's the withstanding of the storm that makes you strong.'

He told her about some of those storms – the bad times as well as the good.

Kate had known that Angus had no children, but had never felt able to ask why. He told her about a daughter that had been stillborn. 'I thought Mary would never get over it. She couldn't have another, you see. Withdrew from me completely for a while. But I waited, and in the end she came back to me. We called the baby Perdita ... It means "lost",' he explained, glancing at Kate. 'She would have been about your own age now.'

They continued browsing through the albums, while emotions moved across his face like the breeze on the surface of a lake. The final photograph showed a stout woman of late middle age in a printed silk dress, grey hair curling about her face. 'My darling girl,' murmured Angus, rubbing a gentle finger across the picture.

That's how she left him, with the albums spread across the sofa and on the carpet, and gusts of river-wind knocking softly at the shutters. She thought he might stay there all night, dozing and waking, crying and remembering – sometimes smiling, too. He was not alone, but in the best company she could think of, with the woman he loved.

Chapter 23

'Concussion, you say?'

'Yes, My Lord,' Rikki answered.

For one unguarded moment Mr Justice Overend's features registered intense amusement, which he attempted to disguise by raising a handkerchief to his mouth and coughing elaborately. 'Dear, dear, how very unfortunate. We must hope that Mr Fonthill makes a speedy recovery. And have I understood correctly that *you* will be conducting today's proceedings on behalf of Mrs Carmody?' His grey eyebrows rose so high at this outlandish notion that they almost merged into the woolly fringe of his wig.

'Carnaby, My Lord. Yes, My Lord.'

Rikki returned the judge's gaze steadily, though beneath his gown his heart was racing – and he hadn't even entered the courtroom yet. Having consulted the judge's usher, he was following her advice to tell Overend privately, rather than in court, that he would be covering for Fonthill today. It was a matter of courtesy to inform the judge in advance about any change of advocate. Accordingly he was here in the judge's chamber, a grand high-ceilinged room that could be used as an informal setting for family-law cases but was also the judge's private office, where he could retire when he wasn't actively presiding, to study documents and reflect. Rikki spotted a clutch of golf bags propped in one corner, a photograph of a sprightlier Overend shaking hands with Mrs Thatcher, and a paperback copy of Robert Harris's latest bestseller, insufficiently hidden under a pile of hefty legal tomes.

'Your client, I take it, is satisfied with this arrangement?' The judge looked dubious.

'Yes, My Lord.' Rikki felt it was better not to quote Cass's actual words, 'Ooh, goody'. It was humiliating to realise that her enthusiasm was not wholly based on his advocacy skills. Fonthill treated him like a skivvy, Cass like a toyboy. Why did no one take him seriously?

It had taken him a while to appreciate that Fonthill's accident had presented him with an outstanding opportunity. Yesterday evening, in the urgency of looking after his babbling senior, its consequences had not immediately occurred to him. While the taxi crawled through rush-hour traffic to Fonthill's house in Highgate, he had been fully occupied in dealing with his unpredictable fellow-passenger, who veered between a comatose slump and telling Rikki what a beautiful pussy he was, he was, he was. Then there had been Mrs Fonthill to contend with, one of those immaculately groomed women of thirty-five going on fifty-five who could freeze blood at twenty paces. She had been on her way to a Pilates class, and was less than pleased to be diverted into playing nursemaid instead. Having reluctantly accepted her responsibilities, she told Rikki firmly that it was the least he could do to stay with her until the doctor arrived. In fact, he'd had a bit of a job escaping from her clutches, once she'd downed a stiff G&T or three. It was only after they had received the doctor's verdict that he had begun to consider its implications: Fonthill was suffering from mild concussion, requiring twenty-four hours in bed minimum, which meant that he, Rikki King, would have to carry the case on his own. 'Who else is to do it?' Justin had said bluntly when, later that evening, they managed to speak by phone. 'If we adjourn we'll have to start the whole case over again, possibly with another judge, and we don't want that. Just try not to mess it up.'

Rikki had already telephoned chambers and persuaded the clerk on night duty to photocopy a sheaf of the most important documents and courier them over to the Holland Park flat. He had stayed up half the night poring over them, making annotations, and highlighting key passages in preparation for his appearance in court today. He clutched them now, still stowed in the jiffy bag in which they had arrived, with hands that were beginning to sweat.

'You may go, Mr King.' The judge waved a hand as if Rikki were a troublesome wasp. 'I shall look forward to seeing how you perform in court. Eh, what?'

While they were talking the usher had slipped quietly into the room and now bent to murmur something into the judge's ear. 'Another one? Oh, very well,' he said testily. 'You'd better show her in.'

Rikki had stood up and was moving towards the door when Kate walked in. He stopped in shock. Their eyes met. She halted, too, but only for a moment. He could read nothing in her face except surprise, swiftly masked, before she strode past him towards the chair he had just vacated, and began talking to the judge. He paused, uncertain whether he should stay or go. Kate was saying something about Angus McLaren – his wife – funeral arrangements. She looked confident and businesslike, her back ramrod straight and her hands clasped in her lap like a schoolgirl's. Then the import of her words trickled through to him. McLaren, like Fonthill, was out of action. She would be taking his place. Today they would be in combat in court, not at one remove but head to head.

'... but there is no alternative, I suppose.' The judge sighed despondently. 'At least you're well matched. Babes in the wood, the pair of you. Off you go, then. And do try to keep your clients under control.'

Class dismissed. Rikki stood aside, holding the door for Kate with elaborate courtesy, and was irritated when, with equally chilly politeness, she gave a formal nod of acknowledgement and stalked past him. Letting the door slam shut, Rikki chased after her down the busy corridor. He grabbed her arm from behind, and swung her round to face him.

'Kate, we can't go on like this. We have to talk.'

'Not now. Not here. And let go of my arm.' She pulled herself free of his grasp. He felt infuriated as he saw her eyes dart round, checking to see if anyone was watching. Typical! Kate always worried about what other people thought – hiding her feelings behind a public mask. Rikki tried to compose himself. The notion of fighting his own wife over the carcase of another couple's marriage made him hot with anxiety and frustration. *Please don't do this*, is what he intended to say, but the words that came out of his mouth were different, as jealous thoughts came flooding back. 'You're not seriously going to defend that – that *clown*.' He stabbed a forefinger in the air.

'Why not? You seem happy enough to do the same for that – that *cleavage on legs*. When you're not too busy whispering and giggling together, that is.'

Silenced by the unbidden memory of Cass's naked body under his hands, Rikki could only clench his jaw and glare.

He noticed that she was rather flushed. Or was it something else? 'You're suntanned,' he said accusingly.

'Yes. Well.' She really was blushing now. 'I had to conduct some business over the weekend in the West Indies. As you would know, if you had been at home last week.'

'Hey, guys. Having fun?' Hayley had stopped beside them, her arms full of bundles of papers tied with ribbon, fizzing with energy as always. 'God, Kate, isn't it awful about Angus's wife? Poor man! But how exciting that you'll be leading the case! Talk about a lucky break. And you, too, I hear.' She turned to Rikki, breaking into an uninhibited laugh. 'I know it's not funny, really, but Fonthill's such a pompous idiot. I wish I'd seen him weaving all over the pavement, spouting nonsense.' She peered over the top of her bundles at her watch. 'Shiterama. Gotta go. Let's get together soon, yeah? And you two shouldn't be conferring, even if you are married. That sort of thing gives barristers a bad name.' She wagged a teasing finger at them, and was gone.

'Well, at least somebody's happy,' said Rikki with an edge of bitterness. He couldn't help contrasting Hayley's bubbly vitality with Kate's coldness. A stray detail drifted into his mind. 'Didn't you say that she was pregnant?'

'The two are not related,' Kate told him crisply. The half-smile she had produced for Hayley had vanished. 'And I must go. My client will be expecting me.'

'Don't let me keep you from your *client*. After all, who am I? Only your *husband*.'

'Now you're being childish.' She turned to go.

'Go on, then. Bugger off back to Benson.' As he gestured angrily, the jiffy bag slipped from under his arm and fell to the floor at Kate's feet.

'Oh dear,' she said, staring at it pointedly. 'Nothing important, I hope.'

Enraged by her coolness, Rikki could hardly bear to kneel down in front of her. 'Why don't you just go?' he repeated.

'I'll go when I'm ready, thank you.' Then, when neither of them moved, she gave an exasperated sigh, and in one neat movement bent and picked up the jiffy bag. '"Mr Rustom King,"' she read from the label. 'That's you, I believe.'

Goaded beyond endurance, Rikki snatched the bag from her hand, turned on his heel and stalked off down the corridor. Unfair! Unreasonable! Wilful, bossy, uptight, unsympathetic! The words tumbled chaotically through his head, and it was a minute or two before he realised he was marching in the wrong direction.

Chapter 24

〜〜〜

'Mr Benson, would you say that you were a good husband?' asked Kate.

She was leaning on the edge of the witness box, gazing encouragingly into Benson's smug face. It seemed to Rikki that she'd given the last two words a subtle emphasis. He folded his arms and set his expression to amused scepticism.

'Course I was,' answered Benson. 'Gave her everything.'

'Money, for example? Is it correct that you had a joint bank account?'

'Yeah, we did, more's the pity.' He grinned and rolled his eyes at the judge, and looked miffed when he got no response.

'Which Mrs Benson was able to draw on freely?'

'"Freely" is the word. I made the money and she spent it. I tell you, that woman can shop for England.'

'Did you ever refuse her anything?'

'Not so far as I can remember. Well, there was that one time she wanted to adopt a baby tiger as a pet—'

'Or try to stop her pursuing her career?' Kate cut ruthlessly across this dangerous waffle.

'Far from it. I was always trying to get her TV work.'

'This is in addition to a singing career which, in fact, you had been instrumental in promoting in the first place. Isn't that correct?'

Benson gave a smile of false modesty, conceding it was so. 'She was going nowhere until I picked her up and made her a true star with her next single.'

'And would you say that, despite occasional differences with your wife, you behaved reasonably? You didn't, for example, ever storm out of the marital home without telling her where you were going?'

Ha! That was a mistake. Benson visibly hesitated.

'To clarify,' Kate continued smoothly, 'you never *abandoned* your wife. You never stalked out and went to live elsewhere, without even leaving her an address?'

'Nah. Anyway, she could always ring me, couldn't she?'

Indeed she could, thought Rikki, aware that Kate's question was another disguised jab at him – just as Kate could have rung *him* at any time, if she hadn't been so wrapped up in this bloody case. He listened now to Kate arguing that Benson had been 'a model husband'. How could she spout such nonsense?

Still, that was the game lawyers played. And as a lawyer, he admitted grudgingly, she was pretty good. Her voice was clear and confident, and if she needed to refer to her notes she did so unobtrusively. Her knowledge of the law was detailed and precise. It was something he had always envied and admired, even if she did sometimes go on a bit about being awarded an 'Outstanding' grade in Bar school. But Kate was not just a lawyer, she was his wife. The hostility that sparked between them like an electric charge was exactly what he had feared when he had begged her not to take this case. His eyes swept round the courtroom, taking in the vaulted ceiling, the judge's dais and the two rows of benches where the two opposing legal teams sat, divided by a central aisle. It struck him that the layout was rather like that of a church wedding, with a vicar presiding and his-and-hers guests grouped on opposite sides. As it begins, so it ends, he reflected.

'... but you yourself did not have an easy upbringing,' Kate was now saying to Benson, her voice dripping with sympathy. 'Your mother died when you were a small boy, and you were brought up by an aunt, and had to share a bedroom with your three cousins. Is that correct?'

Benson assumed a tragic expression. 'Yeah, it was hard. I must have cried myself to sleep every night for years.'

'You did not experience the trappings of privilege. Private education, for example ... foreign travel ... tennis lessons.' *Tennis lessons?* Rikki realised that this was another dig at him. Benson appeared bemused at this line of questioning and the judge tapped his pencil irritably on his desk, but before he could intervene Kate had pressed on to her concluding summary of her client, as 'a man of outstanding talent, energy and enterprise, who is not ashamed to admit that he built himself up from nothing, and who has generously shared his wealth with his wife, even though she made virtually no contribution to it.'

Kate returned to her seat, leaving Benson to preen himself in the stand. Rikki stood up to address him. 'Mr Benson, just before this hearing began yesterday you decided to disclose assets that you had kept quiet about previously. Is that correct?'

'Er, yes.'

'Why didn't you disclose them before?'

'I didn't think that they were relevant. They were part of

a deal that has only just been agreed.' Benson stared back defiantly at Rikki.

'Not relevant? Even though this deal promises to make you – you personally – *one hundred million pounds?*'

'That's only a ballpark figure.'

'I put it to you that you tried to conceal this deal from your wife so that your huge gains would not be reflected in your settlement with her.'

'That's not true.'

'Ah.' Rikki's manner was incredulous. 'What made you change your mind at the last moment?'

Benson exchanged a glance with Kate. 'I was advised that I should do so.'

'By your legal advisors, no doubt,' said Rikki smoothly. 'But hadn't they advised you to do so long before?'

Benson hesitated. 'No.'

'Could you speak up, please, Mr Benson?'

'No.'

'Why not, I wonder?'

'Because I hadn't told them about it.'

'Ah. So it's not just your wife you conceal things from, eh, Mr Benson?'

Benson glared angrily at him.

'Let's talk about your worldwide success, shall we?' Rikki asked. 'Your show is called *Starmaker!*, I believe. Do you remember where the title originated, by any chance?'

'I ... er ... I'm not sure.'

'Let me jog your memory. Wasn't it your wife who thought up the title?'

'I can't recall.'

'You can't recall. What a pity. I put it to you that your wife came up with the title that is the basis of your fortune.'

'She might have done.'

'She might have done. Well, that was worth something, wasn't it, Mr Benson? Your own accounts show that *Starmaker!* earned you twenty-six million pounds last year. I should say that title is worth quite a lot of money. I hope you have it copyright protected.'

'Of course I have.'

'So it is valuable, then?'

Rikki allowed this question to hang in the air, unanswered. He took a new tack. 'In her earlier submission My Friend' – he emphasised the phrase – 'referred to your wife as "mercenary". Do you think that was a fair description?'

'She likes money, that's for sure. Isn't that what "mercenary" means? 'Fraid I didn't bring a dictionary with me,' Benson said rudely.

Rikki ignored him. 'You told us the impressive story of how you made your fortune. When exactly did you begin your meteoric rise?'

'About fifteen years ago, I'd say.'

'So when you met your future wife, you were not rich?'

Benson glanced anxiously at Angela. 'Not really.'

'In fact I think it's fair to say, is it not, that she had considerably more money than you did at the time?'

'Possibly.'

'So to describe her as "mercenary" might be a little unfair, don't you think?'

'Maybe.'

'You told My Friend earlier that you had encouraged your wife in her career.'

'Yes.'

'As a television presenter.'

'Yes.'

'Not as a singer.'

'No. I thought she was getting a bit long in the tooth for that sort of thing. Besides, I didn't want her out on the road once we were married.'

'Can you tell the court about the programme you suggested that she should present?'

'I think that it was a show about shopping.'

'On which channel?'

'It was a cable channel.'

'Do you know how many viewers this channel had? … No? … I'll tell you. Fewer than ten thousand. It's perhaps not surprising that it didn't last more than a few months. Rather different from *Starmaker!*, which regularly draws several million viewers.'

'Eleven million.'

'Thank you. Don't you think that the contrast with the show you wanted your wife to present might have been humiliating for her?'

Benson grunted.

'Can we talk about you now, Mr Benson? It's true, isn't it, that you're considered a very attractive man?' Rikki hoped that Benson's smug smile seemed as repellent to Kate as it did to him.

'It's not for me to say, but, er, well, my face is my fortune.'

'Quite. And it's true, is it not, that you've had a great deal of plastic surgery?'

Kate interrupted. 'My Lord, this line of questioning is gratuitous. My Friend is trying to provoke my client.'

'Please keep to the matter in hand, Mr King,' the judge cautioned. He seemed impatient for the cross-examination to conclude.

'I will endeavour to do so, My Lord. Mr Benson, you are famous for your flashing white teeth, are you not?'

'Maybe.'

'Didn't you accept the prize for the "Biggest Smile on TV" last year at the Independent Television Awards ceremony at' – he consulted his notes – 'the Grosvenor House Hotel?'

'Yes.'

'But you didn't always have good teeth?'

'No. I needed to get them fixed. Cost me loads.'

'I'm sure it did. Do you remember who persuaded you to get your teeth done?'

'Possibly my wife?'

'It was your wife, and it was she who recommended the orthodontist who carried out the dental work to fix your smile.'

Benson was not smiling now. 'What of it?'

'As you said, Mr Benson, your face is your fortune. I have no more questions, My Lord.'

'You may step down now,' the judge indicated to Benson, who seemed disgruntled, perhaps frustrated that he had been denied the opportunity to make his riposte.

Rikki began his summing-up. 'My Lord, in her questions to the witness My Friend has portrayed Mr Benson as a man of "outstanding talent". That is a subjective view. He is certainly a rich one. My Friend attempted to cast doubt on the claims made by our client by asserting that she made no contribution to Mr Benson's popular success. We concede that she played little formal role, but we do claim that she had an important informal influence on her husband's career. It is difficult to establish the truth of such matters when husband and wife present such different accounts.' He paused meaningfully. 'Nevertheless, we contend that Cassandra Carnaby played a significant part in her husband's success, and that this part ought to be recognised in the financial settlement.'

He gave a final flourish of his gown and stood still for a moment, feeling wrung out but triumphant. He glanced at Kate, who looked stony-faced; then at Cass, who mimed applause and flashed him a smile.

'Do I take it that you have finished?' asked the judge with some asperity.

'Er, yes, Your Lordship.' Rikki returned to his seat and had half sat down before he remembered a final formality. He stood up again. 'Does Your Lordship have any questions?'

'The question uppermost in my mind at present, Mr King, is luncheon.' He banged his gavel on the desk. 'We shall reconvene at two o'clock sharp.'

Chapter 25

In the private room reserved for Jez Benson and his legal team, an array of delicacies fit for the pickiest celeb had been spread out on the table by invisible hands: mini-sandwiches and wraps, bite-sized bagels smothered in smoked salmon, chargrilled artichoke hearts wrapped in prosciutto, a platter of crudités flanked by tempting dips. There was fresh fruit and yoghurt for the weight-watcher; teeny brownies and meringues for the greedy; and a little something for each faction of the lacto/ovo/veggie/vegan brigade. In fact, there was everything but the celeb himself. Though the whole purpose of importing food was to protect Jez from the media scrum outside, he had disappeared almost as soon as the judge had dismissed the court, having immediately switched on his phone and found a stack of messages, which prompted him to exclaim, 'Holy shit!' Angela had also 'gone awol', as she would say. Kate sat alone like a black-and-white ghost at the feast, stabbing a square of pineapple with a toothpick. No one had congratulated her on her performance.

She lifted off her wig and set it down next to the tofu pyramid sprinkled with seaweed. That was better. Leaning back, she ran her fingers through her hair, closed her eyes, and blew out her breath. It had been a tough morning – not least thanks to Rikki. She'd heard about Fonthill's accident as soon as she came into chambers this morning – nothing spread faster than gleeful gossip – and found the news un-settling. It was one thing to step bravely into the limelight, with one's husband in the audience, but quite another to find that she was sharing the stage with him – in fact, fighting him head to head. A tiny, cowardly part of her had even half hoped for an adjournment. But that was before she saw him in the judge's room. How could he be so cold – so unfeeling? How dare he tell her to 'bugger off'! She sat up, opened her eyes, and speared a grape, mulling over the sav-agery of his cross-examination. Considered objectively, it had been an impressive performance, certainly a lot sharper and more polished than their first and only other encounter as opponents in Croydon Crown Court – in fact, different in every conceivable way. It was impossible not to contrast the charm and excitement of that first encounter with today's hostility. Every criticism of Jez had felt like a criticism of herself. His sarcastic tone still jangled in her head. Reaching for a paper napkin, she spat out a grape pip. This afternoon it would be her turn to cross-examine the ludicrous Cass Carnaby. She intended to give Rikki a double-dose of his own medicine. The gloves were off.

'Oh, hurrah, you're here,' whinnied Angela, bustling into the room. 'You won't believe what's happened. Old Justin has just coughed up an amazing piece of info.' She waved a piece of paper. 'There we were, worrying that Benson hadn't disclosed all about his assets, but guess what? Cass hasn't either! Apparently she owns a flat in Holland Park. No one knew about it, not even Jez – though she must have bought it with his money.'

Kate jumped up to find a pad and pencil, and returned to the table, pushing aside a bowl of baby tomatoes with smiley faces drizzled in mayonnaise. Ha! So Cass Carnaby wasn't a 'pauper', as she had tried to make out. Nor was she the guile-less, let-it-all-hang-out-man rock chick she pretended to be. Kate was already scribbling bullet points. *Deceitful. Purpose of flat? Income?*

'Justin found out about it literally this minute. Looking rather shamefaced, actually, as well he might. God knows why the woman didn't tell him earlier, or what made her spill the beans now.'

'What's it worth?' Kate asked. 'And do we have any writ-ten evidence that it belongs to her?' She checked her watch. 'Unless we can establish some facts in the next twenty minutes I don't think I'll be able to use it. Damn!'

'I'm working on it.' Angela sat down opposite her, deposit-ing her capacious Hermès handbag on the table. 'Ooh, yum,' she said, reaching for a brownie. 'I've got the office checking Land Registry records' – she paused for a moment to chew and swallow – 'and an estate-agent chum is coming back to me about the value. I've told them both to jolly well put their skates on and get back to me pronto.'

Kate tapped the pencil anxiously against her teeth. 'What's happened to Jez? He does know he's got to be back here by five to two at the latest?'

'Oh, yah. Poor Jez.' Angela rolled her eyes and tried not to let out a splutter of laughter. 'He's in a frightful flap about his prog. Not the UK series, thank God. I think it's the Romanian franchise. Anyway, there's been a bit of a bish over the phone lines. You know they broadcast a different number for each of the contestants, so that the public can phone in their vote? Well, apparently one of the numbers turns out to be an adult chatline! When you ring up you get a message saying something like, "Hey there, sexy guy. Hot, horny girls are waiting right now to talk to you. Lie back, baby, relax."' She hee-hawed with laughter. 'Not that it's funny, of course.' She popped another brownie in her mouth, just as a text message beeped from the depths of her bag. Kate waited while she extracted her phone, read through the message and gave her a vigorous thumbs-up sign.

'The flat's definitely hers. Owned outright by Cassandra Carnaby. No mortgage. Bought eight years ago for 1.25 mill. My PA's couriering over a hard copy of the title register, but quite honestly I don't think we need it.' She looked across at Kate, suddenly sober and focused. 'We've got her bang to rights.'

'Who's bang to rights?' demanded Jez, slithering through the door and shutting it in the faces of the two security bruisers.

'Your soon-to-be ex-wife,' Angela answered. 'Did you know she owned a flat in Holland Park?'

Jez looked startled. 'No, I bloody well didn't.' For some seconds he brooded on this revelation. Then, to Kate's astonishment, a smile tugged at his mouth. 'The little minx. Holland Park, you say? Must be worth a few quid.'

'We're trying to find out. Do sit down, Jez, and have some of this lovely nosh. Mustn't let it go to waste.' Angela took a third brownie. 'I hope your little problem is under control. Not exactly the kind of PR we want at this precise moment.'

'No,' Jez said shortly, plopping himself down next to Kate. 'Is that coffee in the jug? Pour me a cup, will you, darling? Black, no sugar.'

Was he speaking to her? Somewhat put out by this request, Kate slapped her pencil on her notepad, stood up and walked halfway round the table to where various bottles and stainless-steel thermoses rested on a tray. She was trying to think of a way of eliciting some kind of comment on her performance in court when 'God Save the Queen' tinkled through the room.

Angela snatched up her phone. 'Wills, you're an absolute brick. What have you got? ... Heavens! How would I know which side of the road it's on? Does it matter? ... Oh, I see. Hang about.' She scrabbled about for the piece of paper that Jenkins had given her. 'It's number 12 – is that good? Garden Flat, 12 Campden Hill Road, W11.'

Midway through pouring out Jez's coffee, Kate stiffened. *Campden Hill Road.* Her mind flashed back to the jiffy bag Rikki had dropped on the floor this morning. She'd been curious, because the address was unfamiliar. She'd vaguely assumed that it must be Michael's pied à terre.

'Oi, mind my coffee. You're pouring into the saucer,' warned Jez.

'*At least* two and a half million, even in this market,' Angela announced, shutting off her phone. 'Could be over three on a blue-skies day, he says. Quick, Kate! Write that down.'

But Kate wasn't listening. Michael's pied à terre was in north London, she knew that much. Campden Hill Road was in Holland Park. Why had documents been couriered from Rikki's chambers to Cass's secret flat? She could think of only one reason.

The coffee spilled over her hand, scalding hot. There was a sharp rap at the door. 'The judge is ready for you now,' said the usher.

Chapter 26

'Mrs Benson, would you say that you were a good wife?' asked Rikki.

He leaned on the edge of the witness box, gazing encouragingly at Cass, who smiled back and simpered as if she were on a chat show. Kate itched to wipe that perpetual pussycat pout off her face. Such minx-like behaviour was definitely embarrassing in a woman of Cass's age.

Cass's reply, delivered in a slow purr, was loaded with innuendo. 'I would.'

'Indeed.' Rikki bowed his head to hide a smile, infuriating Kate further. *Have you been in her bed, you bastard?* she wanted to shout aloud.

'I'm not perfect, of course,' Cass continued, 'but I always tried to make my husband happy.' It was perfectly obvious what she meant by this. Kate was annoyed to observe Jez grinning in affectionate reminiscence.

'So he had nothing to complain of?'

'I gave him everything he wanted, and more,' Cass responded with a rippling chuckle. Jez started to laugh too, and then stopped abruptly when Angela shot him a disapproving glare.

The afternoon session had commenced with Rikki disclosing Cass's ownership of the Holland Park flat. He described it as her 'bolthole', where she would escape for peace and contemplation – as if she were some kind of New Age Virginia Woolf, Kate reflected bitterly. 'I go there when I need some head space,' Cass solemnly explained, under his direction. *Or when you want a bit of my husband*, fumed Kate.

Following the disclosure Rikki began leading Cass, dressed immaculately in a Dolce & Gabbana suit, through her testimony. Kate was irritated by the way she was playing up to the judge, and positively flirting with Rikki. A spasm of jealous anger shook her. *Don't get mad*, she told herself, *get even*.

Rikki had changed tack. 'You created beautiful homes for your husband. You entertained his friends. Sometimes, I understand, you even performed at your husband's private parties.'

I'll bet she 'performed', thought Kate bitterly.

'We have already established that your husband didn't want you to continue your recording career,' suggested Rikki. Oh God, not that again, thought Kate.

'Mr King,' interjected the judge. 'If a point has already been established, we don't need to revisit it, do we?'

'Quite so, My Lord. And, as we also established this morning, you provided your husband with essential input at crucial points in his career?'

'Right.'

'So, Mrs Benson, you concentrated on your role as a wife and mother ... staying at home, caring for the children, ensuring that there was always a good meal waiting on the table for him?' Kate was incredulous. Surely nobody was going to believe that this Jezebel *cooked*? She turned round in her chair to appeal to Jez, but he was surreptitiously texting and clearly wasn't paying attention to the absurd fibs his wife was coming out with.

'I wanted to make a home for him to come back to.' Cass adopted her butter-wouldn't-melt-in-her-mouth expression. The judge beamed benignly at her.

Oh, puh-leeze, protested Kate inwardly.

'Though, as I understand it,' continued Rikki, 'he would often abandon you and the children to fly off to the Caribbean, where he has a luxurious villa?' Kate was suddenly alert.

'He told me that he has business interests there.'

'You don't sound very convinced.'

Cass said nothing, but lowered her head. Rikki pursued the point: 'But he would usually go there alone?'

'I don't know if he was alone, but I know that he didn't take me there.' Cass dropped her eyes, the personification of a wronged woman reluctantly giving evidence against her cheating husband. The judge regarded her from his perch with paternal sympathy.

Rikki's expression had become very grave. 'I'm sorry to ask you this, Mrs Benson, but did you suspect that he might have taken other women to this ... this *Caribbean love nest*?'

Kate writhed in her seat. Was this jibe addressed to her? Did Rikki assume that she was the most recent of Jez's conquests? The latest notch on his bedpost?

Cass swallowed, as if being compelled to take a bitter pill. 'I am afraid so,' she whispered. The judge was leaning forward, his hand cupped behind his ear in an effort to hear her.

Kate was riled by Cass's blatant posturing. *What about the time when she went off to the Maldives with the twenty-four-year-old lead singer from Night Duty? The one with the leather trousers and shirt unbuttoned to his navel? Had everyone forgotten that episode?*

After a decent pause Rikki continued. 'And meanwhile you pursued your charitable work?' Cass dropped her eyes, as if too modest to acknowledge her philanthropic acts. The judge nodded approvingly. For God's sake, thought Kate, she's an actress! Men are such idiots! Can't they see through her?

෴

'Ms Carnaby,' Kate began. She wasn't going to have any of that 'Mrs Benson' nonsense. 'We heard earlier that you were a successful singer before you were married. And that when you married you gave up your singing career at your husband's insistence. Is that correct?'

'It is.' Cass smiled smugly.

'Hmmph. Do you remember releasing a single called "Gang Bang"?'

Cass's face clouded. 'Vaguely.'

'Let me remind you. You released this single eighteen months *after* your wedding. Unfortunately it was not a success, despite the explicit accompanying video, and failed to register in the Top Twenty, or indeed the Top Forty. I put it to you that your singing career came to an end for reasons unconnected with your marriage.'

Cass said nothing.

'Let's talk about your attempts to make a new career on television, Ms Carnaby. It has been suggested that these failed because your husband was insufficiently encouraging. Isn't it true that you recently approached the makers of *Celebrity Love Kitchen* to suggest that you might participate in their next series, and they turned you down?'

'It was just a feeler.'

'My information is that they rejected you as "not famous enough".'

'No way!' Cass glanced indignantly at the judge, as if inviting him to join in her protest at this slur.

'Maybe, maybe not. Have there been any significant developments in your television career since you separated from your husband?'

'I've been on Woss.'

'As a guest, I think, not a host. Let's move on. Now, I gather that you have imposed dietary restrictions when the children visit their father. There is to be no alcohol, salt or dairy products kept in the same kitchen as their food. Aren't these demands unreasonable?'

Rikki protested that this hearing was not for the purpose of deciding childcare arrangements, and the judge agreed. 'Kindly confine your cross-examination to the issues, Ms Pepper.'

'I beg your pardon, My Lord.' Kate had been expecting the rebuke. She had introduced the subject only to show what a fruitcake this woman was. Turning back to her witness, she took a new tack. 'In your testimony you put great stress on your charitable activities.'

'I'm working for a better world.'

'Quite. And you claim to have raised large sums for charitable causes, for example donkey sanctuaries.'

'I do support charities working to eliminate cruelty to animals. I also support charities helping people, especially women and children.'

'Ah, yes. The Worldwide Adoption Fund, for example?'

'We try to find homes for children who need them.'

'Very laudable. I believe that you recently spent a week in Uganda to raise funds for this charity. How much did you manage to raise?'

'I'm not sure. About fifty grand?'

'According to the records of the Worldwide Adoption Fund, the visit raised thirty-seven thousand pounds, primarily in the form of a fee from a magazine photo-shoot on location. Against that must be set your expenses of forty-three thousand, including ten thousand for the full-time services of a travelling manicurist.'

Cass didn't even look embarrassed. 'It's important to look right for the photographs.'

Kate had to fight down her rising irritation. She was scoring plenty of points, but this shameless trollop emerged from each bout seemingly unscathed. Kate gritted her teeth for another round. 'I'd like to ask you about the details of your claim for ancillary relief. In your letter setting out your position you suggested that you need three million pounds a year "for basic survival". Can you elaborate on this figure?' Out of the corner of her eye Kate noticed Rikki shaking his head violently.

'Well, that includes the cost of looking after the children.'

'Of course. And I see that you have included a figure of one hundred thousand pounds per annum for "Momcierge services". Can you explain this term?'

'A Momcierge?' Cass seemed puzzled that anyone should be unfamiliar with the term. 'Well, she's a concierge who organises childcare stuff: school runs, supervising piano practice, sports days, birthday parties … that sort of thing. Most people have one nowadays.'

'Of course. *Every* home should have one. Can you explain another item on this list of "essential expenses": "oxygen uplift treatment"?'

'That's when you have oxygen blasted upliftingly onto

your face. It's good for the complexion. I usually arrange it when I'm in the gym.'

'What about this estimate of fifty thousand per annum for plastic surgery?'

'Surgery's expensive. I've given Jez the best years of my life. I will need surgery if I'm not going to be alone for ever in penury.'

'A hundred thousand pounds for colonic irrigation?'

'It's a messy business.'

'There's another sum here of ten thousand per annum for pedicures. Does this seem to you to come under the heading of "basic survival"?'

'That includes the dog.'

'Aha. Now, Ms Carnaby, it has been suggested that you have imposed unreasonable conditions on your husband. For example, while you were still enjoying marital relations' – Kate gave a sarcastic emphasis to this phrase – 'didn't you insist that your husband use "fair-trade" condoms?'

The judge raised his eyebrows. Cass grinned. 'They're a bit squeaky at first, but not so bad once you get used to them. We've all got to do our bit for fair trade. I like to think that we make our contribution.'

'Or made?'

'Well, yes. In fact we have several gross unused, still in their boxes.'

'What a waste. Perhaps you'll find some other use for them … Let's talk about this "bolthole" of yours that My Friend told us about earlier this afternoon. I'm right, am I not, to think that you concealed your ownership of this hideaway from your husband as well as from your lawyers?'

'As I said before, I needed somewhere I could escape to,' Cass answered sulkily.

Kate was conscious of a heightened tension in Rikki's posture. 'So, this, er, refuge isn't ... what was the expression My Friend used? ... Ah, yes, a "love nest", is it?'

Once again Cass was looking indignant. 'Certainly not.'

'So when you have "sought refuge" there, you have always sought refuge alone?'

'Always.' Cass stared back at her in defiance.

Kate left a long pause. 'I see,' she concluded, in a tone brimful of scepticism. 'My Lord, I have no more questions for the witness.'

Cass stepped out of the box, looking only mildly chastened; she even blew a kiss at Rikki. Kate struggled to contain her fury as she began her summing-up. 'My Lord, Mrs Benson has claimed that she suffered significant financial loss when her singing career ended after her marriage. We have shown that she continued her career after she was married, and ceased making records only because these failed to sell. Her claim that her husband discouraged her from pursuing a new career in television does not stand up to examination. In fact, her marriage to Mr Benson enabled her to live in a manner extravagant even by the standards of the very rich. Her husband indulged her every demand. In the process she has lost touch with the reality. We contend that her assessment of needs is set absurdly high, and that a far lower figure would be appropriate.'

◦◦

'Jolly well done.' Angela gave Kate an approving nod. 'You gave her a real pasting. Wasn't she marvellous, Jez?' They were gathering up coats and documents in the waiting room, ready to go home.

Kate waited for his congratulations, but to her consternation he was looking aggrieved. 'Poor old Cass. She can't help being the way she is. She's a one-off. And why shouldn't people spend money how they like, if they've got it.' He turned his famous blue eyes on her, but they weren't sparkling as they did on television. 'You don't know what it's like to be really rich.'

'No. No, I don't,' she stammered.

'Or to live together with someone for eighteen years. On and off,' he added.

'No,' she agreed. She realised that it could be uncomfortable to see your companion of almost two decades made to look foolish. Or maybe he was still sore after the mauling he had received from Rikki earlier today.

'She was doing her job, and in my view she did it like a trouper,' Angela insisted. 'Don't forget that Kate is working in your interests, Jez.'

He grunted. 'I'm off,' he declared grumpily. Two burly security men were waiting to escort him out. 'Anje, I'll catch you later, OK?' He held his two fingers to his ear, miming a telephone conversation. 'Something I need to talk to you about.' He turned his back and stomped off, without a word to Kate. Good riddance, she decided.

'Don't worry about him,' Angela assured her. 'He's frightfully protective of his wife, despite everything. I thought you were brill. Of course I'll tell Angus how you held the fort like the best of 'em. He's been on the blower, by the way. Says that he should be back tomorrow to take up the reins.'

Kate was taking off her gown and stuffing it into her barrister bag. Regardless of Jez's reaction, she felt a sense of grim satisfaction. *I was brilliant!* She'd shown up Cass as a spoiled airhead: no way was that hussy going to get a fifty-million-pound settlement, or anything like it. While Rikki had given Jez a thorough working over, she had punished Cass at least as much – even if the silly cow didn't seem to feel it. Kate removed her wig and fluffed out her hair in front of a small mirror that hung by the door. Her eyes glittered, her cheeks were flushed. The adrenalin was still pumping. Maybe she could drag Hayley out for a celebratory drink.

Leaving Jez and Angela to hover by the entrance to wait for their car and security protection, she made her way down the steps into the street. Someone grabbed her arm. It was Rikki. 'Kate,' he insisted, 'we've got to talk.'

Chapter 27

'Let go! You're dragging me.' Kate yanked her arm out of
his grasp.

'We can't go on like this, Kate. It's tearing us apart.'

His eyes glittered in the orange streetlights. Under his coat
he was still wearing his court shirt, roughly unbuttoned at
the neck. She suppressed an impulse to lean forward and do
up a button. Instead she sighed. 'We've been through this
before, Rikki. You're doing your job and I'm doing mine.
Get over it.'

'It's not about the case. It's about *us*.' He was very serious.
'We need to talk. Please, Kate.'

Kate hesitated. She was *not* going to apologise for her
performance in court. The law was an adversarial business.
It was time he stopped taking everything so personally.

'All right,' she responded at last. 'But don't grab me like
that. And please don't make a scene.' She lowered her voice
to a hiss, conscious of the bewigged throng issuing out of the
Royal Courts of Justice and streaming past them, as raucous
as children let out of school.

'For God's sake! They don't care.'

'Well, I do. Let's go somewhere private. And I don't mean a barrister watering-hole where we'll know half the people there.'

They walked down Fleet Street in tense silence, careful to avoid touching each other, passing the restaurant where they'd celebrated Rikki's thirtieth birthday with friends only a few months ago. It had been an evening of laughter and wine and silliness, with dancing afterwards, then home to bed for their own private celebration, before falling asleep wrapped in each other's arms. They had been so happy then. She wondered if he was thinking the same thing.

'What about here?' Rikki gestured down a narrow side street, to a pub sign with a bell painted on it, hanging over a bright doorway. Kate shrugged and turned towards it.

Like most of the pubs around here it was straight out of *The Pickwick Papers,* low-ceilinged and cosily lit, with coloured bottle-glass in the window-panes, wooden settles stained almost to black with centuries of wear and smoke, and plenty of nooks and crannies – but no barristers as far as she could see. Kate made for a private corner and sat down with her back to the wall.

'What do you want to drink?' Rikki asked her.

'Anything. I don't care.'

Annoyed, he turned away from her and headed to the bar. Kate pulled off her coat and waited, hands in her lap, unconsciously twisting her wedding ring round and round. She was dreading another confrontation. A mixture of rage and misery knotted her stomach. She felt sick.

He brought her a vodka and tonic with a twist of lime and lots of ice, and a pint for himself, and sat down opposite her. 'Cheers,' he said sarcastically.

They sipped their drinks in silence, snatching covert glances at each other. He was jiggling his foot under the table. Despite everything, Kate couldn't help thinking how gorgeous he was, with caramel skin over sculpted bones, and the long, dark lashes that almost swept his cheeks as he gazed unseeingly at the table. But up close he looked strained. There were smudged shadows under his cheekbones, and his mouth was tight. She yearned to reach out and touch him – to make him smile at her again – for everything to be the way it was.

He raised his head and gave her a challenging stare. 'Well, that was fun, wasn't it?' he began bitterly. 'Our day in court. Prancing about like actors on a stage.'

'I did not prance.'

'Oh, yes, you did. I was embarrassed for you, actually. You went too far.'

'We'll see, shall we? I thought that you were rather childish.'

'What made it worse,' continued Rikki, 'was that neither of us could resist the temptation to score points off each other.'

'Isn't that what we're paid to do?'

'No.' Rikki was suddenly earnest. 'We're paid to practise advocacy on behalf of our clients, to make a case for them according to the law, not to make digs at each other. To bring our personal squabbles into the court is to bring the law into disrepute.'

'You were just as bad.'

They glared at each other. Then Rikki swept a hand over his forehead. 'Look. Let's not argue. We were both OK.'

OK? With great effort Kate kept her mouth shut.

'But that's not the point, is it?' Rikki continued. 'The point is that we should never have been in this position in the first place. I told you not to take the case. I knew it would mess up our relationship. And I was right, wasn't I?'

'No, you weren't,' she said indignantly. 'Everything would have been fine if you hadn't made such a fuss about it. You *walked out*, Rikki. You've been gone for nearly a *week*. Wouldn't you say that's a bit of an overreaction?'

'No.' He looked uncomfortable. 'Anyway, I tried to make peace with you the very next day, but you were in too much of a hurry to talk to me.'

'You said that I was trying to "sabotage" your case, when I was simply doing my job. I don't call that making peace. Anyway, stop trying to avoid the main issue.' She folded her arms. 'What about Cass Carnaby?'

'What about her?' He raised his beer glass and took a swig.

'You tell me. All that giggling and flirting in the courtroom. It's humiliating.'

'Oh, rubbish. That's just the way she is. Surely even you can see that. It doesn't mean anything.'

It was infuriating the way he tried to shrug it off, acting as if *she* was the unreasonable one. Why couldn't he tell her the truth?

'Are you having an affair with her?' she blurted out.

'Don't be silly.'

'Why is it silly? What am I supposed to think, when you don't come home, and I find you're living *in her flat*?'

He reddened. 'Who told you that?'

'I saw the address on that jiffy bag you dropped. Your name: her address. If my arithmetic is correct, two and two make four.'

'Well, it doesn't. OK, I admit that I've been staying there.' He raised a palm to forestall her accusations. 'But she told me it belonged to a friend. I had no idea that it was hers until this morning. Honestly, Kate. Don't look at me like that.'

'Like what?' Kate was undecided. She wanted to accept what he was telling her, but her doubts remained.

'Like some – I don't know, like some disapproving schoolmistress. Yeah, I know it was a mistake, and of course *the perfect Kate Pepper* never makes mistakes.'

She hated it when Rikki became sarcastic. 'Oh, for God's sake, stop trying to wriggle out of it. I never said I was perfect. But at the very least I would draw the line at accepting such a favour from a client. If anyone found out, you could be *disbarred*. And as your wife, I think I have a right to worry about any other favours you may have received from that ludicrous, self-regarding, middle-aged airhead.'

'Now, come on, Cass – I mean, Kate. Sorry, sorry, sorry.' Appalled by his blunder, he tried to reach for her hand. She snatched it away.

'You've slept with her. How could you?' she burst out.

'I didn't! I swear.' He sounded in earnest, and she wanted to believe him. But something flickered in his expression – some memory, perhaps, or a shadow of guilt. Before she could pin it down, he rushed into a counter-attack. 'You're hardly in a position to make accusations, seeing how you jetted off to Jez Benson's Caribbean *fuck-pad* without even telling me.'

'It's not a fuck-pad. It's a perfectly ordinary … luxury villa.'

'You know, I turned up at the flat the day you flew out. I even brought flowers. What an idiot, eh? There I was, trying to say sorry, and I find that you've … you've …'

'I've what, exactly? Gone out to see my *client* on the express instructions of his *solicitor*? Since when is that a crime?'

Rikki shoved his hand into his hair and tugged it with frustration. 'You expect me to believe that you spent a whole

265

weekend with that preening, lecherous little creep, talking *business*?'

Kate flushed. She tried to blank out the memory of lobster on the beach, warm air on her skin, cicadas chanting, the stars overhead, moonlight swimming. Jez's arms around her in the pool, his hands untying her bikini top. Not to mention the kiss. Well, two, if she was being accurate.

'It was not a whole weekend. It was ... half a weekend,' she finished lamely.

'Stop playing with me.' Rikki banged his fist on the table, making their glasses jump. 'You slept with him, didn't you?'

'Of course I didn't!' Now she was shocked. OK, she probably should not have let Jez kiss her. In fact, definitely not. But she'd been carried away by all the luxury and flattery. And nothing else had happened. Jez hadn't pressurised her, just laughed and let her go. Looking back, she couldn't imagine how she'd allowed things to go even as far as they had. Jez Benson, for Christ's sake! Mr Phoney. She felt a twinge of shame. Surely Rikki couldn't seriously think ... But what if he did? She grasped the edge of the table and leaned forward. 'Rikki, I promise you, I hardly saw him. We had drinks and dinner. That was it. You have to believe me.'

'Why should I believe you? You don't seem to believe me.'

Rikki's point hit home. Was he telling the truth?

'It seems to me that you do exactly as you want,' he went on. 'First the case, then flying halfway across the world without even telling me. Why shouldn't you go to bed with whoever you like as well?'

Kate jerked back as if she'd been slapped. Surely he couldn't mean what he was saying?

'You've got it all wrong, Rikki. The reason I went to the West Indies was to persuade him to come clean about his assets – you know, the Vegas deal he was about to sign. He hadn't told us about that.'

'The Vegas deal?' Rikki looked unconvinced. 'Why was that so urgent?'

'Because we didn't want Fonthill to spring it on him in court, that's why.'

Rikki frowned. 'What made you think that our side knew about the Vegas deal?'

Oh shit.

'I mean, if Benson hadn't mentioned it, how did you know about it? The only reason our side knew was because Cass had peeped at some of her husband's documents . . .' His voice trailed to a halt. He looked at her with dawning, horrified realisation. 'Oh, no, Kate. You didn't. Please tell me that you didn't spy in my case-notes.'

'Of course not.' She could feel herself blushing. 'Well, not deliberately.'

He reached across and grabbed her arm, hard enough to make her jump with shock. 'Did you look at my notes? Yes or no.'

She twisted in his grasp. 'It wasn't spying. Remember, you'd walked out on me. I – I wanted to know what you were doing.' His accusing eyes made her squirm. 'All I saw was a couple of lines. I didn't mean to. Anyway, Angela already had a suspicion that Jez might be holding something back.'

He let go of her arm, almost with contempt. 'I don't understand you. How could you do that? How could you look in my private things? You, of all people.'

'I – I'm sorry.' She couldn't bear the way he was looking at her – not with anger now, although that would have been bad enough, but with deep, bitter disappointment that seemed to shrivel her up inside.

'I didn't want you to take the case because I was afraid of what it might do to us – but I never thought that you would go this far.'

'Rikki, you've got the wrong idea.'

'It's always about you, isn't it?' he said, in a biting, sarcastic tone. 'Kate Pepper. All you think about is getting ahead. You don't care how much damage you leave behind.'

'That's not true!'

'When I got this big case you weren't happy for me; you were jealous. Jealous of me – your own husband! Somehow you wangled yourself on to the other side, working with McLaren, even though I begged you not to.'

'I didn't wangle anything,' Kate protested. 'Angus asked me.'

He jerked his head up again, and the anger in his eyes frightened her. 'I used to admire you, Kate. I still do, in a way. You're a good advocate. I thought you were so clever and confident and sparky. I was proud to have you as my wife. But now – now I see you're just a shallow, selfish person.'

'*I'm* selfish? What about you? Who forgot Valentine's Day? I had a special surprise planned, which you ruined.'

'Really?' His sceptical look was infuriating.

'Yes, really. See, you didn't even notice! You were much more excited by your big case. In fact, I don't think you've thought about me at all since you got it.'

'I could say the same about you. The way you've been behaving, you might as well still be single.'

Kate gasped at the injustice of this. 'I don't know why you're saying all these horrible things. We've just been arguing in court. It isn't as if this was real life.'

'It seems real enough to me. I'm not sure we can go back to the way we were.'

'What do you mean?' She was becoming anxious. 'We've just been through a bad patch. But it won't always be like this. We can make it as it used to be.'

'No.' He shook his head. 'Look at us, Kate. We're fighting in court. We're living apart. Now we're quarrelling in the pub.' He dropped his head, as if defeated. 'Maybe we should never have got married.'

'What do you mean?' She was panicking now. Didn't he still love her?

'Well, it doesn't matter now.'

Abruptly he rose to his feet. He snatched his coat off the back of his chair and stood over her, his eyes as hard as diamonds.

'Wait! Where are you going?'

'It's no big disaster,' he said savagely. 'It's not as if we had kids or anything. We just made a mistake.' He swished his coat like a matador's cape. 'Goodbye, Kate.'

Chapter 28

Kate lay curled in bed, with the duvet pulled right over her head and clutched tightly in her fingers. Apart from her shoes and jacket she was still fully dressed. Sheer willpower had got her home from the pub, but the last ounce of energy had drained away as she unlocked the door to the flat. Dropping everything on the floor, she had stumbled into the dark of the bedroom, not even bothering to turn on the light, and crawled under the covers.

And with her energy had gone her self-restraint. Hiding in the darkness, eyes squeezed shut and curled fists pressed to her ears, she had wailed and howled and snivelled, and eventually put out a hand to grope for a box of tissues, most of which now lay scattered about her in damp balls and tattered shreds. How could things have escalated so quickly? One minute she'd been strutting about the courtroom, feeling confident and in control; the next, the ground had given way under her feet. It felt as though she was still falling, down and down.

Rikki didn't love her. He had done once, but not any more. *I used to admire you*, he'd said: past tense. She pictured his face, harsh with disappointment – with dislike – even revulsion. *I see you're just a shallow, selfish person.*

In one short hour the man she'd felt closest to in the world had turned into a stranger. Never again would he hold her in his arms, with her ear pressed to his beating heart. Never again would she run her lips over the warm, scented skin behind his ear, or her hands over the smooth curves of his back. Never again would he catch her eye at a party and tell her by his smile that he desired and loved her. She'd never have his children. *We just made a mistake.* They wouldn't buy the house they'd daydreamed of together, with a roof-garden and a study each, or drive coast-to-coast across America in a camper van. She'd be a divorced woman by the time she was thirty. *Maybe we should never have got married.* His proposal had been so romantic that it had overcome all her innate caution. But she had always feared that he had married her on impulse and would regret it sooner or later. Well, he was regretting it now. Kate turned her face into the pillow and sobbed.

What was that? It sounded like the entryphone buzzer. Kate stuck her head cautiously out of the duvet. Yes, there it was again. Well, tough: she wasn't answering. The only person she wanted to see was Rikki, who (a) knew the code, and (b) had told her that she was selfish and shallow and that their marriage had been 'a mistake'. The last thing she needed right now was a visit from some loony evangelist or prospective candidate for the Conservative Party. She grabbed another tissue and blew her nose.

Then the doorbell of the flat rang. Kate propped herself up on one elbow and listened intently. Who could it be? It rang a second time. What if a fire had broken out in the building and someone had come to warn her before she was burned to a crisp? (*Then* Rikki would be sorry.) She threw off the duvet, scattering tissues like snowflakes, and stood up. Her hand groped for the light switch. *Ouch!* that was bright. Hobbling like an invalid, with her hair like a bird's nest and eyes like slits from so much crying, she reached the door and opened it.

'At last. Can I come in?'

Kate's jaw sagged. Of all people, it was Cassandra Carnaby, wearing a long mink coat and enough perfume to sweeten the Albert Hall.

'Rikki isn't here,' Kate told her, blocking the entrance. 'As you are no doubt aware. And you shouldn't be talking to your barrister anyway without a solicitor present. It's very irregular.'

Cass raised an eyebrow at Kate's dishevelled appearance and tear-stained face. 'So is spending a weekend with my husband in the West Indies. Anyway, it's you that I've come to see – you personally. And you're not my barrister. It's got nothing to do with the court case.'

'I'm busy.' Kate tried to shut the door, but gave up when she found it blocked by a stiletto-heeled boot, and yielded to pressure as Cass slid inside.

'Rubbish. You need a drink, and so do I.' She pushed past Kate into the living room, stepping nimbly over the debris lying on the floor. 'What have you got? Not more of the vitriol you poured over me in court today, I hope.'

'I, er ...' For once, Kate was at a loss for words. Short of throwing the woman out bodily, she couldn't think what to do.

By contrast, Cass seemed totally self-possessed. She threw off her coat and tossed it over the back of the sofa, revealing a slinky dress in deep purple with a wide, shiny belt. 'Nice little pied à terre you've got here,' she remarked, looking around.

Kate's nostrils flared. *Actually, it's our home, you spoiled cow*, was what she wanted to say, but Cass's reference to her Caribbean jaunt made her bite back the words. Instead, she planted her hands on her hips and said, 'Look, what do you want?'

Cass sat herself comfortably on the sofa and crossed her legs. 'I've come to talk to you about your husband. But I think we'll both feel much better with some good old alcohol inside us. Got any white wine?'

'I thought you were teetotal,' said Kate.

Cass chuckled. 'Don't believe everything you read in the papers.'

In the door of the fridge Kate found a half-full bottle with the cork stuck back in. That would have to do. What on earth could this wretched woman have to say about Rikki? Except to gloat in triumph by gushing about how marvellous he was, how clever, how handsome ... For the umpteenth time she wondered whether they were having an affair. Rikki had reassured her, but a lurking doubt remained. Something had happened, that was clear. So why was she here? Kate couldn't think of any plausible explanation. It was a mystery. She set two glasses on the counter and filled them. After a moment's reflection she drank almost all of one glass, wiped her mouth with the back of her hand, and topped it up again. Then she turned on the tap and splashed her face vigorously with cold water, before patting it dry with a tea towel. That was better. She carried in the glasses and gave one to Cass before seating herself in the armchair.

The two women stared at each other in silence for a moment.

'Cheers.' Cass raised her glass.

'Cheers,' Kate echoed grudgingly. She couldn't really believe that this was happening.

'So, that was a very interesting day in court,' Cass said conversationally. 'I learned quite a lot from it.'

'Really? You surprise me.' Kate was beginning to feel her hackles rise again. This woman was starting to get on her nerves, with her immaculate coiffure and gaping embonpoint. Without thinking Kate began smoothing down her own hair. She hoped that she didn't look too frightful herself.

'I think Jez did too.'

'Excuse me, but where are we going with this?'

Her visitor chuckled. She didn't seem in a hurry to get to the point. Kate suspected that she enjoyed making her wait. 'I suppose,' Cass began at last, 'that I had better explain why I've come to see you.'

'That would be nice.'

'Your Rikki,' she said slowly, 'is a very special man.'

'I know that,' snarled Kate. 'He's my husband.' *Was*, said a voice inside her.

'No, I don't think that you do.' Cass smiled, as if remembering a private joke. 'Marriage is a funny business. I know that I've made a mess of mine, but there was a time when I loved Jez – still do in some ways, the cheesy bastard. Maybe we could have done better, if we'd really tried. But we didn't. It was never really a partnership, just one long, crazy party. I did my thing, he did his, but there was never an "us". Do you get what I'm saying?'

'No.' Kate could not believe that this woman was presuming to lecture her about marriage.

'I've learned from years of therapy that you have to apply yourself to the project of becoming a spouse. You have to find energy for skilled conversations. Sometimes empathy has to be forced. Am I getting through to you?'

'Only as far as my ears. You haven't reached my brain yet.'

'All right, I'll try to put it in terms that you might understand. A good man is worth holding on to.'

'Thank you for telling me that. When I need advice from a halfwit I'll come back to you.'

Far from being stung, Cass simply grinned. 'What would you say if I told you that I tried to seduce your husband?'

'You did what?' All Kate's fears came flooding back.

'Don't pretend that something similar didn't happen in the Caribbean. I know what my husband is like.'

Kate felt rising indignation. 'And don't get your knickers in a twist,' added Cass, 'because to put it bluntly, he turned me down. What do you say to that?'

'I'd – I'd say you were too old and he didn't fancy you.'

'Ouch, that's a bit below the belt. But I'll take it, because I like Rikki and I know something's gone wrong between the two of you. Did he explain to you that he's been staying in my flat?'

'Why are you telling me this?' Kate felt increasingly confused.

'Yeah, it was a little trick I played on him. And he almost fell for it.' She smiled. 'But not quite.'

Kate shook her head, as if to clear it. 'What is it that you're trying to tell me? Because I don't think I can take much more of this.'

'I'm trying to tell you that your husband loves you. Without going into detail, I made myself as available to him as I know how – and let me tell you, that's *very* available – but the silly man refused the offer. I know that he was attracted. I believe that he was tempted. He could even justify it to himself, believing that you were with my husband in his Caribbean "love nest". But Rikki wouldn't play. He told me that there was only one woman for him, and that was his wife. *You*.'

'When was this?' Kate whispered.

'I don't know – last weekend – what does it matter?'

Last weekend: a lifetime ago.

'The point is that you've got a good man there. A man who can resist me is worth having. You should treat him right and hold him close.'

'What if it's too late?' A tear rolled down Kate's cheek.

'Why should you think that?'

'We quarrelled after the hearing today. He made it obvious that he doesn't love me any more.'

'Not true. What time was this?'

'I don't know. About five thirty, I suppose.' What on earth did it matter what time it was?

'Five thirty, eh? Hmmm … You see, I know something else that you don't. Rikki telephoned me around seven this evening and told me that he wanted to drop the case. He said it was putting his marriage in danger, and nothing was worth that. I persuaded him to wait until tomorrow before rushing into a decision. But he is willing to give it up for your sake. Doesn't that suggest that he loves you?'

'He offered to step down?' Kate was stunned.

'That's what I said. He loves you, all right.'

'But what can I do?'

'My advice is to do something to show that you love him, and do it quick. Rikki's a very attractive guy. If you let him go, someone else will grab him. And if you're going to cry, I'm leaving.' Cass stood up. 'That was disgusting wine, by the way.'

She walked over to pick up her coat, and wriggled herself

into it. Forty-five or no, Kate had to admit that she was just what men liked: big tits, long legs, come-on smile, loads of experience. But Rikki had turned her down.

She showed Cass out in a daze, mumbling about taxi ranks until Cass shut her up by telling her that she had a car waiting. Even when the door clicked shut and she could hear Cass's footsteps echoing down the stairs, Kate couldn't bring herself to move, as the enormity of what she had lost – no, *thrown away* – sank in.

Rikki was right, she saw it now. She *was* selfish. She'd expected to marry him and, as Cass had said, enjoy one long, crazy party without making any attempt to adapt herself to what he wanted, or to the kind of person he was. For all his charm, Rikki was a private person. What had Angus said to her, only last night? *Marriage is a private thing. I wanted to keep it to myself.* And that's what Rikki had wanted, too. He'd asked her to stay away from *Benson* v. *Carnaby,* not because he wanted to keep her down, but because for him their relationship was private and special and he didn't want to put it on display. Quite simply, it hurt him to be opposing his wife in an acrimonious divorce case that was so largely in the public eye. What's more, she'd known that, and had gone ahead regardless. *Marriage is supposed to involve some sacrifices.* She had behaved like a single girl when she was a married woman.

She winced at her own insensitivity and self-absorption as other events from the last couple of weeks crowded into her mind. Telling Hayley how ghastly it was to have a baby. Playing around with Michael and Sam because she thought it would be amusing for Sam to surprise her husband in the Ritz – when they were on the brink of divorce. Even Mrs Mitchison had deserved better from her. It was shaming that she had spent the better part of a decade earning a living from divorce cases, and only now, when it was happening to her, could she understand the pain and bitter sense of failure involved.

Rikki had chosen her and he had loved her and been faithful to her, but she had let him down. The tears fell faster now as she walked through the flat, picturing him lying outstretched on the sofa with his feet propped on the armrest or smiling up at her across the kitchen table. In the bedroom she threw open the wardrobe doors and plunged her face among his shirts, inhaling his smell.

It might be too late to make it right with Rikki. But at least she could show him that she wasn't as selfish as he had assumed.

Chapter 29

In the lofty halls of the Royal Courts of Justice, lawyers and litigants were gathering for another day of battle. There were the usual groups of anxious clients sitting with their solicitors and barristers at tables scattered across the splendid tiled floor. Around them, clerks manoeuvred trolleys piled high with documents, and ushers whisked in and out of the courtrooms, checking that all was prepared for the judges' imminent arrival.

Rikki paced the corridors on the lookout for Jenkins, who had rung him at eight o'clock that morning asking him to come to court half an hour early. There had been 'developments' in the case. He would explain in person. Rikki held his wig upside-down by its twin pig-tails, swinging it at his side as he walked. Some might consider such behaviour disrespectful, but today he didn't care. Never had he felt less enthusiastic about appearing in court. His brain was fogged with misery and weariness. Last night he had checked into a bland tourist hotel, with windows that didn't open and an overpowering smell of air-freshener, where he had slept fitfully as scenes from the past week flickered through his mind in a nightmarish jumble. In particular Kate's pale, shocked face haunted him. How could he have said such cruel things in the pub yesterday? He had wanted to make it up with her, but instead he had made her cry. As usual he had gone too far, and said things that he didn't mean. Why did he do that? It wasn't as if he really believed Kate had slept with Benson. In the cold light of day he wondered how he could ever have imagined such a thing.

The prospect of another day like yesterday, scoring points off the woman he loved, was so intolerable that he had actually phoned Cass after the scene in the pub to tell her that he could no longer handle the case. In fact, he had been quite outspoken. Though she might enjoy tearing Jez to shreds, he couldn't bear doing the same to Kate. And why had she lied to him about her ownership of the Holland Park flat? But she'd won him round of course, adding mysteriously, 'I think you'll find that tomorrow will be much easier.' Rikki felt that he could not let her down, though he had no heart for battle.

'Ah, Rikki. There you are.' A hand clapped him on the shoulder, and he turned to find Angus McLaren at his side, looking every inch the QC in his starched wing collar and flowing silk robe. 'Put on your wig, there's a good chap.'

Rikki did so, now feeling somewhat ashamed of his dishevelment, contrasting with the immaculate appearance of his opponent, a man whose wife had died only two days earlier. 'I was very sorry to hear about your loss,' he said inadequately.

'Thank you.' McLaren gave a firm nod, both acknowledging the remark and dismissing the subject from further discussion.

Rikki could not prevent himself from peering past McLaren

in search of Kate, though he wasn't certain whether he longed to see her or dreaded it.

'She's not coming,' McLaren told him, correctly interpreting his gaze. 'No, it's me you'll be contending with today – assuming that there will be any contention, that is.'

Rikki didn't understand what he was getting at, but he was much more interested to know about Kate. 'Where is she?' he asked. 'Why isn't she here?' A sudden anxiety filled him. 'She's not ill, is she?'

'Don't fret, Rikki. I can assure you that she was in perfectly good health when I last saw her, not ten minutes ago. I can explain more fully later. If you'd care to talk over a pint at lunchtime, you'll find me in the Cheshire Cheese. I have every reason to believe that this morning's proceedings will be over in good time.' And with that cryptic statement he strode off down the corridor, leaving Rikki with his mouth half open and his mind full of question marks.

'Conferring with the enemy?' Rikki spun round to see Jenkins at his side. He started to stammer out an explanation, but Jenkins cut in smoothly. 'Shall we have a little word?'

৶

'All rise for the Honourable Mr Justice Overend.'

Together with everybody else in the room, Rikki stood as the judge entered, with a scraping of chairs. Usually, he was reminded of schooldays, when all the boys would stand for the entrance of the schoolmaster, but today the seductive whiff of Cass's perfume from just behind him cancelled this image in his mind. A moment later, once the judge was in his seat, they all sat down again. Rikki glanced at Benson's team. In place of Kate was a tubby man whom he recognised as

Milo Wittering-Coombe. He was looking rather peeved.

McLaren rose to his feet. 'My Lord, I have to announce a development. My client, the husband, wishes to withdraw his petition.'

There was a gasp of surprise from the court officials in the room. The judge appeared startled, and put his hand to his ear. 'Mr McLaren, can you please clarify yourself?'

'Certainly, My Lord,' McLaren continued drily. 'The husband has decided to withdraw his petition, because he wishes to remain married to the wife.'

'Goodness me, this is most irregular. Mr King, do you have anything to say on behalf of the Respondent?'

It was Rikki's turn to rise to his feet. 'Yes, My Lord. The wife has made the same decision.' He glanced at Cass, still only half convinced by this bombshell reconciliation. She gave him a cat-with-the-cream smile.

'We prefer to stay married, Your Honour,' Benson threw in with a smirk.

The judge was still trying to absorb the implications of what he had been told. 'Do I take it, therefore, that there is no further need for these proceedings?'

Before anyone could answer there was the sound of raised voices and scuffling outside the chamber. The heavy wooden door burst open and a figure in black was catapulted into the room. Rikki was astonished to recognise Fonthill, looking wild-eyed and audibly panting. He thrust the door closed behind his back, in the face of a protesting usher. For a moment he seemed disoriented, like an actor who has forgotten his lines. Then, catching sight of the judge, he visibly swelled with self-importance.

'My Lord, I humbly beg your pardon for my tardiness,' he said. 'I regret to say that I suffered a domestic *obstruction*.

282

Or should I say a marital misunderstanding?' He raised his upper lip in a ghastly leer. 'Yesterday I was confined at home for medical reasons. Today, however, I am ready to resume my duties as advocate. I have come to rescue the situation – no matter how disastrous it may appear.' He shot a hostile glare towards Rikki, who was still standing.

'But, Mr Fonthill, delighted though we are to learn of your recovery, I must inform you that the proceedings are terminated,' Overend explained.

'Terminated?' Fonthill looked perplexed. 'My Lord, there must be some mistake. My junior is very inexperienced. Almost a *baby*.'

'Be that as it may, I am afraid that you are too late. The husband and the wife have decided that they wish to remain married.'

'Married?'

'That is what I said,' the judge responded testily. 'Married.' Ignoring Fonthill, he told the court, 'I shall make an order for costs tomorrow. Case dismissed!' He banged his gavel sharply.

The noise made Fonthill jump. He put a hand to his head, looking confused. Seemingly reassured to encounter the familiar feel of his wig, he drew himself up to his full height, threw out an expansive arm and addressed the judge with passionate fervour. 'O let us be married! Too long we have tarried. But what shall we do for a ring?'

'Remove Mr Fonthill from my court,' ordered the judge, gesturing at one of the officials.

'But, My Lord!' Fonthill protested.

Rikki watched as Fonthill was gently led out of the court, thinking that never again, having witnessed this scene, would he feel compelled to act as Fonthill's stooge. It was a liberating thought. Nevertheless, he couldn't suppress a twinge of pity as he heard Fonthill bleating in the corridor about the land where the Bong-tree grows.

◯◯

Outside the courthouse, mayhem reigned. Angela Cross, her face an impassive mask, told the crowd that 'Mr Benson has an announcement to make,' before stepping aside to make way for her client in front of a bank of microphones.

Reporters and TV camera crews jockeyed for position as Benson stepped forward, hand in hand with Cass. Rikki watched from a raised position on the steps of the Royal Courts of Justice, not quite able to believe what he was witnessing.

'I'm sorry to disappoint you, gentlemen and ladies of the press,' Benson announced, flashing his famous smile. 'I know that you like to see a good fight. But the fact is that me and Cass have decided to bury the hatchet.' He paused, and looked sideways at his beaming bride.

There was a clamour of questions, but Benson continued regardless. 'We've had our differences. I won't pretend otherwise. Maybe we've done things we're not proud of. But at the end of day, it's about love, isn't it? I still love my wife and she still loves me. It's taken all this palaver to bring us to our senses. When I saw my wife in the witness box I realised that, as well as being a very special creative talent, she's a wonderful, caring mother who has created a stable family home for Elvis and Apricot. That's what means the most to me. When it comes down to it, the good times outweigh the bad times. So let the good times roll! Thank you very much.'

Now Cass took his place, tilting her profile this way and

that. Rikki noticed that she had changed out of her demure suit into one with a plunging neckline that drew the cameras forward like bees to pollen.

'I just want to say something about my husband,' she began. 'I've said some unkind things about him in the past, I know. His image sometimes lets him down. But the public doesn't know the real Jez. In private he's modest, generous, straight as a die and loyal. My husband is a true gentleman!'

Shaking his head in bemusement at this ludicrous pantomime, Rikki turned away and headed down Fleet Street.

                                               ☊

The rambling rooms of the Cheshire Cheese were packed and noisy as usual, but McLaren had managed to command a small table in one of the upstairs rooms, on which two pints were already standing. Once again, he felt as if he was half a pace behind everyone else. 'Thank you,' he said, sliding into the seat opposite. 'You should have let me—'

'Nonsense. My pleasure. Even though we are to be deprived of a judgment in *Benson* v. *Carnaby*, we have the consolation of collecting our fees. I can still afford to buy the odd pint.'

'Yes. Of course. That is, I'm still not quite sure that I understand what happened this morning,' Rikki confessed. 'Do you?'

'Oh, I think that it's quite straightforward, really. The Bensons have decided that they are better off together than they are apart.'

'Better off?'

'Quite honestly, I think that the accountants played a bigger part in this than the lawyers. The tax implications of divorce are somewhat daunting. And fifty million pounds is a lot of money, you know. Even to Benson.' McLaren raised his glass. 'Cheers.'

'Cheers.' Rikki sipped his beer. Could the Bensons' rapturous reconciliation really be attributable to something as unromantic as tax? Probably. In which case they deserved each other. But the Bensons were not uppermost in his mind. 'Can I just ask …?'

'Kate came into my office first thing this morning, to tell me that she wished to step down from the Benson case.'

'What?' Rikki was stunned. 'I mean, why?'

'As you will be aware, this is most unusual, especially for a junior who has the opportunity to be led by a QC, and especially by an ambitious young woman like Kate. Had the case not been unexpectedly terminated, her decision would almost certainly have been interpreted by others in our profession as a failure, and might well have set back her career. I have to confess that initially I was very surprised. However, I accepted her explanation, as it seemed to me that she had, and has, a good reason – what you and I, in the family-law business, might call a "fact".' He paused, looking intently at Rikki from beneath his eyebrows. 'I expect you can guess what that is?'

Rikki shook his head in confusion. He could only think of acute illness or some catastrophe. Maybe Kate's mother? Or Sam? But Kat was apparently in chambers as usual, so that didn't make sense. Could she have fallen in love with Jez Benson after all, and be heart-broken? He toyed with the idea, but the image of Benson's vapid, grinning face erased this possibility. Perhaps she had met someone else, and was about to run off with him to a foreign country. He didn't believe that either. An inkling of a different explanation did penetrate the periphery of his brain, but he silenced it at once.

'No. I can't guess. What is it – this "fact", as you call it?'

'It's you, Rikki.'

'Me? Do you mean she doesn't want to see me, even in court?'

McLaren burst out laughing. 'Of course not. She loves you, Rikki. She told me that this case has driven a wedge between you. Quite simply, she'd rather have her husband than even the most lucrative and prestigious legal case. Always assuming that she feels that she must choose between the two,' he added drily.

Rikki felt a leap of wild joy, crushed almost immediately by a weight of guilt and shame. He sank his head in his hands. 'Oh God. What have I done?'

Angus McLaren said nothing. But the answers flew into Rikki's own head like so many poisoned darts. He'd accused her of sleeping with Benson. He'd compared her to a school mistress, and told her she was selfish. He'd called her 'Cass'! Then he'd walked out on her.

He raised stricken eyes to McLaren. 'I told her that getting married was a mistake.'

'And was it?'

'Of course not! She's the most wonderful girl in the world. I love her. I was just ...' He struggled for the right word. Angry? Jealous? He leaned across the table, trying to explain. 'The thing is, Kate's so bloody capable. She's organised and controlled, while I'm all over the place. She can do everything I can – and more. I suppose I think a husband ought to *do* something. But I don't know what my role is.'

'Your job is to love her,' McLaren said simply. 'I know that Kate's a headstrong girl. My Mary was the same. Between ourselves, they're the best – not always easy, I grant you, but the best roses are often the thorniest. And they still need tending and supporting in order to blossom. But don't grab them, or they're liable to whip back in your face.'

Rikki, no gardener, was beginning to feel a bit dazed by this analogy. It was a relief when McLaren returned to plain language. 'It strikes me,' he said thoughtfully, 'that you've both been continuing to live as single people who happen to share a bed. But sharing a life involves sacrifice and commitment, and an acceptance of each other's imperfections. You've had the wedding. Perhaps it's time now to turn that into a marriage.'

Rikki could feel a new optimism swelling in his heart and rushing upwards until he felt light-headed. And he had hardly touched his drink yet. He raised the glass to his lips and drank deeply. He was beginning to see how he could look after Kate without bullying her, and how he could draw strength from her without feeling threatened. He wanted to explain all this to her right now. He wanted to kiss her. He ached to go to bed with her. If only she would give him another chance. His expression clouded as he remembered all the terrible things he had said and done over the past couple of weeks.

'How can I ever get her to forgive me?'

McLaren lifted his glass in a salute. 'I'm sure you'll think of something.'

Chapter 30

It had been another bright day, the sky so blue and pure that it made your heart burst. The late afternoon sunshine was streaming through the window of Kate's office, where she sat at her desk studying an article on pension allocation in divorce settlements. At least, she was supposed to be studying. Her eyes moved obediently along each line, and she held a pen in her hand, ready to take notes. But every time she reached the bottom of the first page she realised that she'd absorbed nothing, and was forced to start again. For the third time in as many hours she reached for her dictionary to look up the meaning of 'fiduciary'. She opened it listlessly, then immediately forgot what she was supposed to be doing. Leaning an elbow on the open page, between 'sex' and 'shallot', she stared into space, chin propped in her hand.

That morning she had come into chambers early, and had asked the clerk to inform her as soon as Angus McLaren arrived. She had been up half the night worrying about how to break the news to him that she couldn't continue with the case. A week ago – a day ago – she would not have dreamed of doing such a thing. Now her concern was not for herself, with her career or reputation, but for him. Having just lost his wife, he might have expected to be able to rely on her, if only for practical support. Kate was very apprehensive about his reaction. Acutely conscious of the pain he must be feeling, she felt terrible about letting him down at such a moment. But once she had explained why, he seemed to understand exactly how she felt. Far from disapproving, he had actually encouraged her to bow out. He was relaxed about the whole thing: almost too relaxed, she fretted afterwards. 'No case is worth jeopardising a good marriage, my dear girl,' he had said. 'I should never have bullied you into taking it on in the first place.' The idea of Angus bullying anybody made her smile, despite her concerns. He had reassured her that nobody would think any less of her for dropping the case. 'To be frank, I don't think that anyone will notice.' Kate frowned at this comment, so Angus explained: 'The hard work for a junior has already been done. And the magnificent job you did yesterday more than compensates for your absence for the remaining day or two of the hearing, if indeed it lasts that long. I shall certainly come to you the next time I take on a similar case – though I expect that you will be leading yourself soon.'

Of course she had asked him how he felt: tentatively, because it was not the sort of subject they normally discussed. 'I'm all right, thank you, my dear,' he said, his eyes moistening for a moment. 'It helps to have something to keep me occupied.' And then he had got out his duster and started polishing his already gleaming desk.

From her interview with Angus, Kate had returned to her office in a state of nervous trepidation, feeling that she had done the right thing but still anxious about the consequences. Ahead of her stretched a day empty of engagements, because she had cleared her diary for the court case. Checking her emails, she opened a message from the editor of the law journal for which she was supposed to be writing her article on Hildebrand, regretting that they did not appear to have received it in time for the next issue. Another black mark against my name, thought Kate.

Feeling weary after a night of not enough sleep, she had wandered into the kitchen to make herself a strong pot of coffee. While she was waiting for it to percolate through, WC popped his head round the door. He was wearing his wig and robe, ready for court. 'Mucked up another case, I hear,' he said gleefully. 'I suppose McLaren decided to sack you, did he? Good thing that I'm around to pick up the pieces.' With a nasty start, Kate realised that Angus had asked WC to step into the breach as his junior. For once she found it impossible to come up with an appropriate riposte. It hurt to think of that idiot taking her place alongside Angus. As she sipped a mug of strong black coffee after the smirking WC had disappeared in the direction of the courts, Kate tried to tell herself that he hadn't been selected on merit, but simply because he was the only junior who was free at the last minute. The thought provided a little comfort, but it was a bitter pill to swallow all the same.

By the middle of the day it was unseasonably warm, enough to sit outside in the sun. Kate took her sandwich into the courtyard and ate it on a bench. The lunchtime bustle had begun, as barristers and clerks streamed out of sets of chambers in search of sustenance. Already there were snowdrops and crocuses in the flowerbeds, and daffodil shoots were beginning to force their way into the light. The Temple was coming to life in the winter sunshine, like a sleepy creature waking after a long hibernation. It was a lovely place to work, reflected Kate. But she remembered something Hayley had said to her – when? – only last week, though so much had happened since that it seemed much longer. *It's not everything. If I don't make it, that will be because something else was more important to me. Something* here. Hayley had pressed a palm to her heart. Kate hadn't quite understood her friend then, but she did now.

As she sat feeding crumbs to the pigeons, Kate allowed herself to think about Rikki. She wondered how he had managed in court this morning. She pictured him looking handsome and serious in his wig as he addressed the judge. How could she have called him 'childish' yesterday? He was a brilliant lawyer – way better than that poser Fonthill. And how could she ever have thought that he would sleep with another woman? Especially a client.

She remembered the strain on his face in the pub. He had wanted this case so much, had been so excited about it – and yet he had been willing to give it up, just for her. It was as if there had been a barrier between them, and he had torn it down. The very thought of it prompted her to feel a new surge of love for him. Yet it was almost certainly too late. She had hurt him too much, and perhaps he would never forgive her. She was desolate. Only one thought consoled her: that in quitting *Benson* v. *Carnaby* she had demonstrated that she loved him, just as he had shown his love for her.

Soon after she had arrived back in chambers, Angus had appeared at her door. 'Surprise, surprise,' he greeted her. Bemused, Kate invited him to sit down. 'The case has collapsed, I'm delighted to announce,' he told her, laughing, as he perched on a chair. 'Love has found a way.' Angus was clearly amused at the outcome. 'What a pair those Bensons are, eh? The perfect couple. We must toast their future happiness.' Kate could still hear him chuckling as she listened to his footsteps retreating down the corridor. She was trying to take it all in. How had Rikki reacted to this development? she wondered. It dawned on her that Angus might have known, or at least suspected, that the case was about to collapse this morning, when she had announced her decision to withdraw. No wonder he had seemed so relaxed about it all! And what about Cass? Had she already decided to stay with Jez when she arrived for their little tête-à-tête last night? Was she in fact on her way to a clandestine meeting with her husband?

All afternoon Kate had kept turning over these thoughts in her mind, which was another reason why she was finding it difficult to concentrate on the *Family Law Review* article. Her reverie was interrupted by a beeping from her mobile. It was a text from Sam: Exciting news! Meet me in Ritz Rivoli Bar 6.30 tonight xx

So she would be going to the Ritz after all: but to meet the wife, not the husband. She felt she must go, even though she felt ambivalent about the prospect. At almost any other time Kate would have been excited by an invitation to the Ritz. And of course Sam was always fun. But right now she wasn't feeling in the mood to do anything sociable – least of all to gush in response to Sam's 'exciting news', whatever that might be.

Kate stood up and drifted over to the window. She wondered what had brought Sam to London. Maybe Michael had a new job – maybe she'd been house-hunting – or, God! Could she be pregnant again? Not already, surely? But whatever the exciting news was, her best friend wanted to share it with her and Kate couldn't let her down. She wasn't going to be selfish (as Rikki had accused her of being). Or shallow. Well ...

maybe just a *little* bit shallow. It was the Ritz, after all. Kate summoned her enthusiasm to text Sam back: Can't wait! xx

Having made her decision, Kate immediately felt better about it. She was determined to have a good time, however miserable she felt underneath. At five thirty she shut down her computer, packed away her work, and opened the narrow cupboard in a corner of her office where she kept her emergency party gear: spare tights, plain black shoes with sparkly silver bows and a short, fitted black dress, with buckles on the shoulder straps to give it a sexy punch – a rip-off of one she'd seen Kate Winslet wear at an awards ceremony. She brushed her hair, pleased that she had washed it only that morning, though this had been as much to wake her up as for any other purpose. As she was doing her make-up, she noticed dark circles under her eyes. Eek! But she could do something about that. Once she had finished, she considered the result in the mirror, and decided that she was satisfied. Despite everything, she looked good – in fact, almost beautiful. It felt like a small victory over how terrible she felt inside.

Kate belted her coat and left the office, turning out the light as she left. At the foot of the main stairs she spotted the Head Clerk standing in the entrance and peering out. As she approached he looked round. 'Special night, is it?' he asked, noticing that she'd changed out of her work clothes.

'No. Well, perhaps.'

The Head Clerk courteously held the door open for her, and then stepped outside for a moment. The temperature was dropping fast, and it was already distinctly chilly. He looked up at the darkening sky. 'I think that it's going to be a beautiful night,' he observed, rubbing his hands. 'Good evening, miss.'

૭૭

The cab pulled up by the kerb, and a uniformed man wearing a top hat and gloves sprang forward to open the passenger door. Kate paid the driver, and stepped out onto the pavement. 'Welcome to the Ritz Hotel, madam.' It was already dark. Other cabs were gathering like insects buzzing around a flame, and in front of them stood a vintage Rolls-Royce, gleaming under the streetlights. The doorman led her under the colonnades and pushed open one of the glass doors, holding it so that she could enter the hotel without pausing. She had never been inside before. In the opulent lobby, her eyes were drawn up towards three tiers of circular galleries, their curve matched by the pattern of the luxurious carpet and the shape of the marble desk. Kate couldn't resist a frisson of excitement at being in such a glamorous hotel. She deposited her coat in the cloakroom, and shyly asked a hall porter to direct her to the Rivoli Bar. As she approached down the corridor she could hear a piano playing over a buzz of chatter. The Rivoli Bar was decorated in sophisticated Art Deco style, with lavish use of camphor wood, satinwood, alabaster, gold leaf and Lalique glass. Each table held a vase of exquisite cut flowers. The other patrons were smartly dressed, some indeed looking as if they might have been transported here from the 1930s.

Kate scanned the room, but she couldn't spot Sam. A waiter glided up to her and asked if he could help. 'I'm meeting a friend,' she explained.

'And your name is . . . ?'

'Kate. Kate Pepper.'

'Ah, yes.' He gave her a slightly odd smile. 'I'm afraid your friend has been delayed. May I show you to a table?'

How typical, thought Kate. From the time they first met at university, she had always been early and Sam had always been late, eyes aghast under her fringe.

The waiter led her to a quiet banquette, and Kate sat down with her back to the door, noticing an unopened bottle of champagne cooling in an ice bucket. Sam must have *very* exciting news. The waiter made no move to open the champagne, but immediately brought her a glass of something else delicious, 'With the compliments of the Ritz, madam.'

Kate sat back and sipped her drink. She glanced over her shoulder around the bar. There was a constant bustle of activity, with waiters speeding to and fro and more people coming in all the time. She watched an infatuated young couple sitting on bar stools, knees touching, gazing at each other over a couple of cocktails. Her heart stirred in sympathy. The pianist struck up a familiar tune, and the words began to chime in her head: 'Oh, how the thought of you clings … These foolish things remind me of you.' Suddenly moved, she bent her head, blinking back tears. Why had she never come here with Rikki? She told herself that she mustn't think of him. She mustn't think of romance and happiness – dancing and moonlight – Italy. She mustn't!

'Mind if I join you?' said a voice. And there he was, her beloved Rikki, looking marvellous in a dark suit and the pink shirt she had bought him. His smile was hesitant, hopeful, but above all loving. In an instant she saw the trick they had played on her, Sam and Rikki, and was impossibly moved. Happiness swept through her like a warm, energising tide, setting her heart racing.

'I'm not sure if you should join me.' Her eyes danced with mischief. 'I'm married, you know.'

'Good.' He slid in beside her on the banquette, and put his arm around her shoulder. 'So am I.'

Epilogue

Kate and Rikki lived happily ever after, or as happily as a clever, independent woman can live with a clever, independent man – or as any couple can live with (eventually) three children, a mortgage, ageing parents, setbacks, crises, broken washing machines and unreliable cars.

Any couple, that is, who love each other. At this precise moment they are lying in bed in front of a favourite old film, though they fell asleep in one another's arms shortly after the opening credits.

Jez Benson lost all his money when an offshore bank collapsed, shortly followed by the final collapse of his marriage. He was last seen selling pet products on an Australian shopping channel.

Cass Carnaby founded the online business *toyboyz4me. com*, which she sold to Google for $12.7 million.

Sam and Michael live in Kensington. Sam has become an internationally bestselling chicklit writer, and Michael is her financial manager, working from an office in the basement.

Hayley gave up practising at the Bar and now runs a charity part-time. She has three children.

WC came out when he was forty-five and is a much nicer person. He specialises in civil partnerships and lives in Islington with a pastry chef.

Nicholas Fonthill is now in the House of Lords.

Angus Horatio McLaren is buried next to his wife, under a headstone with the inscription:

I love thee with the breath,
Smiles, tears, of all my life! – and if God choose,
I shall but love thee better after death.

Acknowledgements

My first thanks must go to those people who explained to me how the Bar works and showed me around the Temple, where I lived for a while as a schoolgirl. I should mention in particular the family-law barrister Elizabeth Szwed for generously giving up so much time to talk to me, and for showing me around the Royal Courts of Justice. I should emphasise, however, that responsibility for what I have written is mine alone. In the interests of presenting a dramatic narrative I have compressed the likely timetable for such a court case, and in a few other minor instances, departed from current legal procedure in England and Wales.

I must also thank my family for their forbearance while I have been writing this book and, particularly, my husband, Adam, for his unstinting support throughout.

I'd like to express my special gratitude to my editor, Genevieve Pegg, for her saintly patience and good nature, and for her extremely helpful suggestions on successive drafts of this book. I am also lucky enough to have the best agent ever in Jonathan Lloyd.

While some of the locations in this book are real, all of the characters are entirely imaginary.

Robyn Sisman
February 2010

CherryPicks
Our books.
Your choice.